Booked for Revenge

Books by Karen Rose Smith

Caprice DeLuca Mysteries
STAGED TO DEATH
DEADLY DÉCOR
GILT BY ASSOCIATION
DRAPE EXPECTATIONS
SILENCE OF THE LAMPS
SHADES OF WRATH
SLAY BELLS RING
CUT TO THE CHAISE

Daisy's Tea Garden Mysteries
MURDER WITH LEMON TEA CAKES
MURDER WITH CINAMMON SCONES
MURDER WITH CUCUMBER SANDWICHES
MURDER WITH CHERRY TARTS
MURDER WITH CLOTTED CREAM
MURDER WITH OOLONG TEA
MURDER WITH ORANGE PEKOE TEA
MURDER WITH DARJEELING TEA
MURDER WITH EARL GREY TEA
MURDER WITH CHOCOLATE TEA

Tomes & Tea Mysteries
MURDER MARKS THE PAGE
BOOKED FOR REVENGE

Published by Kensington Publishing Corp.

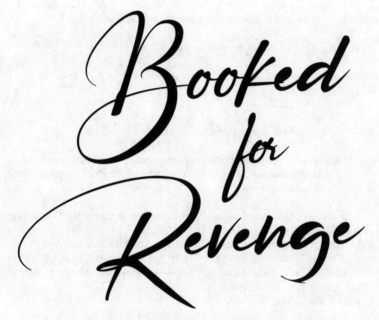

KAREN ROSE SMITH

KENSINGTON PUBLISHING CORP.

www.kensingtonbooks.com

KENSINGTON BOOKS are published by

Kensington Publishing Corp.
900 Third Ave.
New York, NY 10022

All Kensington titles, imprints, and distributed lines are available at special quantity discounts for bulk purchases for sales promotion, premiums, fund-raising, educational, or institutional use. Special book excerpts or customized printings can also be created to fit specific needs. For details, write or phone the office of the Kensington Special Sales Manager: Attn. Special Sales Department. Kensington Publishing Corp., 900 Third Ave., New York, NY 10022. Phone: 1-800-221-2647.

Library of Congress Control Number: 2024951080

KENSINGTON and the KENSINGTON COZIES teapot logo Reg. US Pat. & TM Off.

ISBN: 978-1-4967-4706-8
First Kensington Hardcover Edition: May 2025

ISBN: 978-1-4967-4708-2 (ebook)

10 9 8 7 6 5 4 3 2 1

Printed in the United States of America

The authorized representative in the EU for product safety and compliance is eucomply OU, Parnu mnt 139b-14, Apt 123
Tallinn, Berlin 11317, hello@eucompliancepartner.com

To my niece Sydney, a smart, kind, and amazing young woman. I fashioned Jazzi after her loveliness, liveliness, and independent spirit. I love you, Syd.

Acknowledgments

Thanks to Officer Greg Berry, my professional law enforcement consultant, who always provides the answers to my questions and as much information as I need.

Booked
for
Revenge

Chapter One

Jazzi Swanson often met friends at the food trucks near Belltower Landing's marina. Pontoon boats, day cruisers, and sailboats came and went from the many slips on this side of Lake Harding. With blue sky up above, aromas from falafels, stuffed waffles, pad Thai, and tacos drifted toward the marina and community center on this first day of August. However, she hadn't assembled with the crowd for street food.

Her fit and flare coral sundress lapped above her knees as she approached the judges' table for the special weekend event—Belltower Landing's Gentlemen's Bake-off. She smoothed her low ponytail that was cinched over her shoulder with a butterfly clip. She'd wanted to keep her long black hair in check in case wind from the lake was high.

Her business partner and best friend Dawn Fernsby rushed over to her. Dawn's short brown hair streaked with blond blew away from her high part and covered her eyes. She brushed her bangs over her brow.

"We could have a problem," Dawn warned. "I'm not sure these judges get along. Emmaline and Griffin have been squabbling as long as I've been here. What if they cause a scene during their book signing?"

The book signing event at Jazzi and Dawn's store, Tomes & Tea, had been planned to bring tourism to the resort town as well as more visibility for their bookshop and tea bar. "Maybe it's the crowd that's making them antsy. Or the sun beating down on them. I understand tomorrow a canopy will be set up over the judges' table," Jazzi said.

Jazzi studied the boardwalk that stretched from in front of the community center to the area around the marina and boat supply store. August heat in the mideighties danced off the boards as the crowd waited for the mayor's announcements about the weekend bake-off that would mostly take place at the community center.

The judges' table was covered with a yellow tablecloth. Royal blue swags decorated the front, and name placards large enough to be read from a distance identified the four well-known names from the culinary world.

Suddenly, Emmaline Fox, a famous scone baker now living in Ithaca, pushed herself up from her seat at the judges' table and faced down Griffin Pelham, a popular TV chef who was all over one of the home shopping networks selling his cookware.

Emmaline jabbed her pointer finger at Griffin, who'd risen too. Close to the head of the table, Jazzi heard Emmaline clearly as she berated Griffin in a strident voice.

"You know *Shop Time* is detrimental to the public, who doesn't need even half of what you're selling!"

"C'mon, Emmaline," Griffin snapped. "You realize I'm making money the good ole American way. You've been on my case for the past half hour. Let it go." His voice had risen too, and now some of the crowd had turned in the chefs' direction instead of eyeing the dais, where the mayor had taken his position at the microphone.

Jazzi and Dawn were concerned about all the judges at the table getting along amicably because they'd written cookbooks and would be signing them at Tomes & Tea after this initial introduction to the Gentlemen's Bake-off. The plan was to escort the judges to the bookshop after the mayor's introductions. Jazzi would rather have smooth waters to sail than rippling ones.

As Jazzi's thoughts careened around the idea of a tempestuous book signing, Emmaline and Griffin were still going at it. Emmaline's face, which was almost beet red, was a striking contrast to her almost-white curly hair. She was in her seventies, and Jazzi was afraid the older woman could have a heatstroke. Griffin was in his forties, fit and energetic, and could keep going with his word salad all day.

Stepping practically between them, Jazzi hoped to act as a buffer. With her hand at Emmaline's elbow to stop her flow of complaints, Jazzi suggested to Griffin, "Why don't you explain the benefits of your scone pan to Ms. Fox? It could make her baking easier."

Just as Emmaline sat again and Griffin opened his mouth, the mayor took his position at the microphone.

Rupert Harding, a descendant of Phineas J. Harding, who had founded Belltower Landing, liked to be the center of attention. With his white-and-gray, expensively styled hair making his round face even rounder, he wore a chartreuse-colored shirt, white cargo slacks, and moccasins. By his side stood his thirty-something nephew Charles, who as chief of staff stuck to his uncle like the proverbial glue.

"Gather round," Rupert invited the crowd as the mike made a squealing noise. After Charles adjusted the mike and the feedback ended, Rupert continued. "Welcome to our Gentlemen's Bake-off. Our judges whittled our recipe entrants down to twelve. I certainly hope these men know how to bake the recipes their wives or girlfriends submitted."

Everyone around Jazzi tittered. The mayor *tried* to be a comedian. Sometimes it worked.

"The preliminary round judging of ten entrants will happen

in our community center's own kitchen tomorrow morning. At noon, our judges will choose six men to go forward. Tomorrow late afternoon, the final four will be singled out from those six. Those four will go head-to-head on Sunday."

The mayor went on to explain the tier of prizes for the finalists. Then he introduced the judges.

Jazzi was only half-heartedly listening to the mayor as Dawn leaned into her. "Erica texted me that everything is ready at Tomes. But look at Emmaline Fox. I don't know if she'll be able to walk to the store."

Already introduced, Emmaline was fanning herself with a flyer that had been publicity for the bake-off. She was still flushed.

Jazzi took a closer look at Emmaline. "Maybe it wasn't such a great idea for the judges to walk to Tomes."

Dawn brushed a bead of perspiration from her forehead. "The mayor thinks that's the best way to showcase the storefronts on Lakeview Boulevard, especially if reporters are following and taping. Delaney set it up."

Their friend Delaney Fabron was a public relations specialist and had worked closely with the mayor on this event.

"Still . . . We don't want Emmaline to collapse or worse. Let me talk to Charles," Jazzi suggested.

As the mayor extolled the accomplishments of each of the four judges, Jazzi caught Charles Harding's eye and beckoned to him.

After glancing at his uncle, he hurried to Jazzi's side. "What?" he snapped.

Jazzi lifted her chin toward Emmaline, who had stooped to remove something from her large red designer tote bag. She'd plucked out what looked like a battery-powered fan and secured it on her neck. Jazzi could see Emmaline's hair moving.

"I think Emmaline will need a ride to Tomes. With her cane and this heat, she might not be up to the walk."

Charles glanced at Emmaline, then his uncle. "She shouldn't have agreed to judge if she can't sit through the judging or walk a few blocks." As the mayor's gatekeeper, Charles could be tactless and snarky.

"Her reputation has brought us publicity," Jazzi pointed out. "She is a renowned scone baker." Jazzi knew Charles studied the bottom line, whether in business or politics.

He gave a sigh and adjusted the neckline of his polo shirt. "All right. We don't want anyone collapsing. That wouldn't be a good look. Too many reporters around. I'll provide the gallantry and drive her myself. I'll alert that *Landing* reporter who's covering the bake-off. She wants an exclusive on the judging—first to know and all that."

After another look at the dais, he took his phone from its belt holster, typed in something, and hurried to the mayor.

Fifteen minutes later, Jazzi and Dawn were leading the judges and a group of tourists and residents of Belltower Landing down the tree-lined boulevard to their bookstore.

"I had no idea we'd act as pied pipers," Colleen Cross whispered to Jazzi as they walked.

Colleen, pastry chef at the Dockside Bakery and one of the judges, motioned behind her to the troops of spectators who followed them. Colleen had pixie-cut hair and plenty of freckles, making her look younger than her forty-plus years.

Griffin Pelham, who strode beside them, acerbically commented, "Let's just hope they all buy books to make this weekend worthwhile. I gave up an appearance on *Shop Time* to be here."

Colleen gave Griffin a sharp, chastising look.

"What?" he demanded. "You're here for the same reason, though your little cookbook doesn't stand up to the other judges' books, including mine."

Jazzi watched Colleen suck in a breath. She had worked hard to open her bakery in this resort town, and her drive made it flourish. Her cookbook was a compilation of recipes for her most popular baked goods. Granted, it wasn't as large and glossy as Diego Alvarez's, the fourth judge and a restaurateur from New York City who vacationed in Belltower Landing, but her cookbook sold well too *because* her bakery was right at hand.

A male voice in the bevy of people behind them announced loudly, "Pelham's cookbook was probably written by a ghost chef. All he knows how to cook is rare steak!"

Griffin stopped for a moment, and Jazzi was afraid he was about to confront the pedestrian in the shorts and red backward baseball cap, but then he started walking again. On his *Shop Time* television slots, he often *did* cook steak to tout his cookware.

Jazzi exchanged a long look with Dawn. They understood each other. Not only partners and best friends, they were roommates too, sharing the apartment above Tomes & Tea. Their telepathic message to each other was clear—this weekend could become more complicated than they'd planned.

Changing the subject from Griffin's TV appearance, Colleen asked Jazzi, "Do you know any of the contestants in the bake off? I understand about half are residents and half are tourists."

"A few of the men stop in at Tomes & Tea. Abe Ventrus is an EMT and firefighter," Jazzi said.

Colleen nodded. "He comes into my bakery now and then. He cooks for the fire station."

Dawn leaned close to Jazzi. "Abe is hot. And not just when he's dressed in fire gear."

Jazzi had to admit he was handsome in a rough-hewn, muscled way.

"I know Finn Yarrow," Dawn added, loud enough for Colleen to hear. "He's a photographer and videographer. He comes in to Tomes and worked at the weddings of a few friends."

Jazzi knew Finn too, at least to recognize him. He often sipped tea and studied coffee table books.

The rest of the stroll to the bookstore was uneventful. Everyone walked, chatted, and simply enjoyed the beautiful August day.

When they reached the store, Jazzi opened the door wide to let everyone pass by her and walk in. Once inside herself, she saw that her assistant, Erica Garcia, was settling Emmaline at the book-signing table. In preparation for the signing, Erica had set up a long table with enough room for all four judges to sit with their stacks of books beside them. Wearing her cobbler apron with the Tomes & Tea logo—a teapot sitting on a stack of books—Erica leaned close to Emmaline and handed her a bottle of water.

Erica was the perfect person to see that Emmaline had everything she needed. Erica's shoulder-length wavy hair was dark brown with strands of gray. After all, she did have three kids, two teen sons in high school now. Erica liked to mother everybody, and her sparkling bright eyes were filled with warmth and compassion. Her daughter, Audrey, helped out at Tomes, and she was making certain the other three judges were settled in too. In no time at all customers had lined up to have their books signed. A short time later, Jazzi and Audrey were working at the desk while Dawn circulated to make sure everything stayed on track.

After the first flush of customers had passed through the line, Erica showed Emmaline to the powder room. Jazzi had stopped at the table to make sure each judge had a solid stack of books. There, she heard Griffin say to Diego, "Emmaline's too old to be participating in this kind of an event. Just because she can still bake scones in her home kitchen doesn't mean she should participate in PR events. She can hardly walk with that cane."

Diego Alvarez, with his thick black hair smoothed back, his wide smile, and sparkling coffee-colored eyes, hadn't been overly chatty since the event began. He seemed professional in every look, gesture, and smile. From what Jazzi had heard, he ran his New York City restaurant with aplomb and was a financial success along with the restaurant's success, having a reputation for superb cuisine.

Leaning toward Griffin, he arched his brows. His voice held the wise timbre of experience. "Emmaline is *only* seventy-one. She has a lot of good years ahead of her. We should all wish we were doing something we love at her age."

Jazzi felt like applauding. Apparently, Diego was chivalrous too. She had to admit, a little bit of chivalry went a long way.

As Emmaline returned to the table and Erica made sure she was comfortable, Dawn sidled up to Jazzi. "How would you like to join me and my family on the pontoon boat for a Monday evening cruise? It will be a good break after the bustle of the weekend."

Jazzi liked that idea, but she asked, "Are you sure your parents are inviting me and not just you?"

Earlier in the summer Dawn's parents had wanted Dawn to sell her share of Tomes & Tea. But since Jazzi, Dawn, and their book club friends had suggested ideas that were making the bookstore more profitable, the Fernsbys had been slightly friendlier with Jazzi. The bottom line, though, was they were still leery that Jazzi would influence Dawn in her personal life, not simply in bookstore business. In college, Jazzi had met Dawn at a group for adoptees. They'd connected immediately, becoming fast friends. Jazzi had searched for her birth parents. Dawn hadn't . . . yet. Dawn's parents didn't want Jazzi to influence Dawn to take that step.

"They asked me to invite you," Dawn assured her. "We'll have a good time with the wind in our hair and waves making the boat rock."

Jazzi laughed. "I'd love to come. It's definitely something to look forward to, besides getting home to the kittens." She had found a kitten under their deck, and then she and Dawn had adopted that kitten's sister too. So they had the playful duo around the apartment constantly, giving them belly laughs and a chance to feel like kids again.

Keeping her eye on Emmaline, Jazzi could see she was in her element. Whatever squabble the scone baker had had with Griffin was eclipsed by her love of talking with anyone who wanted a signed copy of *Scones Meant for a King*, which explained basic baking techniques as well as recipes. Jazzi would ask Emmaline to sign a copy that Jazzi had purchased for her mother. Her mom and her aunt ran Daisy's Tea Garden in Pennsylvania and baked a lot.

Jazzi was appreciating the few minutes lull at the register, watching customers take selfies with the judges, when her phone vibrated from the pocket of the Tomes & Tea shop apron she'd donned after she'd returned to the store.

Charles Harding's number was on her display. "Hi, Charles. The signing is going well. The public seems excited about the bake-off."

"We've put a lot of money and effort into this. It had better pay off." He always seemed to be in a gruff mood. Charles constantly searched for publicity to promote the resort town.

"I'm calling about an immediate problem," he said. "Griffin, Colleen, and Diego can reach where they're staying on foot. But Emmaline can't. She actually took an Uber to come here from Ithaca. Something about her car needing repair. Can you make sure she's transported to the Starboard Resort and Golf Center safely and settles in? The town was booked up for the weekend, and that was the only place that had a suite that met her needs. Her luggage is already there. I'm just too busy to be chauffeuring her."

He seemed to be waiting for Jazzi's response because he sighed and asked, "Well, Jazzi, can you do it?"

"Belltower Landing does have Uber service," she reminded him, thinking of the cleanup after the book signing.

"That's so impersonal. After all, you wanted Emmaline at your store for the book signing."

He had a point. She appreciated the time all the judges were giving Tomes & Tea. Emmaline would probably not be comfortable in Jazzi's MINI Cooper, but Dawn's SUV would probably suit for the drive to the Starboard Resort.

"All right, Charles. Dawn and I will take good care of Emmaline."

As soon as she'd agreed, Charles ended the call with a "Great" rather than a thank you.

She had the feeling this was going to be a long weekend.

Chapter Two

Jazzi glanced around Tomes & Tea as she often did to make sure all customers were being helped, not just those at the signing table. Erica stood at the seaglass blue cubicles that were lit by neon blue and green LED lights, helping a customer at the sailboat section. The store's staff had eliminated two of their round tables with the enamel chairs in various colors in order to make room for the judges' table. Jazzi and Dawn tried to keep the shop bright and cheery during all four seasons in New York State.

As Jazzi studied the tea bar, the Sputnik chandelier illuminated the baked goods case as well as the bar where Audrey was serving tea. Audrey was a pet sitter most of the time, but she supplemented her income by working at Tomes & Tea.

The door to the bookshop opened and Delaney Fabron stepped inside. She met Jazzi at the sales desk. "How's it going?"

"It seems to be going well. The rush of customers is dwindling but it's still busy."

Delaney's smile lit up her face. She was usually sophistication personified, with her uneven, wispy hairstyle and false eyelashes. She was a regular member of the Tomes & Tea book club. "Did the mayor stop in?" she asked.

"No. In fact, Charles asked me to take Emmaline to her hotel after the book signing."

"I imagine they're busy coordinating everything at the community center for tomorrow, including bringing in convection ovens to accommodate the entrants. The mayor is determined this event will go off without a hitch. But events like this always have a snag."

"Why?" Jazzi asked.

Delaney shrugged. "We're integrating different promotions. The Spatula Palace stocked up on Griffin's cookware."

The kitchen shop was everyone's favorite for gourmet items, special seasonings, and everyday cookware. "I heard Griffin is making an appearance there later today," Jazzi said.

"Yep, he's on the move as much as he can be."

Just then, Griffin stood from his chair and glared down at Emmaline. Jazzi heard him say in a loud voice that everyone could hear, "You don't have to degrade me in front of my customers."

"I can't help it," Emmaline shot back. "Your customer is complaining about one of your pans. Maybe you should fix whatever the problem is."

Griffin walked off in a huff and headed toward the door.

"Those two have been squabbling all morning," Jazzi said. "I'm not sure what to do about it except separate them at the judges' table. But I didn't want to embarrass either of them."

"Maybe you could find a more comfortable chair for Emmaline and move her to the other end of the table. Just tell her she'll have more room there. I don't know if it will work, but you can try it." Delaney's last words sounded after her as she headed toward Griffin.

Jazzi beckoned to Erica and her salesclerk came over to her. She explained what she wanted to do. "Let's just separate

Emmaline and Griffin," she said in a whisper. "It might help. Delaney is going to keep him from leaving, I hope. I'll bring my desk chair from the break room. If you could gather up Emmaline's stack of books, I think that will work."

By the time Delaney had convinced Griffin to return inside, the changes had been made. He seemed grateful to be sitting between Colleen and Diego, rather than next to Emmaline. Jazzi wondered how Emmaline could get on his nerves so completely. Maybe she reminded him of his mother? So many feelings swirled around the subject of mothers.

Because Jazzi had been adopted, she'd held questions in her heart about her birth parents while she was growing up. When her dad died and her mom moved her and her sister to Willow Creek, Pennsylvania, where she had been born and bred, Jazzi had decided to search for her birth mother. At fifteen, she'd been successful with her mother's help. But juggling her mom and her birth mom's relationships had been a struggle at times. Her mom had tried to make it easier for her by being cooperative, compassionate, and encouraging the bonds. But how could it be easy? Not possible.

Jazzi had a good relationship with them both now. She'd been to Willow Creek for a few days last month. It had been good catching up with her mom and stepdad and the rest of her family. Still, she found she needed to keep a bit of distance between Belltower Landing and her former life in Willow Creek. After all, at twenty-five, she should be on her own and deciding her own life's course, shouldn't she?

Delaney stayed for the next half hour, making sure everything was running smoothly. At one point Jazzi teased her, saying, "The mayor might hire you for his office to help with public relations and brainstorm further promotions for Belltower Landing."

Delaney considered the idea. "I like working for myself, and I don't know if I'd want him as a boss. But this Gentlemen's

Bake-off seems to be more popular than if professional chefs were competing. It was a good idea. I do come up with them now and then."

Jazzi was straightening one of the stand-alone bookshelves, surreptitiously watching the cookbook authors sign books, when the bell announcing another customer walking in took her attention. She looked up and her heart skipped a beat.

The man who had just walked in was Oliver Patel. He owned The Wild Kangaroo pub and had a superb Australian accent. Jazzi and Oliver had gone bike riding over the summer and even shared a couple of food truck waffle breakfasts. But they hadn't gone on a date, and Jazzi still wasn't sure if she was ready for that complication in her life. She didn't know much about Oliver, and the hurts in her past had left scars. But she had to admit, if he asked her out, she could be tempted.

As Oliver spotted Jazzi, he lifted his hand and waved to acknowledge her. Then he went to the signing table, right to Diego Alvarez's line. Oliver wanting to speak to Diego made absolute sense, restaurateur to restaurateur.

She continued straightening books and helping customers until Oliver finally came to her in the back of the store. He was carrying two of Diego's books.

"Hi, there," she said. "Do you plan to read his cookbook twice?" Now wasn't *that* lame? Jazzi thought.

Oliver laughed. "Not quite. My chef asked me to pick him up a copy, and I wanted one for myself. How's it going in here?"

"It's been busy. It's had its ups and downs. Two of the judges don't get along well."

Oliver was at least six-foot-two with short wavy blond hair that was a little bit longish on the top. The style seemed to emphasize his jaw, which was sharp and determined under his scruffy beard. His blue, blue eyes were absolutely amazing.

Jazzi caught the scent of his woodsy aftershave as he leaned closer to her. "I bet I can guess which two," he said with confidence.

"Seriously? Who do you think?"

"Emmaline Fox and Griffin Pelham."

"How could you guess that?" She tried to keep the surprise from her voice.

"The culinary world is as small as any other mix of professionals," he pointed out.

Jazzi knew any professional community could have rumors and gossip running rampant. "So there's gossip about them?"

Oliver gave a nod. "When the chefs for the bake-off were sent invitations, the buzzing started."

"Can you tell me what's at the bottom of this? Maybe I could step in more and help them solve it."

Shaking his head, Oliver sent her a wry smile. "Jazzi, you can't fix everybody's problems."

"No, but I want to keep them civil to each other while they're in my store. And think of the bake-off weekend. What if they're fighting the whole time?"

He studied her, thought about it, then gave in. "The rumor I heard was that Emmaline wanted Griffin to give her a spot on one of his shows and let her bake a few scones in his pans."

Jazzi covered her mouth with her hand. "Oh, my gosh. I suggested Emmaline use Griffin's scone pan."

Oliver chuckled. "I bet Emmaline loved *that* suggestion."

"I can't keep them from squabbling. The mayor set out guidelines for contestants not to interact with judges. But the judges can consult with each other."

"So the contestants can't buy a signed cookbook?"

"They can pick one up after a winner is chosen and ask to have it signed. It's another reason Dawn and I are keeping our eyes on the lines of people speaking to the chefs."

"First prize is one thousand dollars," Oliver mused. "Not

ten thousand. Not twenty thousand. The mayor is treating this as if it were a high stakes competition on the Food Network."

"That's our mayor," Jazzi said sweetly. "And he's right to devote his attention to the integrity of the competition, but sometimes he goes overboard."

"I would have liked to have met the original Phineas J. Harding, who developed the town of Belltower Landing," Oliver offered. "He must have been an overachiever. When I first arrived in this town, I went to the Historical Society just to look up the history of the place. Phineas's ancestors made their wealth off the trains and big oil. When he drew up the plans for Belltower Landing himself, he had some talent about him. His motto was 'A Harmonious and Joyous Life.'"

"Who doesn't want that?" Jazzi asked. "I guess he wanted anyone who came to Lake Harding to have a good time and enjoy themselves and relax. And if they stayed, build a solid life here."

"Is that what you're doing?" Oliver asked, his serious blue eyes almost boring into her brown ones.

What was he really asking her?

She didn't have time to find out because Dawn came over and pulled her toward the sales desk. A customer had a question Dawn couldn't answer.

Reluctantly, Jazzi stepped away from Oliver with her "Excuse me" and his "See you around." But it was hard to tear her gaze from his.

After the book signing had ended, Jazzi and Dawn both thanked each of the chefs for contributing to the fun day. Emmaline opened the gift bag that Jazzi had given her. Each of the judges had received a bag with Tomes & Tea tea in a souvenir box along with imported chocolates. It was just a small thank you, but Emmaline seemed delighted.

Studying the box of chocolates, she said, "My suite is supposed to have a microwave and a refrigerator. The mayor told me someone would be taking me to lunch after the book signing."

That was news to Jazzi. She and Dawn had decided Jazzi could use Dawn's SUV and drive Emmaline to the Starboard. Now it looked as if they'd be stopping for lunch on the way. Jazzi wondered if the mayor was footing the bill for that.

"Where would you like to stop for lunch?" Jazzi stacked up leftover copies of *Scones Meant for A King* that Emmaline had signed. "Belltower Landing has all kinds of cuisines. The restaurants will be busy today, but I'm sure we can snag a table somewhere."

Emmaline looked thoughtful. "Speaking of snags—" She grinned. "I understand The Wild Kangaroo serves barbecued snags with mashed potatoes and grilled onions. Is that true?"

"That's often the special on their menu." Jazzi checked her watch. "The lunch crowd will be in full swing at The Wild Kangaroo right now. Do you want me to call and see if I can reserve us a table?" She knew Oliver would do that for her if she asked.

Emmaline was wearing a caftan with huge red roses on a white background. She adjusted the neckline, then she tucked the small bag of chocolates and tea into her tote bag. In a low voice, she said to Jazzi, "I have to admit, I'm pretty tired. I don't have as much energy as I used to. Do you think maybe we could just pick up lunch and go to my hotel?"

"Of course, we can. I'll call and order those barbecued snags. Is there anything you'd like with it?"

"Do you think we could pick up a sandwich for later? I certainly don't want to have to go out again."

"The Starboard has room service."

"I heard that. But I might be resting. I don't really want to be bothered. I can just stuff the sandwich into the refrigerator and have it later."

Emmaline did seem wan and tired, so Jazzi agreed. "Why

don't you freshen up? I'll order lunch, then I'll go get the car and we'll be ready to go."

"Can you watch my tote so I don't have to carry it into the bathroom with me?"

"Of course."

As Emmaline made her way to the powder room, Jazzi took out her phone and made the call to The Wild Kangaroo. Standing by Emmaline's chair with the tote, she spotted Finn Yarrow speaking with Griffin. Her senses went on alert. As a contestant, Finn shouldn't be anywhere near the judges. The conversation didn't last long. Both men had smiles on their faces, and they shook hands before Finn passed by Jazzi and left the store.

Griffin had a few books in hand as he stopped by the table to pick up his small gift bag. Giving a pointed look at Emmaline's chair, he said, "Thank you, Jazzi. This event went as smoothly as possible with me and Emmaline being forced together."

Attempting to be diplomatic, Jazzi said, "I guess the two of you are just strong personalities."

Griffin laughed. "You could say that. We have a history. I'll just make sure I'm not seated next to her at the judges' table, then we can avoid any conflict."

"Was that Finn Yarrow I saw you speaking with?"

"Yes, it was. I know the judges aren't supposed to converse with contestants, but that had nothing to do with the judging or cooking or baking."

"No?" Jazzi prompted.

"No, not at all. Finn was trying to convince me to use his services for my next cookbook. He says he has a portfolio, and I might take a look at it. Maybe taking wedding photographs doesn't pay well enough anymore since everyone can shoot great photos with their phones."

"That's nice of you to consider it."

"I was going to give him an automatic no, but then Finn claims he has a unique way of shooting food that can capture an audience's notice. I'm always interested in a unique way to sell my products and maybe even another cookbook. That could be a win-win."

Books in hand that he'd chosen to purchase for himself, Griffin pointed his chin toward the sales counter. "I'm going to give you another sale and then rent a pontoon boat for the evening. I want to take advantage of that beautiful lake."

"Have a good evening," Jazzi said as he headed for the sales counter.

Forty-five minutes later, Jazzi had picked up lunch orders at The Wild Kangaroo, and she and Emmaline were riding the elevator up to Emmaline's suite. Jazzi had parked as close to the building with its green architectural-shingled roof as she could.

After Emmaline had used her key card to open the hotel room door, she and Jazzi stepped inside. Jazzi could see the mayor had reserved Emmaline a suite on the second floor for a reason. It wasn't as posh as the executive suites on higher levels. Delaney had described those. This one was still well equipped.

Emmaline's gaze swept over the teal sofa. It faced a corner fireplace with a TV mounted above it. Jazzi guessed the fireplace was electric for mood rather than warmth. French doors led to a balcony. The kitchen did have a small refrigerator, a microwave, and a two-burner stovetop. A teal glassy backsplash sat between the upper white cabinets and the lower ones.

"I'd better make sure my luggage is here." Emmaline headed toward the single bedroom.

Jazzi peeked in behind her and saw the statement wall was painted teal. The room was simple, with a queen-sized bed and a nightstand with a lamp. A small dresser sat against one wall, and Jazzi could see into the en suite, which had a wide door leading from the bedroom. There were grab bars on the shower, which was elegantly tiled. The plate glass doors slid on chromed rollers, and the single vanity would probably give Emmaline enough room to lay out her toiletries.

"I'll set out our lunch." Jazzi crossed to the table for two that sat near the French doors that lead out to a balcony. "I didn't know what you like to drink so I added bottled water to our order. You'll have a couple of bottles for later."

"You're a doll," Emmaline gushed. "There aren't many younger folks like you who like to associate with a senior like me."

Jazzi pulled containers from a bag and set them on the table, one across from the other. The food smelled delicious, and aromas filled the sitting area. "My aunt is in her sixties, and I love spending time with her and my grandparents. I've spent time with my mom's older friends too, having tea and sometimes even scones."

"Then you're a rare specimen." Emmaline came over to the table, checking the barbecued snags, mashed potatoes, and grilled onions.

Jazzi nodded to the other bag on the table. "Do you want me to stow the sandwich in your refrigerator?"

Emmaline sank heavily into one of the padded chairs. "That would be wonderful. I have no energy left. Today really sucked all energy out of me."

"The heat and the adrenalin from dealing with fans probably got the best of you. That adrenalin's probably leaking out about now." Jazzi pushed the sandwich into the mini-refrigerator. "You'll be able to rest this evening and the first judging isn't until ten tomorrow morning. I'll make sure Charles has a ride scheduled for you that will take you to the community center. I think the lounge at the center will be set up so you'll have a place to rest in between judgings."

After Jazzi sat across from Emmaline, she opened her bottle of water and began digging into the snags and potatoes. "You and Griffin seem to have a history."

"We do. Ever since he asked me to come to his show and

praise his cookware, and I said no, he's had a burr up his butt."
She looked embarrassed. "Pardon my language."

Jazzi suppressed a smile. That wasn't the story Griffin told,
according to Oliver. "Did you know each other long before
that?"

"We ran into each other at food festivals and chef conferences.
He always seemed pleasant. But after he developed his cookware
and found spots on shows to sell it, he became more . . . cutthroat. I suppose at his age business is all-important. But it's better not to burn bridges, I guess. I suppose it's his attitude that
bothers me the most. If someone can't help him make another
sale, get further in his career, put him on another spotlight show,
then he has no time or patience for them . . . for me . . . for
anyone."

After they ate for a while in silence, Emmaline looked up at
Jazzi. "Do you want to know what the real controversy has
been that has been sort of kept under wraps?"

Jazzi's innate curiosity took over. "What *is* the real story?"

Emmaline's grin was a bit wicked. "That Griffin stole the
specifications for his rondeau pan from another company."

Rumor? Or an actual charge? "Are there any lawsuits
about it?"

"Not that I know of. Apparently, the other company found
out they had an employee who leaked the information to Griffin. They can't trace any money that changed hands, but I bet
you Griffin paid somebody a pretty penny for those specifications."

"Certainly authorities could trace the money. Police depart-
ments do that all the time." Jazzi knew that because of the murder
investigations her mother had been involved in. Daisy Swanson
had helped detectives solve ten murder cases and Jazzi had
picked up information all along the way.

"Griffin has connections, and apparently this stayed in the
civil realm instead of the criminal realm. Someone has to put

out that money for the civil investigations. Griffin got away with it this time."

"And you expect there to be a next time?"

Emmaline's face crinkled with certainty. "Absolutely. Men like Griffin Pelham don't play by the rules."

Jazzi didn't like the sound of that. "Hopefully, as a judge, he'll play fair and square."

But she wondered, *What if he didn't?*

Chapter Three

Jazzi and Dawn were still straightening up Tomes & Tea from the book signing the day before when the door opened and Farrell Fernsby walked in. Dawn's brother was two years older than she was. He wasn't tall, maybe about five-nine, and had his brown hair buzz-cut short.

"Hey, Sis, I need to talk to you."

Dawn had a stack of Colleen's cookbooks in her arms when he approached. "Give me a minute," she said. "These are signed copies, and I don't want to get them mixed with the ones that aren't signed."

Jazzi extended her arms to Dawn. "Here, I'll take those." She did and moved behind them to a display table.

Farrell gave Jazzi a nod. It wasn't exactly a thank you. Then he asked Dawn, "Can we go back to your break room? This is important."

"I can't go to the break room now." Dawn motioned to the customers who were starting to stream in. "These people want cookbooks before the first judging. We can talk right here."

Jazzi set down the books on the table. She glanced over her shoulder in time to see Farrell's frown. "All right. If you insist on doing it here," he agreed begrudgingly. "I want you to come with me to Naples. I'm considering a space for a satellite store for Rods to Boards."

"Why do you want *me* to come along? It should be Mom or Dad."

"They're too busy with this bake-off. More customers than usual have been coming in."

When Dawn shook her head, her long puka shell earrings swung. "I won't have time until next week. I can't just drive off with you and leave all this." She motioned to the line at the sales desk where Audrey and Erica were helping customers.

"You know it's all *her* fault," Farrell said, pointing to Jazzi. "She roped you in to thinking about your birth parents, and now this store and the idea of a search is all you think about."

"Farrell, whatever gave you that idea? It's not true. I was attending that adoptees' support group at college even before Jazzi was. Yes, we met up there. Yes, we bonded on the issue. Yes, we became roommates because we like each other. Yes, we became partners because we wanted to build Tomes & Tea into a success. But she has no influence over what I intend to do about my biolgical parents."

Dawn glanced over her shoulder and noticed no one was watching them, at least no one but Jazzi.

"I don't believe that for a minute," he protested. "Mom said Jazzi searched for her biological mother and she found her. And that messed up her relationship with her mom who raised her. Why do you think Jazzi lives here, so far away from her home?"

Closing her eyes, Jazzi wanted to curl up into a ball in the corner and pretend she wasn't there. But she couldn't. She was hearing this even though she didn't want to.

"You have your facts all wrong, and if you got them from Mom, then *she* has them all wrong. She knows better. Jazzi has a relationship with both her biological mother and her adoptive mom. I can only hope that's what I would have some day, but I haven't made up my mind yet. If you keep poking at me like this, getting in the way of what I want for my life, then I might go searching even faster."

Farrell looked really disturbed. "Mom and Dad and I are only thinking about your future, and we don't think it's in this bookshop."

Jazzi's best friend spread her feet apart and squared her shoulders. Her apron covered most of her body, but her stance seemed to shout "Don't mess with me." Out loud, she said, "I don't want any responsibility in Mom and Dad's business. I'm adulting. I'm carving out my own life. Isn't that what parents should want for their children? If you want to manage the satellite store and you want to take over the business someday, you go ahead and do it. As you can see, I'm not telling *you* what to do."

"You're impossible," he decided. Shooting a look full of daggers at Jazzi, he stalked out of the shop.

Quietly, Jazzi came up behind Dawn. "I shouldn't have heard all that. I wish I hadn't. Your parents and your brother think I'm interfering in your life."

"Yes, but *we* know you're not."

"If you want to go with Farrell to the satellite store location, go ahead. I'll call in temporary help."

"No, just because he's older doesn't mean he knows best. I just wish—"

Jazzi watched Dawn's eyes glisten over. She was close to tears and Jazzi knew why. "You want their approval. I get that. I think I moved this far away from Willow Creek so I could figure out what I need to do to make my own life. It's not that

I don't love my family. I do. And they love me enough to let me do this, whatever *this* might be." She motioned around the bookstore.

"I'm here for you, Jazzi. For the long haul." Dawn gave her a huge hug.

That hug came with a responsibility for friendship. Jazzi hoped she was supporting Dawn the best way she could.

Jazzi's staff was taking care of the end-of-the-day customers on Saturday at Tomes while she scooted to the bake-off to see who the finalists were. She'd almost arrived at the judges' table under the tent when she heard loud male voices near the community center's main door. Two men were standing under the portico. When she took a good long look, she saw that it was Finn Yarrow and Tim Blanchard, two of the men who were contestants in the bake-off. If they'd been having a discussion, it had turned heated.

Finn's sandy hair had dropped down over his brow, and his hands were balled in fists by his side. Tim's face was red, his shoulders were hunched, and he looked ready to push Finn.

Jazzi spotted Parker Olsen, a close friend, in the gallery of watchers. Then she spotted Oliver exiting the side door of the center from the kitchen.

Tim did push Finn then. She heard him flick the word "immoral" at Finn. Finn had his arm cocked, accusing Tim of being "the problem." Before she could sound an alarm, Oliver and Parker had approached the men, one at Tim's side and one at Finn's. Emmaline, who had stood up at the judges' table, seeming to ignore the dishes in front of her, looked scandalized.

Jazzi heard her say, "I'm going to withdraw from this judging. Those two are ruining this."

By then Oliver and Parker had separated Finn and Tim.

They went their separate ways, but not far. Apparently, they wanted to hear the results of the judging.

Jazzi approached Emmaline but Delaney was already there, saying, "It's over, Emmaline. It's all right. We can go on with the judging now. You can enjoy these lovely desserts."

Colleen, who sat next to Emmaline, said, "I'm surprised by Finn's involvement in that. He's been the photographer of many of my confections at the wedding receptions I bake for. He's never been anything but professional and polite."

Thinking back on her experience at the beginning of the summer, Jazzi knew people weren't always who they seemed to be. She'd certainly been duped. As Delaney soothed Emmaline and the baker sat to taste the desserts in front of her, Jazzi approached Oliver and Parker, who were still standing near the community center's main door.

"What was that all about?" she asked.

"They were growling at each other," Oliver explained. "Tim was accusing Finn of something, but I couldn't catch what it was. I've got to get back to the Kangaroo. The community center's kitchen manager wanted to consult with me about buying supplies." His blue eyes scanned Jazzi's face. "Are you going to be around for the rest of the bake-off?"

"I'll be here for the final tasting tomorrow."

"I'll try to stop over. The band that will be playing at intermission before the mayor announces the winner plays at the Kangaroo. I think you heard them play there. I always tell diners not to let their name prejudice their opinion."

"Let me guess," Jazzi said. "The Snob Barrel."

Oliver's grin held a world of amusement. "They're the ones."

Jazzi was laughing when Oliver turned to leave. She especially noted his broad shoulders, his slim waist, his long legs.

Suddenly a noise rushed her back to the here and now. She recognized that it was Parker clearing his throat.

"You have a thing for him, don't you?"

Jazzi swirled around so fast her skirt twirled around her knees. "I don't have a thing."

"You might not be dating him, but you *do* have a thing. He looks at you the same way you look at him."

"Parker, really. Stop it. Oliver and I got shot at once. That makes some kind of bond, but we're nothing more than . . . friends."

"Friends, like you and I are friends?"

"You and I are good friends. We've known each other for a while. I still don't know much about Oliver."

"But you'd like to."

"Oliver is . . . intriguing, that's all."

Oliver had shared that his parents had divorced when he was young and he'd spent some of his time in the United States and some in Australia. He'd even worked at an animal camp for wildfire rescues.

"Intriguing more than any man you've ever met?" Parker prompted, studying her with more diligence than she liked.

"I don't know, Parker. Let's stop this, okay? You're embarrassing me."

"Maybe because everything I said is true."

She gave a hefty sigh to show her displeasure. "I want to get back to the subject of Tim and Finn."

"Sure, you do. Okay. I'll let you change the subject . . . for now. What about them?"

"You heard them arguing too, right?"

"Oliver was closer."

"Did you feel it was related to this contest?"

"You mean arguing about their baking skills?" Parker looked at her askance, as if he wouldn't even reply to that.

"Well, if not the contest, then what?" Her curiosity was definitely aroused.

"I think it was personal."

"Personal how?" she asked, pushing him.

Parker shifted his gaze away from Jazzi, as if he were thinking about it. "I think it was personal because Tim mumbled something about a problem with Finn's house."

After thinking about that for a few moments, Jazzi said, "Tim is a plumber, right? Do you think he could have done work at Finn's and there was a problem with the bill?"

"I guess that's possible. I really don't know any more than that. I *do* know Emmaline seems serious about cutting out. Then what would happen to your bake-off?"

Jazzi nodded to the judges' table, where all the judges were tasting desserts and marking score cards that had been provided. "Soon we'll know the four finalists for tomorrow."

"Once we do, do you want to get a bite to eat at one of the food trucks?" Parker looked that way.

Jazzi thought about it. "I really should get back to my apartment. I didn't spend much time with the kittens the past couple of days. I didn't even go up to feed them at lunchtime today. Dawn did."

Zander and Freya were now four months old. They had the run of the apartment but still had to be checked on, played with, and cuddled.

Parker appeared disappointed at her refusal to have dinner with him, so she asked, "Why don't you come back to the apartment with me? We can both play with the kittens, and then I'll make us something. I have fish Dawn's dad caught. We've been waiting for the right time to fry them, and we can roast vegetables with the fillets. What do you say?"

"I think that's a great idea."

Jazzi considered the best way to spend a Saturday evening was with Parker, Dawn, and the kittens. They'd probably play board games. They might even break out the new chocolate chip ice cream for dessert. How could anything else compare to that?

The devil on her shoulder tapped her and whispered, "Maybe a date with Oliver?"

As Jazzi sat on her bed early Sunday morning with her laptop open, Zander chased Freya across her bed, and they tumbled onto the floor together. Zander's basic coat of fluffy white fur was as soft as cotton, patterned with dark gray and brown designs from his ruff to his tail. His tail was a sweeping hairy fluff feather. White fur from his coat played from his eyes to his chin, and the black markings along his eyes looked like eyeliner. It always made Jazzi smile when she spied the design in the middle of his nose that resembled a heart.

Oliver had found Freya in an empty box at the back of his restaurant. Knowing Jazzi had found a kitten, he'd brought her over, thinking they were brother and sister. They'd seemed bonded. Freya was all black, precious with fuzzy hair. The kittens grounded Jazzi when she came home after work. For some reason they signified that her apartment with Dawn was home.

Soon she'd have to go down to Tomes & Tea and pick up the things she needed for the book display at the dessert judging. Dawn had set it up under the tent yesterday, and Jazzi was going to oversee it today. The display was added recognition for the chefs and good publicity for the bookstore.

There was a rap on Jazzi's door and Dawn appeared, still looking sleepy. She wasn't as early a riser as Jazzi. Dawn looked around Jazzi's bedroom, with its whitewashed furniture, lilac-and-blue patterned bedspread and curtains, and sun flowing in the window. Jazzi could tell she was looking for the kittens.

"I think they dove under the bed," she said with a smile. "Some of their toys are under there."

"Do you need help carrying everything for the display to the car?" Dawn asked.

"No. I have it all in a box. I should be fine."

"You might even find a gentleman to help you carry the box from your car to the table."

"I won't need help."

Dawn's frown was exaggerated. "You *do* make it hard for a man to fall into your good graces."

They'd had this discussion many times before. Jazzi didn't date and she was totally aware of the reasons why. When she was a sophomore in college, she'd transferred to her boyfriend's college at the University of Delaware. She'd intended to continue her B.S. degree in human services there. But after she'd transferred, Mark had broken up with her instead of forming a tighter bond. That had been a huge disappointment because he'd been her first serious relationship. She'd uprooted her life for him. She swore often to Dawn, "I won't ever change my life for a man again."

Soon after Jazzi had joined an adoption group at college, she'd decided to search for her biological father. She'd discovered that he'd died during military service in Afghanistan. That knowledge, along with her breakup with Mark, had affected her deeply. Whereas Dawn wore her heart on her sleeve, Jazzi tried to keep her heart safe.

Making a life for herself in Belltower Landing, where Dawn lived, had been Jazzi's way of separating herself from her past and growing as an adult. This town was quirky. She enjoyed the lake, learning how to paddleboard and kayak. A monetary gift from her grandparents, who had sold their decades-established nursery business in Willow Creek, had enabled her to buy the bookshop with Dawn. Her sister, Vi, and her husband had been able to put a hefty down payment on a house.

Diverting Dawn's attention, Jazzi motioned to her laptop. *The Landing*, the town newspaper, had posted an article on their home page about the final four contestants who would be judged this morning. The article profiled each finalist.

Jazzi said to Dawn, "The newspaper must have had the profiles ready to go. They give a history of Tim Blanchard's plumbing company. For Finn Yarrow they mention his wedding photography but also the fact that he photographed charity galas here and in Ithaca. They play up the fact that Abe Ventrus has saved many lives as a firefighter and EMT. They mention the fact that Carl West has fitted boats for some celebrities."

The kittens darted out from under the bed and ran into the kitchen. "Did you feed them?" Dawn asked.

"I did, or their meows would have wakened you earlier."

"Does *The Landing* list what the men will be baking?" Dawn asked.

"Oh yes. Carl is baking a strawberry shortcake, and he seems to be the front-runner, but Finn is planning to make a Black Forest cake. That could be hard to beat."

"Abe?"

Jazzi knew that Dawn might be interested in Abe. "Abe is making éclairs."

"And how about Tim?" Dawn asked.

"Lemon meringue pie. That meringue could be tough in the heat today."

"Have you ever made a lemon meringue pie?"

"*No*, but I watched my mom and my grandma make them many times. They're not as easy as they look. If the meringue's not baked just right, in this hot weather it could weep." Jazzi closed her laptop. "Do you think you'll be able to get away for the final judging?"

"I hope so, but I'll see how busy the store is."

"I'll text you when the judging starts."

"Wear something cool," Dawn warned as she left Jazzi's room.

Jazzi slid off the bed and went to her closet, ready for the day to begin.

When Jazzi reached the community center, the bake-off was still going on. Delaney stood near the judges' table and called to her. "We had a delay in starting. They're assembling. You can watch in the kitchen if you want."

The fun of the bake-off was watching the bakers work in the open-concept kitchen and dining area. After Jazzi entered the area, she could see they were all in different stages of assembling their desserts. Most of the onlookers had straggled out onto the boardwalk, where the judges' tent was located. Still many milled around the kitchen islands, watching how the bakers were plating their desserts.

Jazzi stopped at Abe Ventrus's station first. She imagined he was a little more experienced than the others since he cooked for the group at the firehouse. For the most part his section of the kitchen was cleaned up. He was in the process of drizzling chocolate over the top of each éclair. That made her mouth water.

Dressed in a fire company T-shirt and worn jeans, he looked up, his eyes sparkling bright. "Do you have any advice on how I should drizzle my chocolate?" he asked with a smile.

"I'm just watching to see how you do it."

In a lowered voice, he joked, "The word around town is that you know desserts."

She didn't know what the word around town was. Her friends knew her mom and aunt ran Daisy's Tea Garden and were terrific cooks and bakers besides businesswomen. But she'd kept secret her mom being involved in solving murders. It was such a big thing that had overshadowed her life in Willow Creek that she'd decided just to keep that info about her mom private. "My mom is a fabulous baker. My aunt and my grandma are, too."

"Professionally?" he asked with an eyebrow raised.

"My mom and aunt own a tea garden in Pennsylvania. That's where I've gotten my love of tea and baked goods. Hardly a meal went by that we didn't eat something homemade and sweet."

"Then you *do* know how I should dribble this. Right to left or left to right?"

It was easy to see that Abe was used to flirting. He had that cute boy charm along with some macho firefighter personality. That was an attractive mix.

"I'd say left to right, but you need to do what you think is good."

Finished with the drizzle, he lifted his fingers to his lips and kissed them in a gesture she'd often seen cooks make. "Perfection. Creamy, light, and fluffy. The judges will love them."

She laughed.

Moving on to Finn Yarrow's station, she noticed he was stoning cherries on the granite cutting board on his side of the sink. The cake on his portion of the island looked magnificent. Jazzi knew from her history with desserts that Black Forest cake combined chocolate cake layers with fresh cherries, cherry liqueur, and whipped cream frosting. Finn had added his own touches—long shards of chocolate surrounded the entire cake. On top there were whipped cream circles. She imagined that the cherries he was pitting now would go in each of those circles.

He must have sensed her presence because he turned to see her and smiled. "Do you approve?"

"Yes, I approve. Chocolate, whipped cream, and cherries. What's not to approve of?"

He gave an offhanded lift of his hand. "I just hope none of the judges have an allergy to cherries. I have a cousin who does, and her lips swell up something awful if she eats one."

"I can't imagine they'd be judging if they had allergies to anything food related. You never know what a contestant might include in his baked goods."

Finn gave her a knowing look and smiled smugly. "Exactly."

She proceeded on to Carl West's station. He was still assembling his cake. There were three vanilla cake layers, and he was spreading butter cream over a layer.

"What kind of butter cream?" she asked him.

"Swiss butter cream." He ran his hand through his hair. "I'm going to heap those macerated strawberries right in the center."

"And then you'll add them on top too?"

"Yes, I will. This is going to be the winner."

Looking at the unassembled cake, she wasn't sure. But when it was assembled, the judges might just decide it was the prize winner. She didn't know if vanilla cake and strawberries could win over chocolate cake and cherries.

Tim Blanchard was just removing his lemon meringue pie from the oven. It looked beautiful. Candied lemon peels waited in a pan on the stove.

He looked over at her. "As soon as these cool, they go on top of the meringue. The judges are going to love this."

She knew Tim made his own pie shells. Dawn had told her it would be a butter crust. The judges had received copies of the recipes beforehand so they could judge the ingredients when they tasted the finished product.

Dawn waved to Jazzi and joined her. "I'm here. Are you going to watch the judges taste these confections?"

"Is Tomes locked up tight?"

"It surely is. I even popped upstairs to see Zander and Freya. They're fine until we get back."

Jazzi had taken down the curtains in her bedroom and just left up the valance. That kept the little hooligans from climbing up the panels. She and Dawn had tried to catproof the apartment as much as possible.

Fifteen minutes later, while everyone milled around, Jazzi heard the bell ring in the community center. That meant it was time for the contestants to bring their offerings out to the judges. Each contestant carried a large tray with four dishes of dessert. They set their identical offerings in front of each of the judges.

Jazzi stood with Dawn and Parker in a cluster of people close enough to see the expressions on the judges' faces as they ate the desserts. It was hard to tell their opinions as they sampled each one. They seemed to enjoy them all. Who wouldn't like these classic desserts?

As each of the judges handed their score cards to the mayor, Snob Barrel began to play. Tall speakers on the boardwalk projected guitar, drum, and clarinet music across the area. Jazzi suspected what the mayor or Delaney had in mind—gathering more tourists to the event's conclusion.

People came and went during the half-hour intermission while the mayor and his nephew computed the score cards. Jazzi watched as Emmaline went into the community center, probably for air-conditioning and to redo her makeup.

The contestants could mingle with the judges now that the judging had ended. Jazzi watched as the mayor took his place at the podium.

Emmaline emerged from the community center, heavily using her cane. Jazzi supposed she was beyond tired. Following her progress, she noticed Colleen appeared to give her a hand with her chair. Diego walked across the boardwalk, said something to Emmaline, and she smiled. The smile faded when Griffin joined them.

The band was still playing. Mayor Harding, with a wide smile, listened for a while to build up the suspense. Finally after a song ended, the mayor gave the band the sign that the music should stop. Into the mike, he ordered, "Finalists, please approach the dais."

Tim, Carl, and Abe seemed to come from different directions to gather before the mayor.

The mayor spoke into the mike. "This is close, folks." He went on. "Before I announce the winner, I'd like to thank all of the people who made this event a success."

Jazzi knew the mayor was cognizant that as soon as he announced the winner, applause would break out and the crowd would scatter. He wanted a rapt audience, and he had it at least for the next few minutes.

He beckoned Jazzi and Delaney to the dais along with his secretary, and of course, Charles. He took his time enumerating what each of them had done—Delaney coordinating with the businesses in town, Jazzi making sure the judges' books were on sale, and so on and so forth.

Jazzi believed Dawn should be on the podium with her, but Dawn was on the sidelines, waving at her and grinning with her thumbs up. They were in this together. They knew each other's strengths and weaknesses. At another event, Dawn might be the one on the podium with the mayor beside her.

Finally, the mayor was studying the score cards and his notes. He held up the cards. "The verdict is in."

Rupert Harding looked over at the contestants. "I don't see Finn Yarrow. Where is he?"

Jazzi was surprised Finn hadn't appeared.

"Do you know where he is?" the mayor asked Carl, who was right in front of him.

"I don't know. Maybe he's still at his station in the kitchen, cleaning up."

Dawn waved her hand at the mayor. "I'll go check."

Not more than two minutes later, a bloodcurdling scream soared out from inside the open door.

All conversation stilled. The air went silent.

Jazzi was frozen to the spot. She couldn't make her legs move. What had Dawn found?

Finally, Jazzi put one foot in front of the other, stepped down from the dais, and rushed toward her friend.

Chapter Four

Delaney sat in one of the chairs that had been set up around the boardwalk for the contest judging. Her head was in her hands. Jazzi and Parker hovered over her.

Delaney moaned, "I can't believe what happened. I can't believe Dawn found Finn's body. I know what that's like. She could have nightmares. She's going to have anxiety. I want my door locked all the time. I know how it feels."

Jazzi laid her hand on Delaney's shoulder, in shock herself. After she'd screamed, Dawn had come running out, and Jazzi had caught her.

Immediately, Dawn had erupted with what she'd seen— Finn Yarrow lying on the kitchen floor with his head bashed in.

Now the police were stringing more crime scene tape and buzzing around. The forensics team had arrived and the scene was total chaos.

Parker eyed Jazzi over the top of Delaney's head. "Dawn's going to need our support. I don't understand how this could have happened with so many people around."

Almost to herself, Jazzi murmured, "There are ways in and

out of the community center that don't have anything to do with coming through either door from the lounge area or the door from the kitchen. There are also two back doors and a loading dock. Anyone could have slipped in and out. Even contestants and judges. Any of them could have done it, then mingled in the crowd and acted like nothing had happened."

"Jazzi!" Parker sounded horrified.

"You know it's true, Parker. We don't know who was in the other community center areas. There's even a parking lot back there, and everybody's attention was focused out here."

Delaney finally raised her head. "This is such a mess."

Griffin Pelham had come up to them. "At least it happened at the end of the bake-off. It would have been a lot of money wasted and time spent otherwise."

Jazzi felt like punching him, or at least telling him off. But that wouldn't do any good. Griffin was who he was.

Suddenly, a distraught couple came running toward Jazzi. She knew the couple well—Dawn's parents, George and Gail Fernsby.

"Where's Dawn?"

Jazzi pointed toward the marine boat shop that was farther up the boardwalk. "Detective Milford is taking Dawn's statement. He might not let you talk to her right now."

Gail looked that way and started forward, but her husband caught her arm and addressed Jazzi. "A friend called us. Can you tell us what happened?"

George Fernsby was about five-foot-nine, stocky, with muscled upper arms and a lean body. He was a sports enthusiast and it showed. In his fifties, he was tan with lines on his face that were probably deeper because of his time in the sun. His blond hair was streaked with gray and thinning on the top. His jeans and Rods to Boards T-shirt were his usual uniform when he was in the store. Jazzi guessed the couple had come from there.

Since they didn't know much yet, Jazzi summed up what had happened. "Dawn went to find one of the contestants, and she found him in the kitchen—dead."

George looked perplexed. "Dead? Did he have a heart attack?"

"I doubt it," Delaney said in a low voice. "Dawn said his head was bashed in."

"An accident then," Gail determined. "Did he fall?"

Delaney exchanged a look with Jazzi, and Jazzi knew she didn't know how to say it out loud. Jazzi put it in the kindest way possible. "There might have been foul play."

Gail covered her mouth with her hand. "Oh no! And Dawn saw all this? I have to get to her."

George kept his hand on his wife's arm. "We can walk over there but we can't interrupt. Come on."

The patrol officers who had arrived were milling about the crowd, taking down names and addresses. Most of the spectators had already been interviewed and told they could go home. The judges, however, had been commanded to stay. They were going to be questioned more thoroughly, and Jazzi wasn't going anywhere until the detective was done with Dawn. She imagined Parker and Delaney felt the same.

Forever was a term people used lightly, but Jazzi thought Detective Milford had been questioning Dawn forever. The time passed in increasingly small intervals, like a spooky night spent in the woods when you're afraid of what was going to pop out. Jazzi remembered her first night camping with Dawn in the forest after she'd moved here. But she'd gotten used to the sounds and loved camping after the first few times. This, however, being questioned by a detective, wasn't something she or her friends would ever get used to.

Then Jazzi saw Dawn walk out the door of the boat shop and be immediately overtaken by her parents, who hugged her. Parker looked toward the shop, where the detective was ushering Tim inside. The contestants were probably going to be next. Abe was wandering around over there too. Jazzi glanced at Carl, who was talking to one of the patrol officers.

"I don't know if it will help Dawn to go home with her parents," Parker said.

Jazzi glanced up at him. "They love her."

"Yes, they love her. But they're overprotective. Their fawning could just make her feel worse."

"And you think we could do better?" Delaney asked, doubt in her voice.

"She needs support," Parker asserted. "She might need to talk about what she found, not bury it."

Jazzi thought that Parker was probably correct about Dawn's parents. They would try to distract her, maybe take her out on the boat, talk about anything and everything else. Still, she wanted to give them the benefit of the doubt.

"We might be underestimating them," Jazzi said.

When Parker took a step toward Jazzi, he was wearing a solemn expression. "You know I'm right."

Parker, with his analytical mind, sometimes saw things she didn't. But this time she figured that they were in agreement.

Delaney stood. "Instead of talking about her reaction, let's go over there and see if we can help."

To Jazzi's surprise, Dawn's parents were walking away from her, looking reluctant, when there was a cry from a man with an official vest running up from the lakeshore. He headed straight for Detective Milford. The detective raised a hand that he'd heard and started jogging toward the tech. Jazzi watched as they ran together past the community center and down toward the lake. Dawn crossed to Jazzi to watch the detective and tech as the they reached the shore, where a group of other techs were now gathered.

"Your parents left?" Parker asked Dawn, without an inflection of judgment in his voice.

"I told them to go home," Dawn said, her expression unnaturally stoic. "There isn't anything they can do for me. They were cleared to leave since they weren't here at the time of the murder."

Jazzi put her arm around Dawn's shoulders. "How are you?"

Dawn ran her fingers through her hair and her earrings swung. "I don't know." She spun toward Delaney. "How did *you* wipe away the vision of what you saw?"

When Delaney had found a body, it had taken her a long time to get over it . . . if she had.

Delaney's face was serious when she focused on Dawn. "I'm still not over it. Some weeks I dream about it every night. I guess it depends on what kind of stress is happening in my life. Pictures pop up unbidden. I don't know what to tell you, Dawn. Just be good to yourself in the coming weeks, like with bubble baths, chocolates. Laugh when you can and cry when you can. Get your emotions out. That helps. And you know it's safe to do it with us."

Parker gave Dawn a sympathetic glance. "You can always talk to us, or cry in front of us, or laugh with us. You know that, don't you?"

"I do. That's why I sent my parents home. I feel like I have to put up a front with them."

Jazzi noticed Detective Milford striding up from the shoreline. He was carrying something in a large ziplock bag, heading for the forensics van.

"It has to be something important or the forensics team would have just gathered it and taken it to the van themselves."

"Milford must have given them specific instructions," Parker said. "It could be anything, but it sure doesn't look like a stone from the lakeshore."

Recognition hit Jazzi, and she knew exactly what the detective was carrying.

"I don't know what it is," Dawn said. "I don't think I've seen it before."

"I have." Jazzi nodded toward the community center. "It's

the granite cutting board that Finn had been using to stone the cherries for the Black Forest cake. I saw it on the counter. My guess is that the cutting board is the murder weapon."

A half hour later, Jazzi unlocked the door to their apartment, glad to be home. The sleigh bells hanging on the doorknob jingled as Dawn, Delaney, and Parker followed her. Those bells were a protective measure so the kittens stayed away from the door and wouldn't run out. Scanning the living room, Jazzi caught sight of both kittens napping on the sofa.

She and Dawn had decorated the apartment together. Their style was probably Bohemian Lakeview. The sofa was a patterned fabric with a light-blue background and little navy-blue triangles. She and Dawn had found it at a thrift store. The throw pillows had navy and white stripes. The palest-blue walls wrapped around the front windows. She and Dawn had created art with a designer fabric much too expensive to upholster a chair with, but terrific for a wall decoration. The pattern was an abstract of three sailboats on the horizon, and the sky was magenta tinged with gray. After they'd attached the material around a stretched canvas, their friend Derek had framed it for them. It was a striking piece and was hung over their couch. The wicker table at one end of the sofa carried a light with a shade in striped navy-and-white fabric like the pillows. They'd found another funky, yellow-upholstered chair that older folk might have trouble getting out of.

The kittens, always ready for activity, jumped off the couch and ran across the Native American–designed throw rug. That rug featured all the colors in their room, from bright yellow and pale tan to white and navy. Sliding into the kitchen, the kittens stopped against the few navy-colored cabinets. A white-washed table with shelves on the side had a refinished top in the same color of navy as the cabinets. They'd completed their kitchen décor with two low-back, whitewashed chairs.

Dawn scooped up the kittens and took them to the throw rug, sitting on the floor with them. Zander and Freya climbed over Dawn's knees as she petted one and then the other. Freya, black all over and fuzzy, tried to crawl up Dawn's blouse.

Laughing, Dawn disengaged her and set her on the floor.

Zander scrambled over to Jazzi, who took a seat on the sofa. As Parker took the deep yellow chair, he decided, "We might as well talk about it."

"What's there to talk about?" Delaney asked with a shrug. "We don't know exactly what happened, but we sure know the end result. Finn is dead. I just can't believe it."

Dawn raised her head. "I can." She picked up Freya and held the kitten under her chin as if she needed that comfort.

"There's one question maybe the police should find the answer to quickly," Parker emphasized.

Dawn spun around on the floor to look at Parker, the kitten still in her hand. "What question?"

"Maybe you weren't there. I know Jazzi was."

Jazzi caught on to Parker's train of thought. "Tim and Finn almost got into a fistfight at the start of the competition."

"What was it about?" Delaney asked.

"Oliver and I got there when they were yelling at each other," Jazzi said. "I caught Tim hurl the word *immoral*, and Finn tossed back that Tim was the problem."

"Immoral?" Dawn's voice was reedy. "That could have meant anything from cheating in the contest to sexual harassment."

"Maybe it wasn't that serious," Jazzi said. "We're jumping to those conclusions as if that was part of why Finn was murdered. But the argument might have been something simple."

"You mean Tim overreacted?" Delaney guessed.

"Could be. You can bet Detective Milford will hear about the fight. He doesn't miss any detail." Jazzi knew that as a certainty.

"You helped him with details the last time around." Parker's voice was filled with disapproval.

"Only details that fell into my lap." She heard a "humph" from Parker, as if he didn't completely believe that.

Jazzi hadn't gone looking for trouble in May. She really hadn't. Her mom, in addition to running a tea garden in Willow Creek, Pennsylvania, had helped the police there solve ten murder cases. Ten. Yes, Jazzi had picked up some of her investigative skills. Yes, she was curious. But she wasn't looking to get involved with cases as Daisy Swanson had. In fact, she'd learned from her mother in situations like this to do one particular thing that helped.

"How about if I make omelets for us. I have salad greens and cheese biscuits and plenty of iced tea."

"Sounds good," Parker said. "Let's concentrate on food rather than murder."

Food was a remedy her mom used. Sometimes it worked. So . . . Jazzi rose to her feet and went to the kitchen.

On Monday evening, the Fernsbys' pontoon boat slid through the lake water with ease. The lake was busy with summer traffic, but Jazzi appreciated the feeling of floating in the air on a boat with clouds and azure skies overhead. The hour was nearing dusk, but she probably enjoyed this part of the day as much as the sunny mornings.

Gail was situated on a navigator chair and looked straight ahead as her husband manned the boat. The twenty-two-foot pontoon boat had plenty of space for passengers. Jazzi and Dawn sat on the bench seat on the starboard side.

Jazzi studied the Fernsbys, who kept their eyes on the water. Dawn's mom always looked put together in a sporty classic style. She wore her blond hair in a swingy medium cut. It was being tossed a bit in the wind. Dawn's dad at the helm had his denim billed cap with a captain's logo front and center pulled low.

Although the night was balmy and beautiful, tension vibrated in the air. Dawn's parents had insisted Dawn come with them tonight to relax and "get over" her experience. Jazzi knew that wasn't going to happen anytime soon. Dawn had convinced her to come along to act as a buffer of sorts. But Jazzi knew Dawn's mom didn't do anything lightly and she had a reason for this cruise tonight other than simple enjoyment. Everyone was trying to make small talk except for Dawn, who was quiet.

Gail gazed at her daughter with worried eyes. Dawn's dimples weren't visible tonight, and her pointed chin headed down as if she couldn't keep her face up, so she was looking straight at the water. She was folding in on herself, and Jazzi knew that wasn't going to help. Not much would at this point, not even the water and the sky and the swishing reeds around the shore of the lake.

Gail's eyes were green like her daughter's, and now they swept over Jazzi. "I see Dawn hasn't convinced you to get your hair cut yet. Wouldn't it be so much more convenient for water sports?"

Jazzi had had this conversation with Dawn and Gail in the past. Tonight, she'd worn her hair loose. The wind tossed it away from her face.

Jazzi gave a shrug with a smile. "I like the versatility of my long hair. I thought about having a stylist do curtain bangs, but I'm not sure about that yet." Jazzi hoped her smile said she appreciated Gail's opinion, but she was going to do what an independent woman would do.

Gail switched her attention back to Dawn. "When does your book club meet again?"

When Dawn looked up, she exchanged a glance with Jazzi. "Tomorrow evening. Why do you ask?"

Gail turned her gaze toward her husband, but he was staring out at the water. "We know your book club friends played a part in the last murder investigation. We don't want you involved at all in that, especially if those people attempt to play amateur detectives. Maybe you shouldn't go tomorrow night."

With rebellion in her tone, Dawn responded fast. "No one played amateur detective, Mom. Delaney was in the same position I am now, and the book club gave her emotional support. That's all. I'm hoping for the same support."

"What do you mean 'emotional support'?" George Fernsby asked. "*We* can give you that. Use your brother to talk to."

Dawn was quick to answer that parental advice too. "Delaney has gone through this. She understands what I'm feeling. Farrell lives on another planet with the two of you. You think a boat ride and a balmy night are going to make me feel better. It's not. No amount of donuts or picnics or swims in the lake are going to make me forget what I saw."

"Those things, honey, can take your mind off of what you saw," Gail proposed.

Jazzi was *not* going to wade into this conversation. Right now Dawn didn't need someone to tell her what to do or tell her what might help. She needed friends who would be there when she wanted to talk, who would be there when she wanted to be silent, who would be there when she just wanted to cry. Dawn had once admitted to Jazzi she didn't like to cry in front of her parents. When she did, they looked at her as if she were a little girl again. Dawn was always fighting that image.

Gail pointed her finger at Jazzi.

Jazzi suspected what was coming and she braced herself.

Gail's words were staccato, interfering with the calm of the floating boat and the peace of the night. "Jazzi became involved in that investigation so much so that she almost got herself killed."

Closing her eyes for a moment, Jazzi heard her mom's voice in her head, saying, "Silence is usually your best defense." However, with Gail and George Fernsby looking at her as if she were a criminal, she knew she couldn't stay completely silent.

She'd never told her friends that her mother had solved murder cases in Pennsylvania. Detective Milford was the only one in Belltower Landing who knew about her mom. Jazzi was proud of her mom. She was. But she hadn't wanted her life here over-shadowed by the curiosity, questions, and stares associated with the publicity from those investigations.

"Mrs. Fernsby, you know that I'll support Dawn any way I can. We're good friends, we're roommates, and we feel most of the time like sisters." She reached over and squeezed Dawn's hand.

Dawn squeezed back, with a tiny smile playing around her bottom lip.

"We want our daughter kept out of harm's way," George Fernsby proclaimed . . . as if his wishes could make that happen.

Jazzi didn't say she could or couldn't do that. She didn't know what would come in the future. She didn't know what was going to happen tomorrow. She did know it hurt that Dawn's parents believed she'd draw Dawn into harm's way.

She would protect Dawn anyway that she could.

Chapter Five

It was early Tuesday morning before Tomes opened when Jazzi went to the storeroom to sort new titles to put on the shelves. Her phone played "Boat" by Ed Sheeran, her new favorite ringtone. It suited her right now and she repeated the lyrics whenever her proverbial boat rocked. The text was from Erica, who was brewing tea at the tea bar.

Oliver's here. He wants to talk to you. Send him back?

Whenever Jazzi thought about Oliver Patel, she tried to duck away from the excitement she felt when she was around him. With his Australian accent and his tall, lean good looks, she had to admit she was attracted to him. In the past, she hadn't acted on that attraction. She'd put guardrails up all around her heart when she'd been dumped by her boyfriend of three years after she'd transferred to his college.

She and Oliver had been through a traumatic experience in June, and those experiences always bonded folks. At least, that's what she blamed her heart's pitter-patter on as she texted to Erica.

Send him back.

She kept sorting books absently, mounding a stack into her arms to carry them out to the store.

Oliver rapped on the storeroom door and then opened it, peeking his head in. His blond hair had a surfer look this morning. She imagined she liked it that way because he'd once told her he'd surfed in Australia in the summers when he'd lived there with his dad. The stubble on his chin made him look more like a man of the world rather than a hipster.

He smiled and she grinned. When she took a step forward, the books almost fell out of her arms.

In a moment he was there, catching them and laying a few on the table.

Feeling foolish, standing there just holding three books, Jazzi set those on the table as well and faced Oliver's probing blue eyes.

"Of course, I heard about the murder at the bake-off," he said with a frown. "I was delayed in the kitchen and didn't get there for the last tasting. Last night's gossip in the pub was that *you* were there when it happened. Are you okay?"

"Yes, I was there, but Dawn found the body."

"I heard that too," Oliver said, taking a step closer, "But that's not what I asked. How are *you*?"

Jazzi fidgeted with the pocket on her work apron. "I was at the tent with Delaney. We heard Dawn scream—"

Suddenly, Jazzi felt choked up and her eyes became a bit teary. She swallowed, attempting to regain composure.

"Jazzi . . ." Oliver looked as if he was going to reach out and touch her, but then he dropped his hand. "That had to be an awful experience, hearing your best friend scream, then knowing what had happened."

Jazzi sank down into a folding chair at the table. Oliver sat in one across from her. Fighting off her upset, she concentrated on the way his polo shirt stretched across his chest and around his muscled biceps. She wasn't sure whether the concentration helped or made matters worse. "Finn's murder was awful, absolutely awful. And yes, I'm upset about that and about Dawn's emotional state. I'm not sure how she's handling this."

"I'm sure being a good friend to her will help." Oliver's voice was low and gentle with empathy.

"It should, but her parents are afraid I'm going to lead her into harm."

Oliver looked perplexed. "How's that?"

"They're afraid I'll ask too many questions like last time and pull her into an untenable situation."

This time, Oliver did reach for Jazzi's hand and laid his tentatively on top of hers. His hand was large, warm, and comforting. It felt good, wrapping his strength around hers. Maybe too good. Her heart still had those guardrails.

When she pulled back, the moment was awkward. He asked, "Do you intend to ask questions and poke around for answers?"

"I'm not sure if I will or won't. My attention is on Dawn right now and what she needs. I'm also certain that Detective Milford will do his job adequately. He did the last time."

"You got to the killer first."

"I didn't know he was the killer."

Oliver gave a little nod of assent. He knew exactly how it had all happened. That bond of theirs. Still, he pointed out, "I hear a *but* in your voice. Detective Milford can successfully find the murderer *but* . . ."

Because this was Oliver who was asking, she could be honest. "You know the traffic in the bookstore and tea bar. The pub is the same way. As you said, gossip was running around the pub last night. Gossip runs around here too. If I hear anything that makes a difference, I'll tell the detective."

"And you might just ask a few questions of your customers. You have to do you, Jazzi. 'Av a go at what you think is right."

Every once in a while, a bit more of Australia snuck into Oliver's speech. Jazzi almost smiled. Almost. She was aware of the time ticking past and that her presence was needed out in the bookstore.

Standing, she thanked Oliver. "Your common sense has helped. Dawn's going to have to deal with her parents. She's going to be in the middle of this whether she wants to be or not, since she's the one who found the body. All I can do is support her and help any way I can."

"You have book club tonight, aye?"

"Yes, we do, and Dawn's other friends will help her too."

"I might have to drop in on that some week."

Oliver hadn't shown interest in the book club before. "You can get away from the pub in the evening?"

"My kitchen manager is dependable. I started reading through Diego Alvarez's book on running a restaurant that was published before his new cookbook. Maybe I'll bring that along and report."

"Sounds good." Jazzi thought she would like to see Oliver join in with her friends. He worked even more hours than she did. "I'll walk you out. Do you want tea and a muffin before you leave?"

"That will hit the morning spot," Oliver returned with a grin.

They walked to the interior of Tomes & Tea together.

That evening, Jazzi pushed two tables together in the bookstore and arranged chairs around them for the book club meeting. Dawn was brewing tea for iced tea. Tomes & Tea's book club was a little different than most. They didn't discuss one novel at a session. Readers brought in whatever their latest read was to talk about. This way tourists could drop in and join in too. They didn't always because there were so many activities in Belltower Landing for the tourist season. Tourists joining in was more likely to happen over the winter months.

Jazzi was pushing one last orange enamel chair in at a table when Erica breezed in the door. She was carrying a cake pan.

"I brought blueberry lemon squares, so we'll have to get out the forks too. I thought we could use a sweet pick-me-up after what happened this weekend."

It wasn't long before the members of their book club started streaming in. Parker came over to Jazzi and asked her in a low voice. "How are you doing?"

As a software applications developer, Parker was the club's IT guru. From the first computer his parents had bought him when he was ten, he'd dabbled with coding. During his college years he'd created a video game that had gone viral. From what Dawn had told her, that game and his investments had set him up for life if he never wanted to work another day again. Parker wasn't like that. Besides developing cell phone apps, he consulted with companies that needed security work with their software.

Now, all she saw on his well-defined and handsome features was concern. They'd been friends since she'd clerked at Rods to Boards with Dawn during college summers. Good friends. His brown eyes were intense, and his jaw squared even more as he asked Jazzi the question.

Keeping her voice low, she leaned closer to Parker. "I'm okay. Dawn's doing as well as can be expected. We were out on the boat with her parents last night, and that didn't go so well."

"How so?" Parker asked.

"They're afraid she'll get pulled in to some of the intrigue about what happened to Finn."

"Intrigue?"

"Being that we're roommates and best friends, I think her mom's afraid I'll ask too many questions about what happened. I don't intend to, but Dawn does have questions, and I think she's going to want to talk about the murder tonight. I'll just keep quiet."

Parker gave a grudging smile. "I doubt that."

She lightly punched his arm. They *were* good friends.

Soon the book club members sat around the table. Erica served their snacks, they enjoyed while discussing the books they'd read. They were sipping glasses of iced tea when Delaney placed the book she'd brought along on the table in front of her. "We could talk about what happened to Finn. You know we want to." She leaned over to Dawn and bumped her shoulder. "Remember, you can call me in the middle of the night if you have nightmares. I know what it's like."

After looking around at everyone, Dawn sighed. "Just knowing Jazzi and the kittens are in the apartment helps. If I wake up or am afraid, I go find them."

Derek Stewart, who flipped houses for a living, rubbed his beard and mustache. His russet brown hair looked mussed, but his hazel eyes were laser sharp as he asked, "Why Finn? I'd often call him after I had a house ready to sell. He'd take photos that I could use on my website. He seemed like a genial enough guy. I don't know much else about him."

Kaylee Washington, the property manager of the Belltower Landing Camp and Lake Resort, pushed her springy, dark brown wild curls away from her face. She was a striking looking woman with light brown skin, and dangling earrings. "I don't know how genial. I was there on Sunday. He had that fight with Tim. What was that about?"

"No knowing," Jazzi said. "I don't think anybody was close enough to hear."

Parker gave her a look, and she knew why. She remembered telling him she was going to be quiet tonight.

Kaylee added, "Finn often took photos of the resort for *Resort Life*."

Resort Life was a reputable online magazine that also published a pamphlet for summer rentals.

Addison Bianchi, who was usually a quiet member of the

group, spoke up now. "Finn was married. I know his wife, Belinda. We met on the green one day when I was there with Sylvie." Addison was a stay-at-home mom with a three-year-old daughter. She had beautiful golden blond hair and wide hazel eyes. Everyone seemed drawn to her, and Jazzi guessed Finn's wife was no different.

Addison went on to explain, "Sylvie was playing near the lakeshore, and Belinda was sitting on a bench nearby. She watched her and there was this longing in her eyes. I went to sit next to her. She and Finn were trying to have children. She talked to me about wanting to be a mom and Finn wanting to be a dad. Now they'll never have that chance." Addison's voice cracked a bit.

Everyone was silent for a few minutes.

Derek cleared his throat. "Finn and his wife live in a bungalow on Seneca Avenue."

Jazzi knew where that was. It was a modest development with cute little houses.

Dawn, who had been sipping tea and had been quiet up until now, looked over at Delaney. "I know the detectives questioned you pretty hard back in May. Do you remember how many sessions you had with them?"

"Probably four or five," Delaney answered. "Why? Do you think they're going to question you again?"

"I have another appointment for tomorrow at nine a.m." She looked at Jazzi. "I hope you can cover the store for me."

"Of course, I can."

Parker, concern on his face again for Dawn, asked, "What do they question you about most? It's not like you knew Finn that well."

"We had a nodding acquaintance. But I'm the one who saw the crime scene. Detective Milford questioned me over and over again about what I saw on the way to the kitchen."

Addison asked, "In case anyone was lingering?"

"I guess so. I was looking for Finn, but I didn't see anybody else around."

"Is that all they wanted to know?"

"They wanted me to describe everything that was in the kitchen when I found the body. It wasn't like they couldn't go over it themselves. Nothing happened between when I saw it and they arrived."

"They're probably trying to make sure of that. You came back out. Someone else could have been in the kitchen, tampering with the crime scene, I guess," Parker mused.

Jazzi decided Dawn's memory might be the most beneficial asset the police had.

After the book club meeting, Jazzi noticed that Dawn was particularly quiet as they made their way to the apartment and their kittens greeted them. Dawn scooped up Zander and went to sit in the yellow chair. She stroked under Zander's chin and Jazzi wondered what she was thinking. The book club meeting had brought back the events surrounding the murder, and now Jazzi imagined that Dawn was immersed in thinking about all of that.

Settling down on the floor in front of the coffee table with Freya jumping over her knee, Jazzi looked up at Dawn. "Do you want to talk about it?"

Dawn said, "I don't know what *it* is. Do you know what I mean?"

"Sure. Finn, the murder, his life, what's going to happen next. I get it."

"I just wish I could remember more details for the detective because I think that's what they want."

"You can't try to please them, Dawn. That won't give them an accurate depiction of what you saw, what you heard, what you felt. But there are strategies to help you remember more."

Jazzi's stepfather, Jonas Groft, was a former detective, and he had used a strategy with her mom to help her remember.

"Is it difficult to do? I mean, I can't remember more, and I'm already getting anxious about all of it."

"This is really simple. Nothing involved. Basically, you need to relax so you can remember."

"But I can't relax," Dawn groaned.

"Let's try something," Jazzi proposed.

Zander looked as if he were falling asleep in Dawn's lap. That was good. Jazzi would adjust her stepfather's strategy a little and see if it worked.

"I want you to stroke Zander, and each time you do, take in a deep breath, hold it for five, and let it out again. Do you think you can do that?"

"As long as he wants to be petted," Dawn responded with a chuckle.

Zander looked conked out. That was the beautiful thing about kittens. They could be running around, driving you ragged, and then suddenly be asleep.

Freya had settled into the nest of Jazzi's crossed legs.

"First of all, get comfortable in the chair. Just make sure everything is supported so you're not tense any place."

"I'm tense all over."

"Zander's going to fix that."

A smile played across Dawn's lips as she flicked her hand over Zander's head and then began petting him.

"Slower pets," Jazzi said. "Just stroke up by his head and over his body, breathe in and breathe out. Breathe in all that softness and peace, and breathe out any anxiety you're feeling."

Dawn was staring down at Zander, and her breaths were evening out. Jazzi imagined that her heart rate was slowing too. She herself had practiced guided imagery in yoga classes. This was a little like that.

Jazzi could see Dawn's muscles in her arms relax against the chair. Her hands continued to stroke Zander and then lay on his head. He seemed to cuddle into her. Purrfect.

Jazzi began talking. "Zander is going to help you until you relax so you can remember. That's all we're doing. I want you to remember the day of the event. Can you recall being in the crowd ready for the final judging?"

Dawn nodded. "The judges tasted the desserts, then worked on their score cards. The band was playing and suspense built. Then Mayor Harding went up on the dais to thank everyone before he announced the winner," Dawn said, remembering, her hand stroking Zander's cute little head.

"When you went inside the door to look for Finn, did you pass anyone coming out?"

Dawn's eyes fluttered shut as she thought about it. "No one."

"Did you pass anybody, anybody at all as you went through the dining area?" Tables and chairs lined up cafeteria style outside the kitchen area were used for community dinners.

"No. It looked like a few chairs had been pushed away from tables, though."

"Like someone had had a fight in there?" Jazzi asked.

"It was hard to tell," Dawn responded. "Nothing was knocked over."

"Okay. Now as you headed for the kitchen, did you *hear* anything?"

Again, Dawn took a few minutes to think about the question. "You know that big, black door that leads outside from the kitchen?"

"Sure, I know it."

"I think I heard it close."

Realizing that could be an important detail, Jazzi said, "Stop there for a moment and imagine yourself standing at the kitchen. Was it the door closing or some other noise?"

"It was the door closing."

The back of the kitchen led out to a loading area and a parking lot. Jazzi could imagine whoever killed Finn leaving that way.

"Maybe the noise didn't come from that direction," Dawn added. "You know how everything echoes in there, especially when it's empty."

"Can you think of what the noise would have been?"

"Maybe somebody in the lounge area?"

The community center was a large building that even had a gym behind the lounge. The lounge itself was a relaxation area with love seats and sofas where seniors often gathered.

"All right, let's pass on the door for now." Jazzi didn't want Dawn becoming anxious trying to remember. This strategy didn't work well that way.

"Think about entering the kitchen. Think about standing there. Can you tell me everything you saw?"

"You mean what was on the counter?"

"Sure. What was on the counter?"

"It was fairly cleaned up," Dawn recalled. "The finished desserts were still sitting on the counter at each contestant's station with servings removed. Abe's éclairs sat on a silver tray. Carl's strawberry shortcake had wedges cut out. Half of Tim's lemon meringue pie had been served to the judges."

"Was Finn's Black Forest cake on the counter?"

Dawn suddenly sat up and covered her mouth with her hand. "No. I forgot."

Jazzi kept her voice as gentle as possible. "What did you forget?"

"Finn's beautiful Black Forest cake was spread over him and the floor as if someone had dumped it on him."

"Although you just remembered it, the crime scene techs saw it," Jazzi reassured her.

"The thing is, it wasn't just dumped there," Dawn said. "It looked as if some of the cake had been smeared across his mouth."

Jazzi ran through what she knew. Not only had Finn been

hit over the head with that granite cutting board, but somebody also had made a final gesture. That final gesture showed rage that something personal had happened. Accident? She doubted that it had been an accident. The police had appeared so excited about collecting that cutting board. If Finn hadn't fallen and hit his head, then he was murdered because of someone who had a grudge against him. This was possibly a leap, but Jazzi didn't think it was a far-fetched one.

Dawn opened her eyes and sat up a little straighter. Zander started scootching around in her lap. "I'll be sure to tell the detective tomorrow what I remembered, especially the closing of the door."

Jazzi hoped the little that Dawn remembered could help the detective in his search for the killer.

Chapter Six

Jazzi woke up before sunrise the following morning. She hadn't gotten much rest. Zander and Freya had come scampering onto her bed around two a.m. They'd settled in with her, but even petting them and listening to their purrs hadn't relaxed her enough to fall asleep.

After peeking into Dawn's bedroom to see that she was still sleeping, Jazzi fed the kittens and quickly dressed for a bike ride. Maybe it would clear her head and ready her for a busy day. She'd be covering for Dawn this morning while her roommate went to the police station. Jazzi asked Dawn if she wanted her to come along, but Dawn said this was something she had to do on her own.

Dressed in electric-blue bike shorts and a yellow-and-blue-striped racerback tank top, Jazzi left her apartment, jogged down the steps to the back, and headed for the garage that belonged to the property.

Her compact white-and-black-topped MINI Cooper allowed more space on her side of the garage. Dawn's SUV took up the other half. Jazzi rode her bike whenever she could instead of driving her car for the exercise and to save gas.

The garage was an old-time clapboard one that a coat of cream paint and a few repairs had helped refurbish. Her stepdad had helped her and Dawn with those as well as with the cupboards for their kitchen before they moved in. Although a former detective, Jonas was now a woodworker and craftsman. She'd appreciated his help in this as well as his detective skills in helping her find her biological mother when she was fifteen. That search had brought Jonas and her mom together.

Jazzi slid the wooden garage door to one side. She and Dawn had to move this door back and forth to access their vehicles. Quickly, Jazzi moved her bike from its position along her car and wheeled it to the back alley. After she closed the garage door, she adjusted her helmet and hopped onto her purple-and-silver bike.

Sunrise bike rides were the best. The blazing August sun broke the horizon beyond the lake and forests with golden streams. Jazzi had swooped her long black hair into a low ponytail for convenience. Her speed and the breeze blew it back and forth between her shoulder blades.

The bike path along Lakeview Boulevard was convenient and safe as she pedaled toward the marina. Traffic was light in the early morning, though marina activity was already gearing up. Not far from the marina, she could smell the aroma from food trucks that were preparing for another day of tourist activity, from paddleboarding to boating. Maybe she'd stop for breakfast on her return.

As she often did, she headed away from the lake to a development known as High Point.

A half-hour later, after ten miles and pedaling up inclines, she rode back toward the marina, her favorite food truck in her sights. Some of the trucks sold prepackaged food, ice cream, and snow cones. However, others had onboard kitchens where they created their offerings or heated up food that was prepared in an off-site kitchen.

Jazzi pedaled toward the waffle truck. The chef put two waffles together to form a pocket, then filled it with omelet-like stuffing or a dessert filling. She'd just jumped from her bike and was locking it in a bike rack when she heard a deep male voice beside her.

"Hey, Jazzi. Do you want to catch breakfast together?" Oliver Patel was looking down at her as if they'd scheduled this meet-up. Now and then she and Oliver biked together, but they hadn't lately.

She wasn't prepared to see Oliver. She was sweaty from her ride. Along with that, she was aware that as soon as she removed her helmet from her head, her hair would be plastered down. There was no escaping it. As she removed her helmet, she ran her fingers through her bangs to let air rustle through them.

Life was always filled with unexpected turns. Jazzi took a deep breath, then smiled because seeing Oliver always caused her to smile. "The idea of waffles for breakfast must have flown into our heads simultaneously."

"I don't know about that," he said with a grin. "When I spotted you, I knew I had to flag you down. I wanted to tell you I simply didn't blow off the book club last night. I had a situation with two diners at the Kangaroo."

Tucking her helmet under her arm, she walked with Oliver toward the waffle truck. The delicious scent of vanilla, sugar, and butter wafted toward them. "What kind of situation? Can you talk about it?"

He lifted his hand in dismissal. "It was public. It's no secret. I'm sure gossip will be circulating in Tomes & Tea today."

"Now you've whetted my curiosity. Was anyone I know involved?"

"Two of the judges for the bake-off."

Jazzi peered up, straight into Oliver's blue eyes, and almost forgot her question . . . almost. "Which judges?"

With a wicked gleam in his eyes, Oliver beckoned her to the truck and the delicious aromas. "Which waffle pocket for you?"

"You're not going to tell me?"

"While we're eating. Hardy or sweet?"

Although she loved the strawberry and whipped cream waffles, she intended to eat healthy today. "Broccoli, bacon, and cheese omelet waffle." After all, anything with broccoli was healthy, wasn't it?

Oliver ordered the same.

In a matter of minutes their plates were ready. With bottles of water, they carried their breakfasts to a picnic table under a tall maple.

"Okay. Spill it," Jazzi ordered as Oliver took a bite of the waffle pocket.

He set his waffle on its plate. "Griffin Pelham and Diego Alvarez."

Jazzi knew her brown eyes widened. "I suspected Detective Milford would ask the judges to stick around. Griffin doesn't surprise me arguing with someone. But Diego?"

Oliver decided to eat the waffle with a fork rather than his hands. He sliced off a bite. "Eat," he said motioning to Jazzi's plate.

She lifted her fork and dug in. She *was* hungry.

Oliver began to reveal what had happened. "I have to admit I was excited about Diego coming to the pub. He had texted me and asked if I'd save him a quiet table. I think the murder and everything at the bake-off had him ruffled. We had exchanged business cards at the book signing."

"You admire Diego." Oliver had conveyed that impression at the book signing on Friday.

"I do. I was looking forward to a quiet conversation with him. The restaurant business isn't easy. The long hours can destroy relationships. It's a lot to unpack, and Diego is an expert at all of it."

Oliver took a few more bites of his waffle while Jazzi thought about everything he'd said. Had Oliver's hours at The Wild Kangaroo broken up many of *his* relationships?

Those thoughts led her to her next question. "Did Diego have advice for you?"

Grimacing when he shook his head, Oliver laid down his fork. "We never *had* a conversation. I intended to let him enjoy his dinner in relative peace. I'd given him a back corner table away from the kitchen."

Jazzi knew that table well. It was sought after by customers who wanted to have discussions, business or otherwise. "What happened?"

"Griffin is what happened. He'd been sitting at the bar hitting back tequila shots."

It was easy to deduce what was coming. "He was drunk?"

"The bartender was ready to cut him loose. He presented Griffin with his tab. Instead of leaving, he interrupted Diego's meal. He claimed Diego cut him out of a deal that had made Diego millions."

"Millions?" Jazzi had trouble fathoming that one deal could do that.

"Apparently, Diego had been given the opportunity to buy into properties that could be valuable restaurant sites. He took advantage of it. Griffin was practically yelling at him when I stepped in. As I corralled Griffin to lead him out, I heard Diego say, 'You were leveraged too much then. You weren't a good risk.'"

"I can't imagine what either man is worth. They're in a different world."

"Maybe so. But I think Griffin is all bravado, a bludger. Diego is the real entrepreneur."

When Jazzi sent him a perplexed look, he explained, " 'Bludger' means generally lazy. I forgot you don't speak Australian." As Oliver resumed eating, he gave Jazzi a mischievous look. "Diego is an entrepreneur like *you*."

She raised her head and spotted the teasing glint in his eyes.

"I just want Tomes & Tea to be successful, which to me means operating in the black with enough extra for Dawn and me to make a decent living."

"Don't underestimate yourself, Jazzi." His voice carried admiration and she wasn't altogether sure why.

Oliver's total attention on her made Jazzi feel . . . seen and heard. She turned *her* attention back to her breakfast.

Jazzi was busy while Dawn went to the Belltower Landing police station. Serving tea and muffins, helping Erica at the checkout counter, and directing Audrey's choices for the self-help section didn't keep her mind away from what was happening between Dawn and Detective Milford. And when her thoughts weren't revolving around that, she was considering what Oliver had revealed to her about Griffin and Diego . . . about Oliver himself.

About two hours after Dawn had left, she returned, looking worried.

Jazzi took her best friend aside. "How did it go?"

Dawn leaned against the seaglass blue cubicles that displayed the sporting volumes on sailing, boats, kayaking, and paddleboarding. "We shook up my memory last night."

"What do you mean?" Jazzi was hoping the memory exercise hadn't upset Dawn more than she already was.

"During the night, I remembered seeing Emmaline around Finn's station a lot."

"All the judges watched the contestants bake."

"Maybe. But she and Griffin weren't sitting at the judge's table during the time the band played."

Jazzi scanned Tomes & Tea to make sure she and Dawn weren't needed somewhere. "How did the detective react?"

"I had the feeling the observation about Emmaline could be as important as the door I heard closing. Most of all I'm not supposed to talk about the crime scene or what I remember with anyone but you . . . since you already know. He made me promise."

Jazzi fingered strands of her ponytail, understanding that the detective didn't want to reveal murder details to the public.

Dawn suddenly clutched Jazzi's elbow. "But *that* wasn't the most important memory that emerged when I was speaking with the detective."

"So, the detective *helped* you remember?" Sometimes she believed Paul Milford was too gruff because of his experiences in a big city. But he must have been gentle with Dawn.

Laughter floated across the store from two teens examining books in the fiction section. The scent of peach herbal tea brewing reminded her she had to get back to work.

However, Dawn's next sentence brought her attention back to the murder. "I hated envisioning Finn lying in the kitchen. But besides the smear of Black Forest cake on his face, I remembered something else. Finn always wore a thick rope necklace with a gold key hanging from it. But when I remembered his body spread out there—" Dawn's voice hitched, then she continued. "He wasn't wearing it. It was missing when I found him."

Jazzi considered what Dawn had just said. *It was missing.* Just what did that key open?

Jogging up the inside staircase from the Tomes & Tea storage room to her apartment, Jazzi checked her watch. It was almost two o'clock. Hopefully the kittens hadn't caused much chaos this morning in their living quarters. Zander and Freya found trouble easily.

As Jazzi opened the door into her bedroom, the sleigh bells hanging on that doorknob jingled. No fur babies were in sight. But as she entered the kitchen, they both scampered around her feet. Freya tilted her head up and meowed.

Jazzi laughed, which she did a lot around these two. "It's good to see *you* too. I'll have your lunch ready in a minute."

Setting down their dishes a few minutes later, Jazzi listened to the little sounds of slight growling Freya made when she ate. She could gobble her food fast. Zander took his time.

Crossing to the refrigerator and opening it, she heard a knock on the door to the apartment. No one would expect her to be up here this time of day.

Last May she and Dawn had installed a peephole. As she peered through it, she inhaled a breath in surprise. It was Detective Milford standing on the landing at the top of the outside stairs!

After she opened the deadbolt and the lock on the doorknob, she pulled open the door.

The detective didn't smile. He always tried to keep a stoic expression.

"Hi, Jazzi. Can I come in?"

He was dressed in dark slacks, a cream oxford open-neck shirt, and a tan sports jacket. She wondered if he looked professional at home too. She knew he was in his late forties and married, but not much else about him.

"Are you dropping in for a cup of tea?" One of these days she'd coax him to smile.

His brow quirked up. "Nope. Dawn told me you'd be up here."

"Another interview with Dawn? She just saw you this morning."

"No. Not Dawn. I came to see *you*."

Jazzi didn't like the sinking feeling in her stomach. She told herself not to worry . . . yet. "Come in." She didn't extend the invitation with much enthusiasm.

The kittens had ducked under one of the dining chairs at the small whitewashed table.

Jazzi closed the door after the detective. As soon as the bells on the doorknob quit jingling, the felines came out and went back to their dishes.

Detective Milford gave them a side glance.

Remembering her manners, Jazzi asked, "*Would* you like a glass of iced tea?"

"No. Mind if I sit?" He pointed to the ladderback chair at the table.

"Make yourself comfortable. Mind if I have a cup of yogurt while we talk? This is my lunch break."

"Go ahead. This won't take long. I wanted to know what you did to help Dawn Fernsby remember details."

Jazzi froze then, crossed to the refrigerator, and found a cup of lime yogurt. Stepping over to a drawer, she removed a spoon and carried it with her to the table. She sat across from him and slowly opened the top of the yogurt.

Maybe he was impatient because she didn't answer right away . . . because he asked, "Hypnosis?"

She plopped down the yogurt onto the table. "Be serious, Detective. I own a bookstore. I have a degree in human services, nothing else. All I did with Dawn was help her relax. It's a strategy my stepfather used with my mom. He was a former detective."

"That's right. I remember well that your mom helped the police. That's another reason I wanted to talk to you."

The detective kept surprising her. "My mom?"

"In a way it's about your mom. There have been articles written about Daisy Swanson. She's been interviewed on true crime podcasts."

"My mom hasn't been involved in a police case in years. She's happily married, makes baked goods and tea, and volunteers at a homeless shelter. I don't understand what she has to do with my life here."

"Oh, Jazzi. You *are* your mother's daughter."

"I'm adopted," Jazzi responded with no inflection in her voice.

"I know that too. But she raised you, and from what I see, she did it well."

Although Jazzi should feel complimented, she realized the detective maybe knew way too much about her. She'd searched for her biological mother when she was fifteen and found her. That search had partly been in response to losing her adoptive father when she was twelve. Heart holes needed to be filled. At least that's the way *she'd* responded to loss.

Jazzi took a spoonful of yogurt. "She did raise me well. I intend to make her proud."

Detective Milford nodded. "My point exactly. Look what happened to you last June."

"Do you think I wanted all that to happen?"

"Of course not. But as a teen, you learned about murder investigation, police procedures, deductive logic. I know you are Dawn Fernsby's best friend as well as her partner. You want to support her. Do that. But stay out of my way. Stay clear of this investigation."

Jazzi kept silent and finished her yogurt. After she did, she asked the detective, "Are we done?"

He stood then, looking down at her like a parental figure, he said, "One more thing."

She gave a sigh, and she knew he noticed.

"I'm sure Dawn told you what she remembered in her visit with me."

"She did."

"I warned her not to tell anyone else, besides you, what she remembered. We need those details kept secret for the investigation's sake. Don't talk to anyone about it. When we question persons of interest, those details are golden. I don't want them tarnished."

"Understood," Jazzi said as she got up. She started for the door and opened it. The bells jingled, and Zander and Freya scampered toward Jazzi's bedroom.

The silence between her and the detective was awkward.

He repeated again, "Stay clear of this case." He didn't wait for Jazzi to respond but left.

On Thursday morning, the cylinder pendant lights with Edison bulbs glowed down on the blond streaks in Dawn's hair as she stood at the sales counter. She called to Jazzi, her mouth set in a serious line, "Come look at this!"

The weather outside was gray and overcast. Storms were predicted for later in the afternoon. The cloudy day made the inside of Tomes & Tea pop even more. The chandelier over the tea bar as well as the neon green and blue LED lights that lit up the book cubicles coaxed tourists into the bookstore. In the summer, Tomes & Tea provided tourists a distraction on cloudy days.

Dawn had readied the sales desk and was obviously checking something on her phone. The severity of storms rolling in later?

As Jazzi approached the counter and slipped around the edge, Dawn handed her phone to Jazzi. "Just look at this. The mayor is going to want to shut down *The Landing*. I bet he'll hold a press conference."

The Landing was the town's newspaper. It published a physical copy for residents and tourists twice a week, but updated news events on the website for digital subscriptions.

Jazzi took hold of Dawn's phone with its glittery pink protective case. She could see the headline on the front page of *The Landing* before she even pulled it closer.

"Did the Gentlemen's Bake-off Cause a Murder?"

Reading quickly, Jazzi quoted a few phrases out loud. "Competition likely caused the murder of Finn Yarrow, well-known photographer." Next she read, "Competition turned deadly."

She scrolled down the page and read aloud some more. "Chef's cutting board did the deed."

"Did the deed?" Dawn scoffed. "How dramatic is that?

Charmaine Conner needs to return to journalism school and learn that newspapers are supposed to print the news and that means only the facts. Not supposition."

"I'm not sure what she's trying to do except create clickbait to sell more subscriptions." Jazzi handed the phone back to Dawn.

Last summer the reporter had wanted Jazzi to give her an interview after her run-in with a killer. But Jazzi wouldn't do it. The police had kept a lid on who had been involved, but somehow Charmaine had sniffed out Jazzi's name. Still, the police and anyone else involved had kept their lips zipped. Jazzi was grateful for that. If anyone other than Milford had even gleaned a hint that her mom had faced down killers as well, it would have been a media circus.

As Dawn slipped her phone into her apron pocket, customers flowed through the door. Jazzi had been right about cloudy days bringing in tourists.

It was midafternoon when thunder began grumbling outside. There was a storm warning alert posted until seven p.m.

Jazzi was checking the baked goods left in the case when the chandelier above the tea bar blinked. That could mean the storm was imminent. Lightning might have already hit a transformer box.

The lights had steadied again when rain began pouring down. The door to the store opened and a group of women ran in, laughing and taking shelter from the downpour.

One of the women glanced around the store and made a beeline for Dawn, who was wiping down a table near the tea bar. "Dawn Fernsby," she said. "I want to talk to you."

At first, Jazzi didn't recognize Charmaine Conner because the reporter had been turned away from her. But Jazzi recognized her voice. It was nasally, high and distinctive.

Dawn glanced toward Jazzi, looking panicked. Dawn knew who the reporter was because Charmaine always made herself prominent at Belltower Landing events, whether they were newsworthy or not.

Jazzi heard her partner say, "I don't want to talk to you."

"Look, Ms. Fernsby. You found a murder victim. Of course, the press wants to talk to you."

Dawn had received requests from news outlets as far away as Ithaca asking for interviews. She'd turned down all of them, eventually adjusting her phone's setting so she only received calls from her contact list. Charmaine's, though, had been the first she'd rejected.

Charmaine apparently didn't take rejection well. "You *have* to comment. You have to tell the public exactly what you saw."

Dawn left the cleanser bottle and cloth on the table and moved toward Jazzi. The reporter followed.

Next to Jazzi, Dawn faced Charmaine across the counter. "No, I don't have to tell the public anything. In fact, Detective Milford instructed me not to say a word to anyone, let alone the press."

"You're restricting the flow of information!" Charmaine practically squealed. "I need a follow-up to my story today."

"No." Dawn's tone was adamant.

Charmaine targeted Jazzi. "You were involved in setting up the bake-off with the chefs who signed books here. Certainly, they gossiped about what happened. I'm going to track them down. So you might as well give me details."

"No details," Jazzi repeated as adamantly as Dawn. "Anything you print could harm the investigation."

"Or *help*," Charmaine disputed.

"Ms. Conner, we have nothing to say to you." Jazzi's fuse was a long one, but her patience was running thin. She remembered how her mom usually stayed even-tempered when dealing with the press or anyone attempting to dislodge information from her.

"The public information officer will tell me *nothing*," Charmaine complained. "You two are my best source." She leaned forward across the counter. "What if I tell you I can give your bookstore free press and free ads? C'mon. Give and take. Isn't that the secret to success?"

Jazzi exchanged a look with Dawn, though she guessed she didn't need to. They knew each other well enough to expect they were on the same page. Dawn gave a little shrug, as if to say either one of them could answer the question.

Jazzi did. "We don't run our bookstore that way."

Charmaine studied them both, then sneered, "Maybe you should."

She turned in a huff and left, seemingly unmindful of the rain and the storm.

Dawn turned to Jazzi. "I think we've just made an enemy."

Chapter Seven

Jazzi couldn't help but smile on Friday as Tomes & Tea's Pop-Up Parade of Books began. The kids were loving it. The parade had been Dawn's brainchild. She was dressed like Alice in Wonderland. Jazzi had her mom to thank for the cute Alice apron—blue trimmed with white eyelets. Her mom's tea garden had hosted an Alice in Wonderland–themed tea. Today Dawn had also donned a blond wig to accompany the apron.

As Dawn was reading to a group of five children under the age of ten, the mom of a little red-headed boy who looked to be around four approached Jazzi.

The woman pointed to her freckle-faced son. "He loves pop-up or interactive books. That Alice in Wonderland pop-up is beautiful. I'm hoping to keep it in his library for years. I teach him to handle books carefully so they last."

Jazzi grinned. "I still have Golden Books from when I was small. I hope to pass them on to my kids someday."

"Exactly." The woman held out her hand for Jazzi to shake. "I'm Fran Jenkins. Parker Olsen suggested I come with Davie. I'm glad I did. Do you have story time often?"

"This is our first time hosting this event, but the library has story time on Saturday mornings."

"Yes, but I like to buy books for Davie. This is convenient."

Jazzi knew many parents couldn't afford to buy books. Story time at the library could expose them to various authors, and the children could access books with their library cards.

Before Jazzi could put that sentiment into words or consider whether she should, Fran pointed to the tea bar. "There's Parker now."

Parker had stopped at the tea bar and was ordering from Audrey. Dressed in denim shorts and a black T-shirt printed with I'D RATHER BE FISHING, he looked lean, casual, and Jazzi had to admit . . . attractive. Their friendship was very different from hers and Oliver's.

"I hope Davie grows up to be as smart as Parker," Fran said. "I know Parker was homeschooled. But honestly, I don't think I have the aptitude or patience for that."

Jazzi admired Fran for being self-aware enough to realize that. "I went to public school in a small town in Florida and then in Pennsylvania. I had teachers who cared. And my mom stayed involved. She chaperoned many field trips when I was in elementary school."

"Yes, I do intend to be involved," Fran declared. "I've already met Davie's first grade teacher." She nodded toward Dawn. "I'm definitely going to buy the Alice pop-up. Can you recommend others for a five-year-old?"

"If you want a nonfiction pop-up, *The Color Monster* is a book about feelings. A child can learn to identify them with the help of that book. We also carry a pop-up dinosaur book."

"He loves dinosaurs."

"An interactive book is *What Should Danny Do?* It's a series and Danny has red hair."

With a cup of iced tea in one hand and a cupcake in the other,

Parker approached them. "Hi, Fran." He pointed his cupcake at Davie. "He looks enthralled."

"You know he loves books. This was a great idea. I'm going to pick out the books Jazzi suggested." Fran headed toward the preschool bookshelf.

"Thanks for recommending Fran stop in today."

"I play video games with her husband. He often tries out my prototypes. I'm working on a new idea."

"Can you talk about it?" Parker usually kept his new projects confidential.

"Let's just say the game is more fantasy than reality."

"Role playing?"

"Most likely."

Jazzi punched him lightly on his biceps. "Your secrets are safe with me."

He gave her a long look that wasn't at all teasing. "I hope so."

She looked away from his intense studying. "Did you just stop in to see how the Pop-Up Parade of Books was going?"

"That and to ask if you knew what was happening at Vibes." Parker headed for a table to set down his tea and cupcake. He pulled out a purple enamel chair and sat.

Jazzi didn't really have time to take a break. So she stood beside him and asked, "What's going on at Vibes?"

After Parker pulled the paper from his cupcake, he took a bite. Jazzi smiled because he had peanut butter icing above his upper lip. He licked it off, then took a slug of tea. "Anyone who was at the bake-off at the time of the murder can't leave town. Most especially the judges."

"That's to be expected. Anyone could be involved or be a witness."

"Exactly. But the judges aren't happy about it since they had plans to leave as soon as the judging was over. Except for Emmaline." Parker ate the rest of his cupcake in two bites.

"I suppose they complained to Detective Milford. Did it do any good?"

"No. So, they are becoming creative. Diego's specialty is fusion cuisine. He's going to take over Vibes's restaurant tomorrow night. Reservations are necessary. Do you want to go?"

Dinner at Vibes, overlooking the lake, sounded like fun. It would be even more fun if a group of friends enjoyed it together. "Why don't we ask Dawn and maybe Delaney to go with us?"

For a moment, just a moment, disappointment crossed Parker's face. That disappointment bothered Jazzi, and she didn't want to examine it too closely.

But then Parker rallied. His brows evened out and he smiled. "Good idea. I'll make the reservations for the four of us. We'll have good food and excellent company to enjoy it."

Jazzi hadn't wanted to hurt Parker's feelings. But his invitation had sounded too much like a date.

Experiencing the meal with friends was a safer route to take.

Vibes was very different inside than on its more laid-back deck outside overlooking Lake Harding. For the lunches Jazzi had eaten at Vibes, she and friends had sat on the deck, with its black enamel tables and gray-and-white-striped umbrellas. She usually avoided the high-priced restaurant because it simply *wasn't* her vibe.

Tonight, however, she and Parker, Dawn, and Delaney were met by a tuxedoed maître d'. He accepted the reservation cards that Parker presented to him.

"The place is befitting of Diego Alvarez, don't you think?" Parker asked.

Jazzi tried not to be too obvious about scanning the space from the front desk, which was black marble all the way down to the terrazzo-tiled floor.

Dawn nudged Jazzi's arm. "I told you we had to dress up tonight. Aren't you glad you did? This place is classy."

Jazzi had listened to her roommate. But when Dawn had chosen a sequined-top cocktail dress from her closet, Jazzi had pulled a one-shoulder wrap dress in shades of raspberry from hers.

"It is classy," Jazzi agreed. "I don't think I've ever seen tables like those."

Parker leaned close to Jazzi. "Those are Gallus dining tables in black concrete. The side tables are alabaster concrete. Haven't you been inside before?"

She shook her head. "No. I've only ever come to the deck entrance. The upper deck has a great view of the lake."

Her focus swept to the black bench under a row of windows that had a curved silhouette. Pillows decorating the bench were fashioned in an abstract design with a band of gold at the bottom.

As they walked through the restaurant to a table, Jazzi spotted a few people she knew.

After the maître d' had seated them, she said to Parker, "This had to cost a pretty penny. Thank you for buying the tickets."

"Anything to have three beautiful women join me," he quipped. "It raises my status with guy buds."

He was grinning, but she knew nothing was further from the truth. Parker was kind and generous to his friends and rarely made decisions according to anyone else's opinion.

Dawn nudged Jazzi. "I'm looking forward to the cocktail social out on the deck after our meal. It will be fun to mingle."

The aromas of dinners being served at neighboring tables made Jazzi's mouth water. The sommelier stopped by their table and asked if they preferred red or white wine with their meals.

Parker said to the group, "I ordered the seafood dinner since I know you all enjoy it. Scallops for our appetizer and Chilean sea bass for our entrée. White wine?"

All three women nodded.

Jazzi heard a high-pitched voice she recognized and turned to catch a glimpse of Colleen and Emmaline at a table behind them. "I guess Emmaline is joining the fun."

Delaney rearranged her napkin on her lap. "Colleen brought her. I spoke with her at the bakery yesterday. She said she'd stopped in to visit Emmaline, and she was complaining about being cooped up. So Colleen bought a ticket for Emmaline and surprised her. She looks happy to be here."

Emmaline was leaning forward with animation, obviously contributing to the conversation at the table. Jazzi was happy to see that. On the few occasions she'd spoken to the older woman, Jazzi had suspected she was lonely.

Once the dinner course started, the diners' attention was all on the food. First course—seared scallops with garlic butter, sweet and perfectly seared and caramelized.

"I wonder if Diego cooked these himself or one of his sous-chefs." Dawn rolled her eyes in delight at the taste of a scallop.

"He's probably executing and making sure every dish turned out is perfect." Parker lifted a scallop to his lips, enjoying the look of it as he did.

Every dish *was* perfect. Jazzi had never tasted anything as good as the seared fillet of Chilean sea bass served on wilted sesame spinach and topped with a sweet-and-sour sauce.

As they all savored every bite, Parker revealed, "I heard this dish was inspired by Diego's trip to Vietnam last year. When the menu was posted, chat rooms were filled with suppositions on which of Diego's travels inspired which dish.

"He's been around the world," Dawn said with a sigh. "Wouldn't you love traveling from country to country and tasting native dishes?"

"In my spare time," Parker jibed with a wicked smile.

Jazzi laughed, knowing exactly what Parker meant. Traveling would be nice, but it wasn't what she'd want for her *real* life.

After the table finished their dessert—mangos a la canela, created with mangos and a cinnamon-and-sugar cooking sauce—Jazzi leaned against her chair back, her scoop of vanilla ice cream with the mango concoction now only a memory.

She studied the faces of her friends. "Just imagine dining like this in Diego's New York restaurant maybe once a week."

"Food nirvana," Dawn agreed. "Every meal would be memorable."

Laying her napkin on the table, Jazzi stood. "I'm headed to the ladies' room to freshen up before the social."

"I'll come with you." Delaney rose to her feet.

In the ladies' room, with its quartz counters, Jazzi freshened her lipstick alongside Delaney. Delaney's white sleeveless sheath with its low décolletage set off her tanned skin. Her layers of bracelets rattled as she fluffed her hair.

She shot Jazzi a sidelong gaze. "Why didn't you just come with Parker tonight? Why ask me and Dawn along?"

"I knew you'd enjoy the dinner too."

"Um," Delaney grunted.

"What's that supposed to mean?" Jazzi asked.

"It means that's the answer I expected from you rather than the real reason—you didn't want to give Parker the impression it was a date."

Jazzi kept silent.

"It wouldn't hurt you to date him. He wants to date *you*."

Turning to face her friend, Jazzi shook her head. "That's the problem. I don't want to hurt him. I don't want him to think—"

"That you care?"

"He knows I care. I just don't know if I care in *that* way."

"Fair enough," Delaney agreed. "But *someone* is going to snap him up. He's a catch."

Did the idea of Parker in a relationship with someone else bother her? Maybe.

When the women left the bathroom, Jazzi pointed to the left. "Let's take a peek into the kitchen. I've always wanted to see how a famous chef works. I can't imagine Diego shouting like Gordon Ramsay."

Delaney laughed. "I think this kitchen has an open door policy. Let's check."

Heading for the kitchen location, they heard the clatter of pans and utensils as well as voices. After they rounded a wall, they stopped short.

The voices Jazzi had heard were men's voices, rising as a conversation barreled back and forth between them. Those two men were Diego and Griffin, so engrossed in the dispute they didn't notice Jazzi and Delaney peeking around the corner.

Jazzi couldn't decipher every word. Griffin was doing most of the talking.

She heard Griffin say "Finn." His voice went lower, and she caught the word "agreement." His tone raised as he asked Diego sharply, "What are we going to do?"

Delaney grabbed Jazzi's arm and yanked her toward the main area of Vibes once more. But not before Jazzi saw Diego turn his back on Griffin and say a sharp, "We'll do nothing."

Neither Jazzi nor Delaney said a word as they made their way back to their table.

It only took a glance at their faces for Parker to say, "What's wrong?"

Delaney grabbed her glass of wine and took a healthy swallow.

With brows arched and real concern in his brown eyes, Parker stared at Jazzi. "What did you see or hear?"

Parker's IQ radiated much further than his ability to solve mathematical calculations and computer issues. Parker often complained that he wasn't that social. But Jazzi understood he could read her and their friends better than most.

She kept her voice low. "We heard Diego and Griffin having an argument."

"About Vibe's kitchen? I didn't think Pelham had anything to do with tonight."

"Not the kitchen," Delaney said in a tense voice. "About Finn."

Dawn's face seemed to go pale at the mention of Finn's name.

Parker still didn't understand so Jazzi laid it out. "We didn't hear all of it. I could only catch certain words. But they were arguing about an agreement they had with Finn."

"Maybe you misheard. Is that possible?"

"There was a lot of kitchen noise," Delaney admitted. "But we heard Finn's name clearly."

Dawn was shaking her head at the idea the three men were involved. "I don't understand what Finn would have to do with them business-wise. After all, he's a photographer, not a chef."

"Still. Finn approached Griffin about photographing his cookware," Jazzi reminded her.

Parker rearranged his fork on his dessert plate. "Diego has a spotless reputation. He's aboveboard in his business dealings. I've been to his New York restaurant when I'm there for business. He's even known for treating his employees well."

Jazzi turned to look at Delaney. "Maybe we read too much into their dispute."

"Maybe," her friend agreed, but with uncertainty. "But we both got the same shivery feeling from it."

"What about Griffin's image?" Jazzi asked Parker. "What have you heard about him?"

"I don't know much. I'm not as attuned to shopping channel celebrities as much as good restaurants to dine at in New York City. But since the bake-off, I have heard he's jumped around a lot in his career. From a line chef to cookware to home shopping. But that's not unusual for chefs trying to make a name for themselves. It's all in who they meet, who they come to know, who will invest in them and their career."

Two questions still played in Jazzi's mind. What did the three men have in common? And could either Griffin or Diego have murdered Finn?

Jazzi and Delaney strolled along with tourists as they aimed for the town hall on Sunday evening. Lakeview Boulevard was a mecca for visitors. They ambled, stopped in at restaurants, and enjoyed the beauty of the roses on the median.

But Jazzi wasn't concentrating on the view tonight. The mayor had called a meeting at the town hall. Since she and Delaney had been on the planning committee for the bake-off, they had been summoned to the meeting. Charles had stated their presence was mandatory when he'd phoned them both.

Delaney pulled open one side of the heavy wooden double door that led into the building. "The mayor probably wants to discuss the prizes for the bake-off and what we should do about them. He takes votes on everything. This isn't any different. I'm torn between the idea of simply forgetting about the prizes altogether or donating them to charity."

Delaney took a few steps into the first floor of the structure, which smelled like old wood, lemon polish, and years of history.

Jazzi rarely had reason to visit Belltower Landing's town hall. It was one of the oldest structures in the community and almost resembled a church, but without a steeple. The brick two-story building, with its white clapboard fish-scale adornment inset at the pointed roof, had served multiple purposes. In the early history of the town, meetings had been held on its first floor when residents sat on pew-like benches. However, now those town hall meetings were called at the community center near the marina, which was larger. The mayor's and town administrator's offices occupied the second floor here.

"Everyone is here," Delaney commented as they walked up an aisle toward the front of the open first-floor meeting room.

The first two benches of hardwood oak were filled. As soon as Delaney and Jazzi were seated, Delaney leaned close to her. "How is Dawn really coping?"

Delaney finding a body last May had affected her deeply, Jazzi knew. "Dawn's spending more time with her family. I believe she's trying to avoid thinking about what she saw. She's busy every minute, and that's her way of dealing with Finn's death."

"She'll have to face her feelings about it eventually. I thought

I did, but I still have nightmares." Delaney's voice was filled with resignation. "I just hope my mind and heart will eventually move on."

Jazzi leaned her shoulder against Delaney's to show her support.

Rupert Harding and his nephew descended the stairs and took their place at the table facing the benches. They didn't sit. Today the mayor was dressed in khaki pants and a burnt-orange and green plaid blazer with a peach-colored shirt. Charles was wearing his typical gray linen suit.

The mayor seemed to nibble on his lower lip. The lines under his eyes seemed deeper. With a sigh, he ran his fingers through his white-and-gray mop of hair. He seemed to have aged a decade since the bake-off.

"I had believed we'd meet today to discuss the best way to proceed with coordinating the end of the bake-off and tying up loose ends. But, as mayor, my nephew encouraged me to make a decision and not take input. Still, I'd like you to vote on what I've decided."

Jazzi felt herself holding her breath, hoping whatever decision the mayor had come to would be compassionate for everyone involved.

"I believe we should award the prizes for the competition. All in favor, please raise your hands."

Charles nodded his approval, as did everyone when hands flew into the air.

The mayor looked relieved. "I'm glad that's settled. Finn won first prize, Carl second, and Tim third. I could announce it at a town meeting or—"

"Mayor, I have a suggestion," Jazzi said.

"And what would that be?" Charles asked.

Jazzi addressed the mayor rather than Charles. "Maybe members of the committee could give the prize winners the news privately . . . individually."

"To avoid the press getting hold of this," Charles ruminated. "That new reporter tries to make everything a controversy."

For once Jazzi agreed with Charles.

"I know Abe," Delaney said.

"Carl often comes in to my store," Jazzi offered.

Another committee member said he'd contact Tim.

The mayor spoke again. "And I'll visit Finn's wife, Belinda. I'll make sure she understands we all send her our condolences."

Jazzi thought about the fact that Finn had won first place with his Black Forest cake. Would that acclaim give his wife any consolation?

Jazzi doubted it.

Chapter Eight

The front window of the Dockside Bakery was stuffed with pastries such as profiteroles—a cream puff with a filling of custard. Beside those sat napoleons, layers of puff pastry filled with pastry cream. However, what usually interested Jazzi and was her favorite was the opera cake—almond sponge cake soaked in coffee syrup, then layered with buttercream and covered in a chocolate glaze.

She sighed.

Today she was passing on all of those goodies. The long line of customers weaving into the bakery even in midafternoon were counting on buying Black Forest cake, created especially in memory of Finn Yarrow.

Giselle Dubois, a friend of Jazzi's and a member of the Tomes & Tea book club, stood in line behind Jazzi. "I think this is a wonderful thing Colleen is doing."

Community minded, Giselle owned and operated a cleaning service for expensive lakeview homes. She hired women who had been down on their luck and needed a hand to climb back to their feet.

"It's generous of Colleen to donate ninety percent of the

proceeds toward the scholarship Finn's wife is setting up."
Jazzi admired Colleen for wanting to help in some way.

"I understand the scholarship will go to a high school senior who is interested in photography or making movies." Giselle's heart-shaped face was full of approval.

The sun was beaming down on them. Jazzi pushed her Dutch braid away from her shoulder. "I think the kids will have to submit either a portfolio of stills or a movie they created. The scholarship could reveal real talents."

In the past, Giselle hadn't wanted to discuss anything to do with the murder. Jazzi didn't blame her. But to Jazzi's surprise, Giselle asked, "How is Dawn? I haven't seen her since book club, and she seemed much quieter than her usual bubbly self."

Moving forward in the line, Jazzi said, "She's coping. I don't know what to do for her except listen. She's the one who suggested I use my break to buy Black Forest cake for us and our staff. She wants to be supportive of the project but didn't want to come here, where she might be asked all sorts of questions. That happens enough at Tomes."

Giselle moved forward with Jazzi. "I hope this experience doesn't mess with her mind. I've seen women who've experienced trauma have problems moving on."

A high-pitched woman's voice from behind Giselle soared over to Jazzi. "It's hard to move on when the detective keeps interviewing us over and over again!"

Giselle frowned as she looked behind her. In a low voice she murmured to Jazzi, "Can I move ahead of you? I don't want to get caught up in a conversation about Finn's murder."

Immediately, Jazzi let Giselle step in front of her and go through the door. Then she faced Emmaline, who had apparently jumped the line. She had her cane in one hand and her large red tote bag in her other, so Jazzi suspected customers in line had let her move before them. Jazzi hadn't noticed Emmaline as the line had formed.

Jazzi wore a pink floral sundress today. Emmaline, however,

looked as if she were dressed for fall rather than summer. Her red dress with a black print had three-quarter sleeves and a high-buttoned neck. She looked hot.

Emmaline dug into her tote bag, dragged out a tissue, and mopped her brow while her cane stood on its three prongs beside her.

Jazzi asked her, "Did the detective question you again?"

Emmaline's frown caused long lines on either side of her mouth. "Yes, he did. And he made me come to the police station."

"He couldn't interview you at your hotel?" Jazzi wondered if the older woman had stood up for herself or just done what she was told.

"When I protested coming to the station, he said he'd send a patrol car for me. I said 'forget it' and called an Uber. Like I want anyone seeing me in a patrol car." Emmaline sounded outraged and seemed to want to protect her image.

Jazzi said, "I suppose Detective Milford believes interrogating anyone at the station will pull out the truth quicker."

"That's hogwash. Just because they sit me in a hard chair in a hot room doesn't lead me to cooperate more. Really. Just wait until he gets old enough for his bones to hurt."

Sympathetic toward Emmaline, Jazzi laid a hand on her shoulder. "It's over for now."

Emmaline put her own hand on her cane once more. "It won't be over until they figure out who killed that photographer. And interviewing the likes of me isn't going to do that."

Deciding to change the subject, Jazzi asked, "How will you get back to your suite?"

"I'll call another Uber. I should send the bill for my rides to the police department. Just imagine me riding in a patrol car. How humiliating would that be?"

"Maybe a slice of Black Forest cake and a cold drink will make your trip to town worth it."

"I certainly hope so. I might buy two slices. Once I'm back at the resort, I'm not going out again." Emmaline's harrumph put an exclamation point on that.

The line moved forward, and both Jazzi and Emmaline stepped into the bakery and its air-conditioning. Emmaline breathed a sigh of relief.

There were ten small, round, white wrought-iron tables in the bakery, and they were all filled both with tourists and local residents.

"I couldn't eat here if I wanted to. Is it always this crowded?" Emmaline inquired.

"It can be." Jazzi spotted Derek Stuart and Parker at one of the tables. She beckoned to them. While Derek finished his slice of Black Forest cake, Parker came over to her.

Jazzi said, "Can I ask you for a favor?"

He cocked his head at her with a questioning smile. "Sure."

"Will you let Emmaline sit with you while I buy her a slice of cake and a drink? I think she needs to sit."

"Of course." He turned to Emmaline. "Would you like to sit at my table? Derek and I are just finishing."

Swinging around to Jazzi, Emmaline beamed at her. "Thank you, thank you, you dear girl. I won't forget your kindness. And you too, young man."

Parker grinned. "My pleasure. I'll get rid of our plates while Jazzi picks up yours."

When he left to do that, Emmaline pointed to a glazed granite cutting board on the counter behind the glass case. "Do you see that? That detective kept focusing on what I remembered about a cutting board. Can you imagine what that weighs? I could never lift that."

As if her comment wasn't completely out of left field, she added, "Thanks again for being so kind."

With that, Emmaline used her cane to walk toward Parker and Derek, looking happy to be welcomed to the table.

Jazzi watched Emmaline. She was in her seventies and seemed frail. But was she? Her tote bag could weigh as much as the cutting board, and she carried that without a problem.

Could Emmaline have hit Finn with the piece of granite? If so, why?

Tomes had been so busy all afternoon that Jazzi and her staff hadn't had time to eat their Black Forest cake. After the store had been closed and the digital sign on the door said as much, Jazzi pulled the bag of cake slices from the mini-fridge in the storeroom and carried it up to their apartment. Dawn had already gone up with Audrey and Erica to settle in.

As Jazzi made her way through her bedroom, Zander and Freya scampered in to greet her. They rounded her ankles, their fur brushing above her ankle strap. Then they scampered under her bed to play hide-and-seek amid the bedspread and folds.

Once in the living room, Jazzi saw that Erica and Audrey were seated on the sofa.

"I have a pitcher of berry-flavored herbal tea," Dawn offered from the kitchen.

"I'll take a glass," Audrey called.

"Me too," Erica seconded.

Heading for the kitchen counter, Jazzi placed the bag of desserts there and reached to a top cupboard for plates. They owned four Polish pottery dessert dishes they'd found at a secondhand shop. One had a chip, and that's why they'd been discounted.

Dawn said, "I already fed the kittens. They ate and ran."

Jazzi laughed. "That's their MO. They're under my bed with the dust bunnies."

After adding the poured iced tea glasses to a tray patterned with sailboats, Dawn carried it to the oval coffee table near the sofa. Audrey and Erica each took a glass. Dawn set hers on a coaster on the side table.

"I saw Giselle at the Dockside, Dawn. She asked about you." As Jazzi pulled a chair from the small dining table, she turned it to face her friends.

"What did you tell her?" Dawn asked a bit defiantly.

Jazzi distributed forks and the plates of cake from the counter until they each balanced one. "I told her you were coping."

Deflating a little, Dawn nodded. "That's about right."

Erica flashed Dawn a concerned-mom smile. "Talk to us whenever you need to. Get those pictures out of your head."

Jazzi could see Dawn shudder. Then spotting Zander, who'd run into the room with his sister, Dawn caught him under his belly and held him up in front of her nose. "This little guy hears about my feelings all the time. I repeat myself constantly and ask, 'Who would do that? Why would they do that? What kind of upbringing did a murderer have?'"

Not having heard Dawn express that last question before, Jazzi asked, "Did you and Zander come to any conclusions?"

"Not exactly." Dawn lowered the kitten to her lap as Freya climbed the chair to join her brother. "Maybe someone who has an anger problem."

"Or poor impulse control," Audrey added.

She looked as if she was going to say more but didn't. Jazzi wondered why. This group of women was usually open with each other.

To fill in the gap of silence, Jazzi said, "I ran into Emmaline in the line at the Dockside."

"Was she just walking around town and saw the special?" Erica took a forkful of her confection—cherries, chocolate cake, and whipped filling. She closed her eyes to savor the flavors.

Slicing off a bite of her cake, Jazzi slid her fork under it. "The detective insisted on interviewing her at the station."

"Really?" Erica seemed disgusted with that idea. "I can't understand Detective Milford's interest in her. She can't even get around that well. If she wanted to clobber someone, she'd probably do it with her cane."

"Maybe he thinks interviewing us at the police station gives him more street cred. I know it's intimidating to sit in that interview room knowing you're being recorded." Dawn quickly ate a few bites of her cake and washed it down with swallows of tea.

"Emmaline says what she thinks. I don't believe she was intimidated. At least not much. She made a point of telling me she couldn't lift that piece of granite. Too heavy. But I think her tote looks just as heavy." Jazzi's glass was sweating on its coaster. She picked it up.

Zander and Freya had scooted in between the yellow chair's arm and Dawn's hip. They were a pile of furry cuteness.

"That tote bag is an Yves St. Laurent calfskin," Audrey pointed out.

"What does that mean?" Erica asked her daughter.

"It means it was originally worth about fifteen hundred dollars. And Emmaline wears Jimmy Choo shoes. I notice clothes. I can't afford fashion like that, but I sure can view runway shows online and check out new styles each season."

Erica glanced at her daughter. "But you mostly wear leggings and jeans."

"While I'm pet sitting, I have to be comfortable. But I buy an expensive piece here and there when I can afford it. I guess Emmaline can afford that stuff because she's a famous baker. But I heard last weekend that she's looking for paid gigs."

"Really?" Jazzi asked. "Then I'm surprised she accepted coming here for the bake-off. The chefs are supposedly doing this for publicity alone. And because Belltower Landing is one of their vacation spots." She couldn't imagine that participating in judging the bake-off would result in real money flowing into their pockets. But who knew?

Audrey's brown eyes were bright as she looked around the group. Appearing to make up her mind about something, she revealed, "Tim Blanchard and his wife are my clients. They have two dogs—a German Shephard and a dachshund."

"You don't usually name your clients," her mother noted.

"No, I don't. But I was talking with Tim. He thinks the bake-off was rigged. He believes Finn modified one of Diego's recipes and that's why his Black Forest cake won. Something about the secret is in marinating the cherries," Audrey added.

Jazzi imagined the type of liqueur made a difference in taste. Was that what Finn and Tim had argued about at the bake-off? Jazzi expressed the question out loud.

Jumping right in after she did, Erica added, "Tim is a friend of my brother's. And I've used his plumbing service for years. He's an honest guy. Maybe he was right about Finn. But I can't see Tim being involved in the murder."

Dawn suddenly pushed herself up from her chair, disturbing the kittens. "I think we need cheese to go with this dessert. Maybe I can throw together omelets for all of us so we don't have sugar highs. What do you say?"

Jazzi exchanged looks with Erica and Audrey. Dawn obviously needed to change the subject.

Audrey piped up first. "Let's do it. Dessert first is a new trend."

For now they'd set aside talk of murder. But it would come up again.

When Parker arrived at Tomes & Tea at midafternoon the following day, he asked Jazzi, "Are you ready?"

Jazzi had been serving at the tea bar. Now she smiled at Parker as Audrey took her place to relieve her for her break.

"I'm ready. Let me grab my purse and Carl West's gift certificate."

In their storeroom, Dawn was unboxing new titles for their shelves. "Do you think you and Parker can find Carl?"

"Carl's wife, who schedules his workday, said he was working at the docks, maybe bringing an outboard to the boatyard after looking it over. When Parker brought his boat in last evening, he ran into Carl. Carl told him he'd be working at slip eleven today. If we don't find him, we'll both get some exercise."

"You could simply stop at Carl's house tonight," Dawn said as she used a ceramic box cutter to open a new carton.

"I know. But then my evening would be tied up. It will be nice to have a leisurely dinner with you and play with the kittens, maybe stream a movie. I don't want to think about tomorrow." The next day would be heart tugging for anyone who had known Finn or wanted to pay their respects.

"Do you think Belinda's doing the right thing, having Finn's memorial in the high school auditorium?" After removing an armful of books from the carton, Dawn set them on their break table.

"Finn knew so many of the students and their parents from shooting class photos to senior pictures. So many residents in Belltower Landing knew him, at least professionally." Jazzi took her purse from a cupboard next to their mini-fridge and checked to make sure the gift certificate from Rods to Boards was inside. It was.

Dawn sagged against the table. "Finn's had the high school contract for at least the past five years. I know tomorrow is necessary but I'm dreading it."

Jazzi stepped closer to her best friend. "You *don't* have to go."

"I know I don't have to. But I should. Even my mom and Farrell are going. Dad's going to hold down the shop."

Dawn looked so sad that Jazzi gave her a hug. "*If* you go, I will be with you."

Giving Jazzi a hard squeeze, Dawn finally stepped away. "Take your walk with Parker and grab some lunch on your way back. It will almost be like a date."

Jazzi rolled her eyes at her friend and left the room.

As Parker and Jazzi walked, they didn't talk. Not until they passed The Wild Kangaroo and the leather shop beside it.

Parker glanced at her. "Have you seen Oliver lately?"

His question surprised her. "No. Not since last week. Why?" She remembered exactly when she'd seen Oliver last—at the waffle truck.

"Just wondered."

"Parker, I'd tell you if I was dating someone." Wasn't *that* what he wanted to know?

"*Are* you thinking about dating him?"

"No!" The word blew out of her mouth much more vehemently than it should have.

Parker didn't comment, but with her sidelong perusal of him, she saw his lips tighten and his jaw jut out.

They didn't talk again until the marina came into sight. Sunbeams bounced off the tin roof of the boat shop building. They crossed the boulevard at a light. Their shoes clomped on the boardwalk as they followed it around the store to the dock.

There were three sections of sixteen slips each on their side of Lake Harding. They walked down the first pier to slip number eleven.

Jazzi would never tire of the diamond sparkles on the lake, the breeze catching the hem of her sundress, the sun beating down on her loose braid. These were all reasons why she loved living in Belltower Landing. Even the briny smell of fish and the musk of the bulrushes added to the appeal of this tourist town.

As soon as they neared the slip, Jazzi recognized Carl stepping off a hard-topped boat with his clipboard.

"Hey, Carl." Parker called to the man so he wasn't surprised by their appearance.

Carl adjusted his ball cap so the bill protected his eyes from the sun's rays. "Hi, Parker." He tipped his head. "Jazzi." Returning his attention to Parker, he grinned. "Are you going to buy another boat? This one is in good shape. Just a scratch or two in the gel coat."

"No. Not another boat. Mine will do."

"This one is bigger." Carl motioned to the length of it.

"I'm good. Remember, I like to fish alone. I just accompanied Jazzi on her walk. She has something for you."

Carl flipped off his ball cap and poked it under his arm. "Did another mystery come in for my wife? You're hand delivering?"

Jazzi laughed, then opened her purse. "No. The mayor asked me to bring this to you. It's your second-place prize from the bake-off."

After blowing out a breath, Carl stuck the clipboard under his arm with his cap. "I never expected the prizes to be given out after what happened." He accepted the envelope from Jazzi's hand.

Opening the envelope, he slipped out the gift certificate. "I can always use credit at Rods to Boards." His smile faded. He took his clipboard in hand again and added the certificate under the clip.

Seeming to debate with himself, Carl finally studied Jazzi. "Are you in on this investigation? Do you know who the suspects are?"

Jazzi didn't know how close Carl and Finn had been. "No. Why would you think I would be?"

"Since Dawn is your roommate." As a second thought, he added, "And since you were involved with the last murder, I thought you might have an in with the police. Like in those TV mysteries."

"I don't, Carl. I'm sorry. The detective is questioning anyone who could be involved."

"I didn't know Finn Yarrow that well. But I am friends with Tim Blanchard. He believes he's the detective's number one person of interest because he had that fight with Finn in plain sight."

A horn farther down the pier startled Jazzi. A day cruiser headed toward slip number thirteen.

Carl raised a hand in greeting.

Jazzi adjusted a strap on her sundress that had slipped sideways, and then she asked the question uppermost in her thoughts. "Do you know what the fight was about?"

She could see Parker was listening for the answer too.

Carl shrugged. "Tim said it had something to do with the bake-off. That's all he would say. He was upset about the murder and all the questioning, so I didn't press."

And if Carl had pressed, would he have found out the argument *was* about the bake-off? Or about something more personal?

Chapter Nine

When Jazzi and Dawn stepped into the lobby of Belltower Landing's public high school, Jazzi was hit by a stream of memories from her own high school days back in Willow Creek. Somehow schools everywhere smelled the same. Maybe it was the floor wax.

Other residents of town were streaming along with them, passing trophy cases, plaques on the walls, and the ambience of a new school year starting at the end of the month. Jazzi imagined teachers had already prepared their classrooms.

Two sets of double doors led from the tiled foyer into the auditorium. Cranberry-fabric seats fifteen across lined the middle section. Rows of ten ran down each side. Jazzi was surprised to see that over half of the seats were filled and more people were filing in.

Two large video monitors were positioned on either side of the stage. A stream of Finn's friends and clients formed a reception line which flowed down the right-side aisle, stopped to gaze at the photo collages on the first monitor, then crossed in front of the stage to the second monitor.

Dawn caught Jazzi's arm. "Did you expect to see the auditorium so full?"

Jazzi pulled her phone from her crossbody bag. "I'd better text Erica to tell her we might be here longer than we expected. We really should give our condolences to Belinda, and that could take a while." Finn's wife sat in the front row before the stage. Friends stopped as they passed the monitors to express their grief and share hers. Jazzi could see many tears as women and men embraced Finn's wife.

As Jazzi texted Erica, Dawn followed Jazzi down the side aisle. "We should think about hiring temporary help. We can afford it now, don't you think?"

"Do you believe we'll need it once tourist season is over?" Tomes & Tea was more financially solvent since spring with the special events they'd planned. The store had a larger social media presence, because of highly visible guests and celebrities who'd stopped at the bookstore and given a shout out to their followers.

"We'd need someone willing to work a few hours a week. Maybe we can talk about it at book club. Addison's little girl will be starting preschool. Maybe she'd consider it."

"That's a great idea." Dawn was pointing at the monitor to which they were headed. "These photos are all personal."

On the screen, Jazzi watched the photos express sentiments about Finn and Belinda as a couple. One flashed of the two of them in a kayak. The next appeared to be a wedding day photo, with Belinda in white satin and Finn in an elegant black tux. There were photos of the couple on a mountaintop and another in D.C. at the Vietnam Veterans Memorial. The city photos looked to Jazzi like pictures she'd seen of New York City— Rockefeller Plaza at Christmas, the Metropolitan Museum of Art.

In most photos Finn had his arm circling Belinda's waist, or they were leaning in for a kiss.

Standing in front of the monitor, Dawn pointed to photo

after photo. "Those aren't selfies. I guess Finn set the timer and let the camera shoot."

Seeing that Belinda was speaking to someone, Jazzi and Dawn strolled toward the other screen. As she watched the stream of photos, Jazzi nodded. "That was him putting his expertise to work. They all look professional."

One element of this memorial was the dark wood table on center front of the stage. A black ceramic urn sat there. On lower stands to both sides and back of the table stood arrays of floral bouquets, from lilies to roses to carnations to exotic-looking arrangements. The scents of the flowers wafted down, creating a perfume of mixed smells. It was almost . . . cloying.

Jazzi heard the woman talking to Belinda say, "We so wanted Finn to videotape our wedding. Ralph wished he could come today but work took him to Ithaca."

"I can recommend someone else." Belinda brushed her long brown hair away from her face, either in habit or a nervous gesture.

"I don't want you to think about that right now." Her friend patted her shoulder. "We'll find someone. I heard Claude Fenton is on par with Finn."

"He is," Belinda answered her.

Jazzi guessed Belinda was simply being polite. She probably wanted to say, "No one is on par with my husband."

Heading a few steps away to where Dawn was standing, Jazzi saw her friend seemed mesmerized. Many of the photographs featured couples. However, some pictures of cute children with chubby cheeks and shining eyes flashed by. The slideshow continued with artistic photos mixed with themes of light and dark, lightning flashes, moon phases. All part of Finn's body of work.

Since Belinda was free for the moment, Jazzi tapped Dawn's arm and motioned toward her. Jazzi's low braid patted along her back as she walked and stopped to greet Belinda.

"Jazzi and Dawn, right? I've stopped in at Tomes & Tea but we never formally met." There was sadness but warmth in her voice. "Thank you for coming."

"We're so sorry for your loss." Dawn leaned in to Belinda to give her a hug, then Jazzi did the same.

"From the looks of the friends gathered here, Finn was well loved." Jazzi nodded toward the seats that were still filling.

"I hope I can get through the eulogy after Finn's friends and colleagues speak." Belinda gazed toward the podium at the right side of the stage. "I'm just glad our minister will speak after me."

"You'll do fine," Dawn assured her. "Everyone will understand your grief."

Dawn's encouragement caused Belinda to frown. "Not everyone. Finn's murderer is still out there somewhere or even *here*. When his friends or clients wish me well, I can't help but wonder if one of them did this."

"I think about that, especially in the middle of the night," Dawn said.

"It had to have been awful for you to have found him. I can't imagine." Belinda's eyes grew glassy with tears.

"Detective Milford will find who did this." Jazzi's voice was gentle. "And the scholarship fund is a wonderful idea. I imagine many of the people here are students and parents who admired the photos Finn captured."

"*Captured* is right." Belinda's smile was soft and hardly there. But she went on. "Some of those teens he photographed for senior pictures didn't want to be part of what their parents wanted for senior pictures. They tried to convince Finn to photograph them in raggedy clothes, baggy pants, and cropped tops. But Finn always made sure they had their parents' approval. He said their parents were paying and they had say. He'd even call them right from the shoot. And don't get me started on class photos and all the shenanigans."

"He must have had a lot of stories to tell," Jazzi prompted.

Belinda wasn't looking as drawn as she shared memories about her husband. "He surely did. I'd like to see more than one student be awarded the scholarship, but we'll have to see what funds come in."

"Will you have restrictions on the scholarship? Like they have to be enrolling in college?" Dawn asked.

Belinda frowned, lines that showed her age going deeper around her eyes and the sides of her mouth. Maybe she was older than Jazzi had guessed. Maybe closer to forty-five than forty?

"We'll include provisions for art schools. And there will be a limit on parents' income. I'd like to see a student who couldn't afford college or art school otherwise receive it."

A couple came up behind Jazzi and Dawn, so they knew they had to move on. Jazzi motioned to a few empty seats on the left aisle. Most people wanted to sit in the center to see better. But Jazzi was okay with listening. Apparently, Dawn was too.

They skittered up the far aisle and side-walked into the row where Colleen was sitting. She smiled in welcome.

Before she sank down onto the padded seat, Jazzi caught sight of Tim and Abe in a row farther back. Carl sat on an end seat in the center aisle. As she took a last glance at Belinda, she noticed Griffin approaching her. Jazzi couldn't help but think, "Most of the suspects are here."

Suspects? Really? She shouldn't be categorizing *anyone* that way.

"The gang's all here," Colleen commented when Jazzi turned and sat.

"Excuse me?" Jazzi wasn't exactly sure who Colleen meant or what the sarcasm in her voice was supposed to convey.

With a lopsided shrug, Colleen explained, "Everyone who participated somehow in the bake-off is here today except for Emmaline. I haven't seen her."

"What about Diego?" Jazzi hadn't spotted him in the crowd.

"He came through before you arrived. He spoke with Belinda but didn't stay."

Jazzi remembered the conversation she'd heard between Diego and Griffin. Just how intertwined were the chefs and the contestants?

"I suppose Diego is the busiest of everyone in that group," she said. With his New York City restaurant and global travels, she imagined he couldn't just take a vacation in the midst of all that.

"Could be. But I heard the detective cleared him to leave. He's headed back to New York City today with the understanding that he'll be available for further questioning." Colleen watched the row of Finn's friends climb the stage's side stairs to the podium.

Jazzi looked that way too. "I guess none of the other contestants were considered Finn's friends?"

Colleen nodded toward a man in a cream sports jacket and khaki slacks. "Just Leon Avila. He almost made the second cut with chocolate pecan pie."

Jazzi hadn't recognized Leon dressed as he was today. He was a stay-at-home dad who'd worn a T-shirt, jeans, and a ball cap to bake.

"Everyone says Finn was well-liked, so I assumed he was friends with most of the contestants," Dawn mused.

"Don't assume." Colleen's expression said that because she was fifteen years older than Dawn, she had more wisdom. Probably she did.

"Any competition can turn friends against each other," she continued. "Remember the fight between Tim and Finn?"

Jazzi nodded.

"They were supposedly friends before that. In fact, Belinda asked Tim to speak today, but he declined. I spoke with her before friends started filing in. I think she was hurt he wouldn't share his memories of Finn."

It sounded as if Colleen had been close to the couple. "Did you know Finn well?"

"I did. And Belinda asked me to speak, but I felt my story was too personal to share."

Jazzi didn't know whether Colleen would share or not. But she waited. Sometimes silence was the best persuader.

With a glance over her shoulder and then lowering her voice, Colleen leaned closer to Jazzi. "My son was bullied at school. He turned to drugs. After rehab, Finn mentored him. Hank had always been interested in photography. With Finn's help, Hank learned so much about the art, light, and positioning of subjects. He's been selling photos online for a while now and videotaping constantly. He's attending film school in Atlanta. Finn's death hit him hard. But I think he's on solid ground now thanks to Finn."

From everything Jazzi had seen and heard about Finn, he'd been well respected. Colleen's latest revelation about him added another layer to his good-guy persona.

"I think the sales of the Black Forest cake were so high because Hank's story isn't the only one like it," Colleen added. "Around high school students as much as he was, Finn mentored others too. You'll probably hear about it when his friends eulogize him."

That was probably going to happen in the next few minutes.

Jazzi suddenly realized she wasn't the only one who would be listening intently to stories about Finn Yarrow. Detective Milford had strode down the side aisle and was standing at attention near the stage stairs. Maybe he wanted to be close enough to see the expressions on Finn's friends' faces. Maybe he wanted to pick up the strains of grief in the air. Maybe he wanted to absorb an inkling of Finn's personality through his friends.

Or maybe he was searching out signs that a murderer was in the auditorium, pretending to be grieving.

* * *

Pushing two round tables together, Jazzi scanned Tomes & Tea. She was ready for the biweekly book club meeting tonight. The days since Finn's memorial had been busy. She and Dawn had even managed a relaxing paddleboard excursion over the weekend. She'd brought along the most recent Lisa Jewell thriller to discuss. She never knew what other members would bring since they were a diverse club that conversed about whatever book a member was reading. All participants in the book club were exposed to fiction, nonfiction, self-help, and how-to books.

While Dawn was brewing herbal tea—strawberry pomegranate—to ice for the meeting, Jazzi placed their chairs in an oval around the tables. She was arranging two chairs at the top of the oval when the *ding* of the door opening sounded. When she looked up, she found Oliver striding toward her.

As usual, her stomach did a little flip. She'd changed after work into lotus-blossom-patterned harem pants with a side slit and a white gauzy boyfriend blouse. Casual. That's what the mood usually was here.

Oliver's blond hair looked damp as if he'd showered recently. He was wearing slim-legged denim shorts and a royal blue T-shirt with a jumping kangaroo.

His very-blue eyes sparked with humor and his expression was charmingly unsure. "Am I in the right place?" he teased.

Surprised to see him, she blurted out, "You're taking the night off?"

Leaning closer to Jazzi, he pretended a low conspiratorial whisper. "I'm the boss. I can do that now and then."

She knew she was blushing furiously. The heat in her cheeks alerted her. Out of habit when she was nervous, she pulled her braid over her shoulder and fingered the swath of hair below the braid tie.

Pulling herself together, ignoring the very pleasant scent of cologne or aftershave that he used, she gestured to the arriving members of their club, who caused the bell to ding three times. "Everybody usually arrives in a bunch. We should be ready to start in about ten minutes. You're welcome to pick up a cup of iced tea and grab a seat.

"This place looks different at night." He motioned to the neon lights in the cubicles. "More like a club but without the sweaty bodies."

Oliver still stood relatively close. She found she didn't mind at all. "I don't know. We can become embroiled in sweaty, vehement book discussions."

"I guess men and women get riled over their opinions of characters and book plots."

"Have you joined other book clubs?" Jazzi found herself wanting to know so much more about this man.

He gave a one-shouldered shrug as Jazzi looked up at him. "I have two friends who make Australia their home. We connect once a month and book titles come up." Oliver was holding a book down by his side.

"What did you bring?"

He lifted the volume to show her the cover. "Instead of Diego's book, I decided to stray from restaurant discussion. I brought *Old Cowboys Never Die* by William W. Johnstone.

"Good one!" The words came out in a burst of spontaneity.

"Have you read it?" He looked surprised.

"I have."

They found themselves staring at each other for a very long moment.

The entrance bell dinged again as Derek, Parker, and Delaney flooded in, laughing.

Parker stopped cold when he saw Jazzi and Oliver standing close together and talking.

Erica broke the spell when she rushed in, a large Tupperware container in her hands. "Pecan sandies tonight," she cheerily announced.

"Does Erica often bake for the group?" Oliver was studying the cookie container.

Coming forward, Parker answered, "She does. Though Addison and Giselle often bring snacks too." Parker gestured to the two women as they came through the door in a flurry, carrying tins. He added, "Addison thinks we enjoy the same snacks as her three-year-old. And we do."

Parker sometimes had an attitude about Oliver, but now he made an attempt at a smile.

Dawn waved at everyone from the tea bar. "Iced tea is ready. Come and get it."

Jazzi introduced Oliver to other book club members, though most knew him by sight at the Kangaroo. Everyone picked up cups of iced tea and settled into chairs. No tourists or other residents of town joined them, and she was glad about that. She wanted to run something by the group after book discussion.

Once settled, she found herself between Oliver and Parker, not sure how that had happened. Dawn kept giving her an expression with raised brows and a teasing smile. Jazzi told herself to concentrate on the books they were discussing. For the most part, she could. But she was keenly aware of Oliver's arm sliding against hers and Parker's glances at the two of them.

They all talked about their books. Derek was reading the latest C. J. Box about a game warden who bagged criminals in the Wyoming wilderness. Parker discussed *Control Freak*, in which Cliff Bleszinski wrote about becoming a video game innovator. Giselle, a Danielle Steel fan, was reading her latest.

The group snacked, sipped tea, spoke about what they liked about the books they were reading and what they didn't. Jazzi was always curious about why a reader picked up a particular book. These discussions always aided her understanding of her customers and their preferences.

After each member's book had been the center of discussion, talk turned to community activities like the Get Out and Dance event that was planned for an upcoming weekend as well as a Movie Under the Stars night on the green.

Derek plucked a cookie from the container, then passed it around the oval of chairs. "Do you think the turnout will be worthwhile for community activities after what happened to Finn?"

Giselle suddenly stood, picked up her handbag, and motioned to the door. "I have to get home," she mouthed to Jazzi.

Jazzi knew exactly why Giselle was choosing to leave now. She did not want to talk about murder. She'd made that expressly clear last May.

Jazzi slid from her chair and followed Giselle to the door. She didn't know much personal history about their friend. Giselle didn't share much on a personal level. Now Jazzi wondered if someone had been murdered in her past to cause this reaction. Or maybe she was tenderhearted and could be affected by the motives of a killer.

"Are you okay?" Jazzi asked at the door.

"I'm fine," Giselle answered with a smile. "I have an early meeting with my cleaning staff in the morning."

Jazzi placed a hand on Giselle's shoulder. "If you ever want to talk, I'm here."

After studying Jazzi's face, Giselle nodded. "I know that. Thank you."

The door closed behind Giselle and Jazzi headed back to the group. When she spotted Dawn's expression, Jazzi knew her roommate probably didn't want to talk about Finn's murder either.

"Finn's service was moving," Addison claimed. "I was in tears, and I didn't even know him well. But he'd taken our family photos after Sylvie was born and again last Christmas. He was so good with Sylvie during both sessions. Didn't get impatient at all."

Agreeing, Erica gave a sad smile. "He was around kids so much with school photos. I think he understood all ages."

Audrey looked thoughtful. "Finn made taking senior photos easy. I think my junior year was when he was contracted as school photographer. When he said I could have more than one change of scenery for my senior pictures, I was delighted."

"He often came in to the Kangaroo," Oliver said. He switched his attention to Dawn. "Are you okay talking about Finn?"

Jazzi should have asked her best friend that question. She appreciated Oliver doing it.

"I'm okay." Dawn picked up her tea as if her hands needed something to do. "As long as we stay away from the day it happened."

Jazzi gave Dawn a hug as she came around her chair and took her seat between Oliver and Parker. "We will stay away from that." Knowing it was hard for Dawn not only to remember but also to keep what she'd remembered to herself, Jazzi changed the course of their conversation.

"Watching all the photos on the monitors at the service, I had a thought."

"Uh oh," Parker said under his breath but loud enough for her to hear.

She ignored him. "What if Finn's murder had something to do with his photography rather than the bake-off?"

Oliver shifted toward her. "You mean competition had nothing to do with it?"

"At least not a baking competition." Jazzi's gaze met his, and she saw that he understood where she was going with her logic.

A pensive expression stole over Dawn's face, and she expressed her thoughts. "Carl and his wife used Finn. I know of another couple who also used Finn to videotape their wedding and reception. They bought the wedding video but not the reception video."

"Do you know why not?" Addison asked.

Dawn leaned forward to the group. "I do. Their relatives had too much to drink and caused a scene. Their behavior permeated the entire video. They didn't want to remember *that*. They paid Finn for his time by purchasing tons of still photos from the wedding."

Jazzi exchanged a look with Oliver, and he expressed what she was thinking. "Finn probably kept tons of videos from all types of events."

"Exactly," Jazzi agreed. Following the dots, she posed the question on the group's mind. "What if Finn photographed or videotaped something that could damage a client's reputation. Or worse yet, was criminal?"

As the group pondered that, Jazzi wondered if Detective Milford's investigation had been diverted to that track too.

Chapter Ten

Jazzi stepped into the Lakeview Boulevard restaurant, not knowing what to expect. The Silver Wave Eatery beamed silver and blue with an upbeat atmosphere. The wall-sized mural of an outboard-motored boat skipping over a wave was impressive and inviting to anyone who enjoyed a lakeside community. The selections of American cuisine at inflated prices even drew in residents of Belltower Landing as well as tourists.

Gail Fernsby, Dawn's mother, waited for Jazzi at a back booth. Last evening Gail had texted her, asking Jazzi to meet her here on her break for a late lunch. That was surprising in itself. Even more surprising had been the last line of her text.

Please don't tell Dawn.

Jazzi's thoughts had run amok overnight, catastrophizing about what Gail might have to say. She was about to find out.

Jazzi slipped onto the bench across from Gail. She smiled, hoping this was a pleasant rather than disastrous lunch.

Gail smiled back, but Jazzi thought Dawn's mother appeared a little uncertain. "Order whatever you want." Gail motioned to the menu on Jazzi's side of the booth. "Lunch is on me."

Jazzi wasn't sure where to go from there, but the manners her mom had taught her took over. "You don't have to do that."

Gail's smile was a little easier this time. "I know I don't have to. But I can buy my daughter's best friend lunch, can't I?"

"Sure," Jazzi relented. Then she decided honesty should accompany manners. "I was surprised when you invited me, especially without Dawn."

The waitress, dressed in a blue short skirt and a pale gray blouse, brought a tray to the table with drinks. She set glasses of lemonade beside their water glasses.

"I remember how you enjoy real lemonade. That's what this is."

"Thanks." Jazzi narrowed her eyes at Gail, not liking the feeling she was being *buttered up*, one of her aunt Iris's favorite phrases when she suspected someone wanted a favor.

"We had good times when you worked at Rods to Boards." Gail dragged a finger down her sweating lemonade glass.

The college summers she'd worked with Dawn's parents at their outfitters shop had been fun and eye-opening. "I'd never been on a boat or a paddleboard until that first summer. The lake and Belltower Landing was a whole new world to explore."

"We were glad to introduce it to you. You were excited to be here. And your friendship with Dawn is so special."

Was this lunch about her friendship with Dawn or their partnership in Tomes & Tea? Uppermost on Jazzi's mind was the fact that this past May, Dawn's parents had wanted their daughter to sell her half of Tomes & Tea. They'd wanted Dawn to take over management at Rods to Boards. They'd used the excuse that the bookstore wasn't profitable enough.

As Gail studied Jazzi's face, she must have read her thoughts. "I have to congratulate you . . . and Dawn, of course . . . on how much better Tomes & Tea is doing financially in just the past few months." She looked up at the waitress, who'd appeared at their table to take their order.

The waitress asked, "Do you need a few more minutes to decide?"

Jazzi had the feeling that she didn't want this lunch to last any longer than necessary. She remembered the menu offerings from the last time she'd been here. "I'll take the fish and chips with coleslaw on the side."

Smiling up at the waitress, Gail gave her order. "The broiled crabcake for me. No fries. Broccoli on the side."

The waitress took their menus from them and slipped away.

Jazzi returned to their conversation. "We had good luck with celebrities and social media this summer. Online sales have quadrupled, and we might have to hire temp help to deal with that."

Frowning, Gail readjusted her place mat. "Dawn is working particularly long hours."

Jazzi couldn't help but quip, "Isn't that what Gen Z women are encouraged to do? We're building our future and meeting our goals."

Lifting her glass, Gail let silence linger while she took a few swallows. "Dawn doesn't have as much time to go out on the *Sunny Days* with her family."

The name of the pontoon boat was the description of most days the Fernsbys took her out on the lake.

Feeling as if she was walking on the proverbial eggshells, she reminded Gail, "Dawn wants Tomes & Tea to succeed as much as I do."

"Perhaps," Gail drawled. "But we still want Dawn to play a major role when we reorganize Rods to Boards to include a satellite store in Naples. Farrell wants to manage the new store with her. That could still happen if your bookstore doesn't continue to earn a respectable profit."

Now Jazzi felt she had to push back. Manners or not. "And who decides what a respectable profit is? My name and Dawn's are on the line. We own the store. We pay the bills. We're mostly frugal." Jazzi didn't add that Dawn was the one who appreciated designer clothes and shoes.

Backing down a bit, Gail sighed. "I understand that."

Maybe Gail did and maybe she didn't. "I truly believe Dawn wants Tomes & Tea to succeed as much as I do."

Gail's lips tightened. "That's possible."

Their waitress returned to their table with a tray that held their platters and side dishes. Jazzi and Gail were silent as the waitress arranged their plates appropriately, then told them to enjoy their meal.

Staring down at the fish and chips, one of her favorite meals here, Jazzi felt no appetite for food at all. She wished she could leave now but realized she couldn't for many reasons. She wanted her relationship with Dawn's mother to remain amicable. She knew the Fernsbys' influence was still an important factor in Dawn's life.

However, Jazzi was attuned to the fact that Gail might not have finished discussing why she'd brought her here.

Both women began eating. After she picked up a piece of batter-fried cod and dipped it into tartar sauce, Jazzi took a bite and her stomach growled. She *was* hungry despite the discussion. Spraying ketchup on her chips—thinly fried potatoes—she turned her attention back to Gail. "Have you considered when you'll remove *Sunny Days* from the lake for winter storage?"

Gail looked up. She'd been preoccupied with her crabcake. Maybe. Or maybe she was considering how to approach another subject with Jazzi.

"We'll probably take it out at the end of September. But it depends on the weather patterns. Last season we left it in until mid-October. That's climate change for you." Suddenly, Gail laid down her fork.

"Here it comes," Jazzi thought.

"I invited you to lunch to ask you if Dawn has decided to take up the search for her birth parents. Since she found Finn Yarrow's body, she's much quieter than usual. She's not talking to me or to her father or brother. Can you tell me what's going through her mind?"

Jazzi felt compassion take over instead of the annoyance she had been feeling over this lunch date. Gail was a mother who cared about her daughter and Dawn's emotional well-being.

Wiping her fingers on her napkin, Jazzi leaned forward. "Finn's death and finding his body has affected her. The detective's interviews have too. When she's quiet, I think she's mulling over all of it."

"I didn't realize she knew Finn outside the context of the bake-off." Gail seemed surprised that she hadn't known this about her daughter.

"Apparently, she knew Finn from when he photographed her friends' weddings and the times he came into Tomes." Jazzi paused a few moments. "But, Gail, about a birth parent search, I think you should ask Dawn that question."

"All right." Gail seemed resigned to the fact Jazzi wouldn't divulge Dawn's confidences. "I'm only asking because her father and I want to be prepared if she *does* search."

Gail resumed eating.

Jazzi didn't understand how the Fernsbys would prepare if Dawn followed the road to her birth parents. More troubling right now for Jazzi was the question, *Should* she tell Dawn about this lunch?

On Thursday morning, Oliver had texted Jazzi at six a.m. He knew she was an early riser.

Bike ride? Dif route. I'll come to you.

She had to smile. They usually biked east into forested developments. It looked like today would be different.

Both kittens had climbed up the spread and onto her bed. Zander landed on her hand holding the phone.

She plucked him off with her other hand and he meowed at her, obviously indignant. "I'll feed you in a minute."

Taking hold of her phone, she quickly texted back.

6:30?

She needed time to dress and feed the felines.

Oliver texted back a thumbs-up emoji.

Jazzi checked her phone for the morning temperature— fifty-nine degrees.

After she fed Zander and Freya in the kitchen, as quietly as she could, she returned to her room and chose electric-blue biking leggings from the chest's drawer and a yellow T-shirt her sister, Vi, had gifted her with that said BEST SIS EVER. Jazzi suddenly missed her family. Maybe she could get away for a long weekend in October when the activities at Tomes & Tea died down.

After she slipped on her sneakers and brushed her hair into a long ponytail, she grabbed a protein bar. As she took a bite, she saw Dawn's bedroom door was open a crack. Freya and Zander slipped inside. They hated closed doors and would make a meowing ruckus if the door wasn't open. After they ate, they usually groomed and slept.

On the small outside landing, Jazzi locked the apartment door behind her. She quickly jogged down the stairs that hugged the wall of the building, enjoying the sun on her head.

Instead of sliding open the larger garage door, she slipped in the side door, grabbed her bike with her helmet hanging from the handlebars, and lifted it out the side and over the step. She wheeled it along the paved path that led to the walk out front. Oliver was standing there.

He looked *so* good. Not hot in the *GQ* category. More like hot from an *Outdoor Life* magazine. He was wearing black cycling shorts. His jersey was pale lime green. Carrying his helmet under his arm, he held his bike with the other. His blond hair was long enough to flutter in the breeze. With his defined jaw covered with trimmed stubble, he appeared ready for a race or a leisurely ride.

Jazzi walked her bike beside her. Wheeling it toward him, she stopped when he smiled. That smile caused a hummingbird to take flight in her chest.

Rolling her bike close to his, she smiled back and said the only thing that came into her head. "So, you want to head out?"

"Only about as far west as the campground. What do you think?"

What she thought was that Oliver could be dangerous to her heart. But what she responded with was, "Sure. That's about five miles out. I have time for that."

Soon they had crossed the boulevard. After they put on their helmets, they climbed on their bikes and entered the bike lane. Jazzi followed Oliver as the breeze from the lake swept over them. The scent of mown grass on the green spread with it. Joggers jogged along the lakeshore while a couple stood under the arch of the bell tower. A few people who had probably watched the sunrise lingered on benches.

Oliver sped up as they rode past the police station, the firehouse, and the steepled stone church. Once they'd biked past a sprawling funeral home and then turned off the boulevard, they ended up on a wide paved bike path that circled around part of Lake Harding. Oliver slowed so Jazzi could pedal up beside him.

They rode through forests dense with fir trees and caught quick glimpses of the lake, its serene blue water sparkling in the sun. As they approached a clearing that led to the lakeshore, Oliver held up his hand. Jazzi slowed and stopped beside him.

"Want to head down to the shore for a few?"

Jazzi checked her watch. "I have time. We got an early start."

Oliver removed his helmet and hung it on his handlebars. "Some mornings I like to ride for the exercise. And others . . . let's just say I need my attitude rebalanced after a busy night."

"Did anything in particular happen?" She could only imagine juggling staff, food, finances, and tourists.

"Nothing in particular. Just crowd control. I had customers out the door who were not happy about wait times. At the end of summer maybe I should go reservations only. But we're not that kind of place." As he talked, Oliver wheeled his bike through a patch of sedges. They rounded a cove away from the main body of the lake.

Jazzi stared out over the water instead of being intrigued by Oliver.

He moved closer to her until their bikes were pressed together between them. In a quiet voice he said, "Look over there."

Jazzi saw he was nodding toward his left and farther out in the cove. Among the bulrushes she spotted a great blue heron. The gray-blue bird stood at least three feet tall. She knew the wingspan on these birds could be six feet wide. This one stood silently on a floating log, the plumage of feathers on its chest and back ruffling a bit in the lake breeze.

"It's majestic." The wildlife here awed her.

"This is why I ride out here." Oliver stood absolutely still so as not to disturb the bird.

"I guess I don't ride this way often *because* it's more secluded. I'm more careful than I used to be." Jazzi stole a glance at him.

As if he sensed her looking, he turned to her. "That's why you need a bike-riding buddy. I know Dawn is your paddleboard bud."

"She is. But we haven't done much of that this month. We were getting ready for the chefs' book signing and then . . ."

"The murder happened," he filled in. "It's good you're cautious. But you can't be afraid to live enthusiastically. Do you know what I mean?"

She shifted her feet in the reeds. "I do. But Dawn's really been affected by what happened and that has affected me."

"We pick up other people's energy. I know that. When my parents told me they were going to divorce, I was five. Up until then, I think I'd picked up vibes from their unhappiness. But the divorce brought out the worst in both of them, and I was in the middle."

"Where were you living then?" She wasn't sure how hard to press, but she wanted to know more.

She and Oliver were facing each other now. His eyes held sadness from unhappy memories. "Their marriage was complicated. My mum met my dad in Melbourne when she was touring there. They came back to the states to marry because her family insisted. But they returned to Melbourne to live because of my dad's work in search-and-rescue in the bush. I was born there. But when I was five, they divorced and I came to the states to live with my mum because the judge gave her sole custody."

"Did they divorce because your mom missed the U.S. and her family?"

"I suppose that was part of it, though they don't talk about it . . . ever. Victoria is a wonderful place. My father ran a search-and-rescue unit in the mountains and the bush. He loved doing it and had survival skills I could only dream of. My mum's family live in Colorado, and she wanted Pa to look for search-and-rescue work there. But he insisted that wasn't the same."

"I imagine it was difficult splitting your time between your mom and dad."

"Since the judge gave my mum sole custody, she let me spend time with my dad for a few weeks every summer. But trips back and forth from Australia became more and more expensive. So they diminished over time."

Studying Oliver, she could see the boy who had looked to both parents for love, wanting to live with both mom and dad. "Then what happened?" Because she suspected a change had.

"I moved to Australia for college at seventeen. I had skipped a grade. I lived with my pa. When he went away on SAR trips and I was on break, I surfed, hiked, and learned how to scuba dive."

"What was your specialty in college?"

"Electrical engineering—navigation systems."

"And you gave that up to own a pub?" She knew the long hours he worked now.

"I learned when my parents divorced that I should set a goal and do what I liked, where I liked. I came back to the U.S., partly for my mum. I worked in engineering for a while, making good money, living on the least amount so I could save most of it. The Wild Kangaroo is an investment, just like your bookshop. But the draw here for me was the lake and water sports. My manager has been in training for over a year. This winter, and even when the tourist season begins again next spring, I'll take off more than one day a week."

"With the bookstore opening at ten, I have leisure time if I get up early. This morning I needed to ride and think."

"Are we messing up your thinking time by talking?" Oliver's expression was part teasing and part serious.

Embarrassed, she felt her cheeks heat. "Not at all! I'm enjoying this—" Unsure what *this* was, she waved at the blue heron, still straight and sure on the log.

He laughed. When he sobered, he took a looser grip on his bike and swiped down the kickstand. Coming around her bike, he stood at her side. "You can put your thoughts into words if you like."

The branches of the sycamore shading them rustled. Glancing up, Jazzi caught sight of a blue jay.

"Only the blue jay and heron will overhear," he said. "I don't think they're sticky beaks." At Jazzi's questioning look, he explained, "Nosy."

A smile curved her lips. "Maybe your opinion will help."

"'Av a go at it."

Oliver's accent was even stronger when he was relaxed. He'd shared with her, talking about a painful time in his life. She could ask his opinion about Dawn and Gail.

Mirroring Oliver's action, Jazzi swung her kickstand down and made sure the bike was steady. "Dawn's mom asked me to lunch."

Oliver eyed her, looking a bit perplexed. "That wasn't good?"

"There's been tension between us for a couple of reasons. One was that her parents thought I went looking for trouble with the murder investigation in May."

"But you didn't. Not on purpose." He sounded sure of that.

"I didn't. Still, that's hard to explain."

"Was the lunch about Finn's murder?"

"Gail is worried about Dawn, like I am. We have that in common. Then the real reason she invited me came up. She wanted to know if Dawn is considering searching for her birth parents. I tried to be tactful during lunch, but with that question, I told her she has to ask Dawn."

"I take it her mother doesn't want her to search." It wasn't a question.

A raptor soared on the thermals high above them, and Jazzi's focus rose up, maybe to pull her thoughts together. Gazing into Oliver's eyes was a distraction.

"Dawn and I met in college when we both attended a group

for adoptees. Many of us searched for biological parents. My story's a bit complicated."

"I understand *complicated*," he said.

Jazzi took a deep breath, then dove in. "I lost my dad to cancer when I was a preteen. My future stepfather helped me search for my birth mom with my mom's support. Then in college my boyfriend broke up with me. I was wrecked because I'd even transferred to his college to be with him. I was in a bad place."

Oliver placed a hand on her shoulder, and she felt heat to her toes. "You met Dawn around then?"

"Yes. And when she learned I wanted to search for my biological dad, she supported me. She wasn't ready to search, and I understood that."

"Did you find your birth dad?" Oliver's eyes were filled with compassion as if he realized how necessary knowing her roots would be.

"My birth dad was killed during his service in Afghanistan."

After a beat to give that background the respect it deserved, he said, "That had to have been a blow."

"It was. But my mom married a really good guy. He's there for me when I need him, though I'm trying to stand on my own."

"You are."

"Dawn's trying too. She hasn't talked about searching lately. She knows it can be disappointing. Questions sometimes lead to answers you don't want. Finn's murder might have her looking at her life and that hole most adoptees have. My problem isn't just about that. Gail didn't want me to tell Dawn about our lunch. I didn't. And it's eating at me. I don't like keeping secrets from her."

He removed his hand from her shoulder. She immediately missed the weight of it there.

"If I was Dawn, I'd want to know." Oliver's tone was definitive. "If you don't tell her, it could affect your friendship, I reckon."

She had to tell Dawn about the lunch with her mother.

It was noon when Jazzi considered telling Dawn about lunch with Gail. But Dawn was helping a customer, and Jazzi decided she'd wait until after work when they were alone in their apartment.

The bell at the door dinged when Emmaline entered Tomes & Tea. Everyone there seemed to turn to look at her. Emmaline was a presence, at least when she entered a room. Maybe it was her cane and her big red tote. Maybe it was her colorful shawl and midi-length flowing dress. Whatever the reason, Jazzi was glad to see Emmaline and relieved she wasn't simply sitting in her hotel suite. She'd heard Emmaline had decided to vacation here, the same as Griffin had.

Jazzi had been checking inventory in the sailing section of volumes. The number listed in the computer didn't match what was on the shelf. A mistake? Or shoplifting?

Her gaze tracked Emmaline at the baked goods case and then at the tea bar. Finally, Emmaline sank down into a chair at a table in the center of the store.

Jazzi forgot about the sailing manuals for now and went to join Emmaline. She motioned to the chair across from the scone baker.

Emmaline smiled and nodded. "Please sit. It's nice to have company. Tourists actually checked out of my hotel because of the murder. There's no one else on my floor."

Jazzi sat back and studied the older woman. "Have you been able to enjoy your stay here in spite of what happened?"

"As long as I don't run into the other chefs, especially Griffin. I've never met a more annoying man." Emmaline picked up the blueberry muffin she'd bought and peeled off the protective paper.

"Are you two like oil and water?" Jazzi suspected the chefs couldn't agree that the sky was blue even on a beautiful day like this.

"He thinks he knows everything about everything." She split the top of the muffin from the bottom and bit into the layer of cake. Then she sighed. "He does know a lot about patents and TV ads."

Leaning forward, Jazzi prompted Emmaline, "Does he know anything else?"

"I think he knows more about Finn's murder than he's letting on." Emmaline lowered her gaze to her muffin.

Avoiding eye contact? Did she want to reveal more or less? "What makes you say that?"

Emmaline set down the muffin but picked up her cup of tea. She still didn't meet Jazzi's eyes. Her charm bracelet jingled as she lifted the cup of tea to her lips and took a sip.

Afterward, she lowered her voice. "He has way too much energy for a normal man. Type A or not."

"Maybe he drinks gallons of coffee or Red Bull," Jazzi joked.

"Perhaps. Or . . . perhaps he takes something more than that. Think about it. He blows up over nothing. I visited his TV set one time when he didn't know I was there. He blew up at the producer and offstage at the host who was hawking one of his pans. Just doesn't seem normal to me."

"Did you see that happen during the bake-off?" At times it seemed Emmaline tried to goad Griffin. Was that on purpose so others would see his temper? With what result? Simply to reveal Griffin's character?

"I saw him argue with Diego. And with Finn."

"Did you hear what it was about?"

Emmaline shrugged. "I was never quite within hearing distance."

"Certainly, Griffin's true character would show when the

detective interviewed him." Jazzi knew Paul Milford didn't pull punches and would use whatever tactic he needed to.

Could Emmaline have a valid point about Griffin? Possibly, she was merely a lonely older woman who liked to gossip for attention. Jazzi could give her a little more time. "Why don't you tell me about your latest scone recipe?"

A grin spread across Emmaline's face. "It has coconut and nutmeg."

Jazzi settled in to help her feel important . . . at least for a few minutes.

Chapter Eleven

Last night Jazzi had wanted to tell Dawn about having lunch with her mom. But Dawn had gone to dinner with Delaney and then Delaney had taken her to a new club. Jazzi had been asleep when Dawn returned home.

This morning, Dawn had been late getting started and Jazzi had come to work first. She had been jittery around Dawn and hoped her friend couldn't tell she had something on her mind. A busy store kept them all going in different directions. Tonight, Jazzi thought, they'd have a serious talk about Dawn's mother.

Sitting on the floor in the children's section of Tomes & Tea, her phone vibrated in her apron pocket. Still cross-legged, she lifted out her phone and saw the text from Erica.

Be on alert. Trouble coming. Charmaine Conner.

Before Jazzi could push aside the books that she'd propped on her knees, Charmaine stood at the bookshelf, looking down at her.

"That woman at the sales desk said I'd find you back here."

Jazzi took in Charmaine's appearance. Dressed in black

skin-tight joggers, pink Crocs, and a gray tank top with one side slipped from her shoulder, she fidgeted from one foot to the other.

After Jazzi set the books aside, she rose to her feet.

Charmaine's hair was straight, medium brown, and lank. She was pale with no lip gloss or makeup. Her wide mouth would make her pretty if she smiled. Her golden brown eyes were large, but she had bruising circles under them.

"We can talk," Jazzi said patiently, not wanting to cause a disturbance. "Just let me pick up these books—"

Charmaine cut her off. "Can't you just leave them on the floor?" She cast a look over her shoulder. "I'd rather go in your back room or someplace where it's quiet."

Jazzi stooped to pick up the books. She wouldn't leave them on the floor. At eye level with Charmaine once more, she laid the books on a nearby cart, then motioned to an empty table. "We can easily talk here and have a glass or cup of tea if you'd like."

"I don't drink tea."

When Jazzi was a teenager, she knew a reporter who'd become friends with her mom. He would have done almost anything to get a story, including drinking gallons of tea.

"What do you want to talk about? I told you before I won't discuss any details." Jazzi figured they might as well reach for the bottom line.

"Your partner just ducked out when she saw me come in, so I can't talk to her."

Jazzi knew Detective Milford had warned Dawn about speaking to reporters or talking to anyone about what she'd seen and remembered. Jazzi was concerned about this reporter's intentions.

Charmaine snapped, "I need details about the murder."

"Details that will lead to apprehending the murderer?"

Charmaine looked flustered. "Possibly. Possibly not. I can't find a killer. But I can tell the public exactly what happened and how it happened."

"Those details might be valuable to the police. If they get out to everyone, the police lose leverage when they question suspects."

Charmaine seemed puzzled.

"Are you familiar with the true crime genre? Forensic shows on TV? Even mystery fiction?"

Charmaine's hand came up and brushed the questions away. "I don't have time for that."

"You don't have time for research?"

"Not that kind of research. I'm interested in what's true here and now. I used search engines to research the chefs and your partner. Not much turned up. So, I'm trying in-person interviews. But no one wants to talk to me."

Jazzi could see why Charmaine was confrontational. But if she didn't create rapport, she would never accomplish her goal.

"*You* haven't told me anything," the reporter groused.

"I don't know anything you can use."

"Tell me what the atmosphere was like the day of the murder," Charmaine demanded.

"Everyone was excited to find out who the winner was." That fact had been obvious to onlookers who stood around the judges' tent.

"Is it true the competition was cutthroat? I heard even the chefs didn't get along."

Jazzi wondered who had told Charmaine *that*. "They acted professional about the judging."

"Fine. But didn't two of the contestants fight—Finn Yarrow and Tim Blanchard?"

Jazzi parried with "I don't have a comment about that."

"You're stonewalling me." Charmaine's cheeks had reddened, and she was obviously frustrated.

"Ms. Conner, I don't have anything else to say."

Erica was beckoning Jazzi toward the sales desk and a customer standing there.

She turned to Charmaine. "I have to get back to work." She started for the desk.

Charmaine grabbed her arm. "I could camp out outside your apartment upstairs."

Apparently, the reporter's research had paid off in that respect—she'd found Jazzi's address online. Jazzi stared down at Charmaine's fingers around her forearm and then over to a nearby customer in the romance section who was looking their way.

Charmaine let go.

Her voice low, Jazzi said, "If you camp out outside my apartment, I'll have you cited for illegal trespass." Then she walked over to the customer waiting at the sales desk.

Charmaine had no sooner left when Jazzi spotted Colleen Cross scoot in the door with a double box of baked goods. Erica must have texted her that they needed more.

After Colleen handed over the boxes of goodies, she aimed toward Jazzi at a quick pace. "My baking for the morning was done, and I needed to step out from the mayhem. Enough staff today to do that."

Jazzi nodded. "Your day starts much earlier than mine."

"Just a few hours. From what I've heard, you're an early bird too."

"Most days." Jazzi had to wonder if the shop owners in Belltower Landing were aware of how *all* the other shop owners were living their lives, not simply the business owners they personally interacted with.

"Was that Charmaine Conner I spotted? She paid me a visit too." Colleen looked none too happy about that fact.

"That was Charmaine. I think she was looking for a sensational story." Jazzi still had books to shelve, and she picked up a few of them.

"As if a murder isn't sensational enough. She was fishing with me for details that haven't been publicized," Colleen complained. "Detective Milford warned me not to share anything I'd witnessed. What about you?"

"Same. I don't think the detective believes in crowdsourcing."

"Come again?" Colleen looked puzzled at the term.

"It's when a group of people put together the bits and pieces of what they've seen and heard. Some crimes have been solved that way."

"Like when the police start a tip line and ask the public for help?" Colleen's green eyes were curious.

"Sort of. In that case the detective is fitting the pieces together. Only he and his staff are aware of what comes in."

"I see," she murmured. "He doesn't want the bake-off chefs and contestants putting their heads together and coming up with the wrong conclusions."

Colleen's phone beeped and she slid it from her jeans pocket. Then she popped it back in. "Nothing urgent. I have at least another five to take a deep breath. I tell myself I can relax over the winter." She let out a short laugh, then followed up with, "Who am I kidding? I hope the bakery is as busy in the winter too."

Jazzi knew the mayor and his staff ramped up activities in the winter to draw snow-sport lovers to the area as well.

"Before I go, there was something else I wanted to ask you."

Jazzi didn't know Colleen well, so she had no idea what was coming.

"Have you seen Griffin?"

That question seemed to have come from left field. "No. I haven't seen him for over a week at least. Why?"

"The detective didn't want him to leave town."

"But Detective Milford let Diego leave." Jazzi assumed that was public knowledge.

"I know. And that ticked off Griffin. He felt he should be given the same courtesy."

"The detective's reasoning could be simple," Jazzi suggested. "If Diego left, he'd be at one place he could be found—his New York restaurant and apartment. The impression I got is that Griffin moves around a lot."

"Griffin doesn't stay in one place very long. That's for sure."

Something in Colleen's tone told Jazzi that she had more than passing general knowledge about Griffin. "Do you know him well?"

The baker's face took on a dreamy expression. "I once did. We had a fling when we were in culinary school." She shrugged. "We've been on-again and off-again friends since then. I was the one who suggested his name to the mayor to be a judge for the bake-off. If Griffin knew, I'm sure he wouldn't thank me now."

When Colleen's phone beeped again, she threw up her hands. "That's it. The bakery is apparently going to fall apart if I don't get back. If you see Griffin, tell him I'm looking for him. Apparently, he's letting all calls go to voicemail."

As Colleen left, Jazzi wondered if Griffin was ignoring all calls or simply Colleen's.

The other question that tweaked Jazzi's curiosity was, Why wouldn't Detective Milford let Griffin leave town? Was *he* a prime suspect?

A few minutes later, Tomes & Tea was suddenly flooded with a line of tourists who had arrived on a tour bus. The rush kept Jazzi and her staff all terrifically busy for over an hour. While Dawn served baked goods and tea, Jazzi kept pace at the checkout desk and answered questions about books and Belltower Landing.

One forty-something woman with a large straw sun hat and tons of freckles smiled at Jazzi as she laid three boxes of tea shaped like the bell tower, a white bag of muffins with the price written on the outside, a Western historical romance novel, and a YA mystery on the sales desk.

"We love this town." The woman slid a credit card from her

smartphone case. "I'm Meg," she revealed, her green eyes sparkling with good humor.

"I'm Jazzi." Jazzi rang up the tea and started on Meg's other purchases.

"Oh, I know. My family takes this bus trip every year. We started the same year you opened the store. Your partner over there pointed you out."

"You have a good memory."

"Not so much," Meg said with a laugh. "My daughter particularly liked your name."

Taking her bar code tool in hand, Jazzi ran it over the codes on the books while beside her Erica did the same for another customer. "How old is your daughter?"

"She's twelve going on twenty."

Jazzi exchanged a knowing look with Meg. "A handful?"

Meg shrugged, "Not most of the time. But she's becoming more combative over little things."

"More independent," Jazzi guessed.

"Yes. She wanted to know all about the murder that happened here. She's seen Griffin on that shopping network."

"He's popular," Jazzi's tone was noncommittal.

"He has good deals on his cookware. Sometimes I watch too. Mostly when he's cooking to demonstrate."

"How did your daughter find out about the murder?" Jazzi hadn't thought much about the news of murder spreading farther than the surrounding area. But, of course, it had.

"She likes to search Belltower Landing to decide what activities she wants to do. We're only here for the day so she has to be selective. She chose kayaking for this afternoon. That's what she and my husband want."

"It's a beautiful day for it." Jazzi didn't particularly want to discuss the murder with a stranger.

"It is. She found out about the murder when she was online.

My husband and I think one of the chefs did it." She stared curiously up at Jazzi as if she could confirm or deny her opinion.

But Jazzi stayed clear of that swamp hole. She smiled and quickly finished bagging Meg's purchases. After she handed them over, she sent Meg a genial nod. "You have a wonderful day in Belltower Landing."

Erica finished up about the same time Jazzi did. A lull spread quietly over the store as customers perused books and sipped tea.

Leaning toward Jazzi, Erica murmured in an undertone. "I heard some of that."

"She was friendly."

"No, I mean about the murder. I've been wondering about the chefs myself. But why would they kill Finn?"

Jazzi remembered Griffin's conversation with Finn, as well as Griffin's conversation with Diego. No one knew anything about motives yet, except maybe for Detective Milford. "I don't know. And maybe Detective Milford doesn't know either."

After rolling her shoulders and moving away from the desk, Jazzi stopped at a few tables to chat with customers, most of them regulars. The bus crowd mostly had moved on to other stores along Lakeview Boulevard.

The bell tower on the green chimed noon. Jazzi noticed one of their regular tea customers who stopped in most mornings having a discussion with Dawn at the tea bar.

Jazzi was about to return to the sales desk when she noticed the expression on Dawn's face. Her brow was puckered, her eyes were wide, her shoulders straight, tense and taut. She served the customer a cup of hot tea with a forced half smile.

Then she torpedoed straight from behind the bar to Jazzi. "Magda said she saw you and my mom at the Silver Wave having lunch. Is that true?"

Dawn's expression was a combination of hurt, disappointment, and fury. Jazzi suddenly realized Oliver had been right.

She should have told Dawn as soon as it happened. Her friendship with her best friend wasn't something she wanted to sacrifice to maintain a tactful relationship with Gail. She had to fix this. Maybe she could convince Dawn to understand.

She pulled Dawn behind a bookcase. "I was going to tell you tonight."

Yanking her arm away, Dawn shook her head with disbelief. "I bet you were."

Jazzi knew she had to relay the facts, not get caught up in a defensive back-and-forth conversation. "Your mom texted me and asked me to meet her for lunch. She asked me not to tell you."

"And you thought that was a good idea?" Dawn's voice had risen, and customers stared at them.

Jazzi lowered her voice, hoping Dawn would do the same. "You know my relationship with your mom hasn't been the best, especially since she advised you to sell your interest in Tomes & Tea."

"I told you I *wouldn't* sell because we're friends. At least we *were*." Dawn looked close to tears.

"We *are* friends. Best friends. Dawn, I'm sorry. Your mom is just worried about you. So am I."

"So, you thought talking about me behind my back would make the situation better? Well, it hasn't. Everybody is putting pressure on me for *something*, and I've had enough!"

With that Dawn spun around, mumbled something about going for a walk, and dashed across the store and out the door.

Jazzi started after her, but Erica stepped into her path. "Let her go, Jazzi. She needs to blow off steam. She's still upset about finding Finn, and she's overreacting to a lot of life."

Jazzi took a very deep breath and tried to gather her own emotions into some kind of order. She'd see Dawn in a little while when she returned. Then Jazzi would fix this.

She hoped.

*   *   *

The rest of Jazzi's workday was a mixture of waiting on customers, stopping to peer through the bay window for Dawn's return, and chastising herself for not telling Dawn about the lunch with Gail. Anxiety built as she waited for Dawn to reenter Tomes. It wasn't like her to ignore Jazzi's text messages. Even Erica had tried to text and call and was met with silence.

When Dawn *did* return around five p.m., Jazzi went to her immediately. But Dawn just gave her a hard stare and held her hand up with a jerky motion that caused her pretty watch to slide down her arm. "I don't want to talk. Just leave me alone."

"Dawn, I'm sorry. I should have told you."

"Yes, you should have. You betrayed our friendship. I never expected that of you."

Jazzi was about to say more, but Dawn walked away, sliding behind the tea bar where Audrey had taken over.

Jazzi felt Dawn's rejection in the pit of her stomach. But she wasn't going to accept the fact her friendship with Dawn was irrevocably changed. Somehow, she'd make amends.

Hoping to see Dawn and speak to her privately that evening, she was disappointed when Dawn didn't return to the apartment after work.

As Jazzi fed the kittens and let them scamper around her feet, she plucked a container of Greek yogurt from the refrigerator, dished it up, sliced a peach on top, and took her dish to the sofa to eat. Zander nosed under her hand and ended up with a spot of yogurt on his nose. His curiosity made Jazzi smile.

Freya climbed up the sofa as if she wanted a taste too. Jazzi dipped her finger into the remaining yogurt and held the tip of it out to Freya. She sniffed at it, took a lick, and then scampered off quickly as if yogurt had no place in *her* diet.

After the kittens climbed up onto the stuffed yellow chair, they began washing each other's faces and then settled in a furry pile to nap.

Jazzi felt anxious and almost panicky that her friendship with Dawn was ruined. She couldn't sit here and stream a movie as if nothing had happened.

She was only going to step outside onto the landing for a few minutes. But as she stared across at the lake, breathed in the damper evening air, and heard the bell tower chime, she knew she couldn't go back inside.

After putting her phone in her pocket, she made sure she had her keys and locked the door. She just needed to walk off her angst.

Loads of tourists still walked along Lakeview Boulevard, even though many stores were closed. They were stopping at the ice cream shop and simply taking in the sights of Belltower Landing, including the lakeshore. Jazzi headed that way.

Where had Dawn gone? To Derek's? To Delaney's? Jazzi could call around but didn't think Dawn would appreciate that.

The mistiness settling over the lake drew Jazzi farther down the green. Tonight, she'd like that mist to swirl around her and just stop her thoughts for a little while.

On a bench nearest to the shore, she spotted a lone figure. She was certain she recognized that profile—Detective Milford.

She wasn't sure whether she should approach him. Nevertheless, his sensitive detective radar must have sensed her presence. He turned toward her.

His hair was mussed. The top two buttons of his tan shirt were open, and his striped tie hung off to the side. Even in the dimming light she could see that the crinkle lines around his eyes and mouth cut deep. He was a man with the world on his shoulders.

"Hi, Jazzi. Are you taking a late evening stroll?"

"Something like that. Would you mind company?"

"Company is fine. Just trying to decompress before I head home to my family for a few hours."

If Jazzi read the subtext of that correctly, his workday wasn't through.

She took a seat on the bench next to him. "Are you going back to the police station tonight?"

"Most likely. But I want to see friendly faces, grab a meal, and get a shower."

"That makes sense. You'll be able to think more clearly after wiping the slate clean for a few hours."

They both stared out at the darkening lake and the few people strolling along the lapping water.

She had to ask, "Are you letting the pieces of the case fall into place?"

He didn't answer right away. "The cops here learned a lot from our case back in May."

"Learned what?" She could guess but wanted to hear what the detective had to say.

"The team here had never handled a murder. They were lacking in investigative skills that cops in big cities learn from experience or mentors. But I've held a few seminars this summer and brought in experienced detectives I've met over the years of my career to talk to them. I had hoped the department here wouldn't need to know much of it, but here we are again, and I hope the workshops helped. Actually, I know they did."

"I haven't heard of any leaks this time." Erica had tried to pry information out of a friend on the force but absolutely couldn't.

"Exactly. That's one way to protect the investigation. Only info we *want* out there gets out. That's why I wanted you and Dawn Fernsby to realize how important it is not to tell anyone about what she heard and saw."

Jazzi sighed and turned toward the detective. "Dawn minds not being able to talk about it. The whole thing is affecting her. Her mom is worried too."

Even in the dimming light, Jazzi could see the sharpness in Paul Milford's gaze. "Has she told her mother anything?"

"Not that I know of. But I don't know how long she can bottle up her emotions and what she knows."

"Talk to her. Tell her my team is working as fast as we can. We'll catch Finn Yarrow's murderer, Jazzi."

From the seriousness on the detective's face, the determined line of his mouth, and the set of his jaw, Jazzi knew he was making her a promise of sorts.

She was going to pray he could keep it.

Chapter Twelve

The night captured Jazzi in its dusky arms after the detective left the bench. She suspected he'd be working all night—tracing leads, comparing phone logs, studying financial records. In some ways he reminded her of a detective she'd known in Willow Creek who was now married to her aunt Iris. He couldn't relax or take much of a break until the crime had been solved.

The sky was full of at least a thousand pinpoints of twinkling light. She heard voices around the arches of the bell tower, but they were a far-away murmur. The chefs involved in the bake-off and the contestants occupied her thoughts. What if Finn's murder had something to do with a personal conflict with a neighbor or friend and nothing to do with the bake-off?

She spotted a man and a woman along the lakeshore, bobbing lights glowing in front of them. They were strolling with flashlights. She hadn't done that for a long time.

Jazzi's phone played. Taking it from her pocket, she saw Delaney's name.

Dawn's back home. I thought you'd want to know.

Jazzi texted back.

Be there soon. TY

Standing, taking one last look at the shore and the lake beyond, Jazzi took a full breath of night air. She wanted to make things right with Dawn and hoped that she could. The most direct path from the green to the boulevard led her past the bell tower. It chimed nine o'clock as she walked faster.

The traffic on the boulevard zipped by as she waited for the light to turn green. She was at her apartment five minutes later. As she jogged up the steps, Delaney exited the apartment.

"I was worried about her," Jazzi said without preamble.

Delaney nodded. "I figured you would be. When she showed up at my place, she was full of pent-up angst."

"I'm glad she had you to turn to." Jazzi leaned against the landing railing.

"I was surprised when I opened my door. She said she'd walked."

"Did she tell you what happened?"

"She did. She said you went to lunch with her mother. I don't get the big crisis. But I listened and didn't say much. I told her I'd drive her home."

"I'm going to try to make things right. Thanks for bringing her home."

After a hug, Delaney descended the steps.

When Jazzi opened the door, the bells on the knob jingled. Slipping off her sandals and brushing them aside, she spotted Dawn on the sofa, the kittens in her lap.

She wasn't sure how to start. "Delaney said she drove you home."

Dawn took a deep breath and nodded. She seemed as awkward as Jazzi felt. "I . . . I went over to her place for a while."

"You walked to her condo?" Delaney lived over a mile away.

"I just started walking. When I was near her building . . . I decided to see if she was home."

Jazzi settled in the chair near the corner of the sofa where Dawn sat. "I'm glad you had someone to talk to. I want you to talk to *me* too. I'm so sorry I didn't tell you about lunch with your mom. I was going to. But you found out first."

Dawn ducked her head and then looked over at Jazzi. "I'm sorry I reacted the way I did."

Before Jazzi could say she understood, Dawn continued. "I'm on edge. All the time. About everything. I should have been cross with my mom. Not *you*." Dawn stroked Freya's back, and the kitten turned over on her side and stretched over Dawn's leg.

"Your mom is worried about you."

Zander came awake and yawned. He climbed over the sofa arm and hopped onto the arm of Jazzi's chair. She picked him up and settled him close.

"Mom always worries about me. I wish she'd worry about Farrell more. It's like she can never forget I'm adopted and wants to make up for it."

"Don't you think that's natural?"

"You said *your* mom treated you and your sister the same," Dawn protested.

"You can't compare. It might have been easier for Mom to do that since we're both girls. There are so many factors, Dawn. The important one is that your mom and dad want you to feel loved." While Zander purred against her stomach, Jazzi rubbed one of his ears. There were so many components to loving, and it was so complicated.

"Finn's murder really messed me up. Not being able to talk about it freely hasn't helped."

"I spoke to Detective Milford tonight on the green. He reiterated how important it is to keep the details among the three of us. He claims there haven't been any leaks in this investigation, and he wants to keep it that way. I think he questions subjects with that in mind to see if they spill a detail they shouldn't know."

"I wish someone would soon slip."

Dawn still sounded dejected and down, and Jazzi realized that wasn't like her at all. "We still have time to enter the kayak race on Sunday. Do you want to do it? The weather should be good after rain passes through tomorrow."

"Oh, Jazzi. I don't know if I'm up to a kayak race."

"Sure, you are. We haven't been out on the water together for a while." Jazzi was hoping the old feeling of teamwork would return out on the lake.

Reading her mind, Dawn smiled. "We don't have to kayak to be good friends again."

After a beat, Jazzi asked, "*Are* we good?"

Dawn didn't hesitate. "We are. Maybe kayaking will help me relax. I know something else that will too. I'm hungry and there's a pint of peanut butter crunch ice cream in the freezer. Want to share?"

Jazzi definitely wanted to share—the store, the apartment, a sister-close friendship. "I do." She shifted Zander onto the chair cushion and stood. "I'll get spoons."

After Dawn moved Freya to the sofa, she rose to her feet and gave Jazzi a hug. Jazzi hugged Dawn back, praying the detective could keep his promise and find Finn's killer sooner rather than later.

The next morning when there was a lull in activity at Tomes & Tea, Erica rounded the tea bar and met Jazzi at the sink. She washed her hands and grabbed a paper towel to dry them. "I'll take over here for a while if you need to do something else."

Jazzi did need to price books she was going to discount. "Okay. I've filled the baked goods case, and we should be ready for the lunch crowd. A storm is coming through. Tourists could take cover in here." Jazzi had noticed how the red sunrise sky this morning had now turned steel gray.

Erica checked the glass case. "I noticed you and Dawn were talking this morning. I take it you reconciled?"

Glancing at her best friend, who was working at the computer at the sales desk, Jazzi said in a low voice to Erica, "I hope we did. But I'm worried about her. She's not sleeping well. I hear her in the kitchen in the middle of the night. And the kittens have been sticking close to her as if they know she needs comfort."

"Maybe they're just lonely and want to cuddle."

Erica wasn't as much of an animal person as her daughter. "I believe it's more than that. Animals are intuitive. We don't give them enough credit. Especially cats." The two cats she and her mom and sister had adopted had seen Jazzi through some rough times in her teens.

Erica straightened the stack of paper plates on the counter. "Audrey often says the same thing. Though she's an equal opportunity animal lover."

Both Jazzi and Erica laughed. Jazzi knew how much Audrey enjoyed her pet-sitting duties when she wasn't working at Tomes. "I'm going to head over to the sales table and sticker more books."

Jazzi was carrying a stack of books to a table near the sales desk when she saw Diego Alvarez hurry through the door. She could see spots of rain drops on his white oxford shirt, though his black hair wasn't mussed and didn't look damp. In well-creased black slacks, he still looked elegant even though the coming rainstorm had chased him inside. Scuttlebutt had spread the word that he was back in town, though no one knew why. Had Detective Milford called him back to Belltower Landing?

Before Diego could take a breath, a customer who had been perusing the cookbook table that had been set up since the bake-off hurried over to him. "Can I take a selfie with you?"

Diego's face brightened automatically, and he smiled. "And why would you want one?"

Jazzi knew Elsa. The curly haired brunette was a regular customer who lived in Belltower Landing.

"If I take a selfie with you, my Insta Feed could blow up with hundreds more followers," Elsa explained as if Diego didn't know the workings of Instagram.

"And that's something you value?" he asked in his leisurely deep baritone.

"My kids think it's cool. It gives us something to talk about." Elsa had her phone in hand and stooped to set her purse on the floor.

"How old are they?" Diego appeared genuinely interested.

"Twelve and fourteen."

"I see." His expression was amused. "I have a seventeen year old. You have an adventure ahead of you. Let's take that selfie. Jazzi might give you a discount if you post it with #tomes&tea." He winked at Jazzi.

She hadn't suspected he knew she was watching. But apparently, he was people-aware.

Since Jazzi had an interest in the photo, she stepped forward. "Would you like me to snap it?"

Elsa was grinning broadly. "That would be great."

"In fact, Jazzi," Diego offered. "Why don't you squeeze into the shot too. I have long arms. I can fit us all in."

Jazzi slipped between Diego and Elsa, and he took two photos in case one captured them better than the other.

Jazzi motioned to Audrey, who was at the sales desk, and held up five fingers. Audrey knew that meant a five percent discount.

As Diego handed Elsa's phone back to her, Jazzi said, "You'll receive a five percent discount on whatever you buy today. Audrey will ring you when you're ready."

Elsa gave Jazzi a hug and blushed when she expressed her thanks to Diego.

After Elsa had moved away to look over the cookbook selections once more, Jazzi said to Diego, "Thank you. That was gracious of you."

"Through the years, I've found it's just as easy to be friendly as impatient. And the interchange can brighten a fan's day as well as mine."

Jazzi didn't know if Diego's time was limited. "Is there anything I can help you with?"

"Two things, really. I had some time today and wondered if you needed to have me sign more books. I would have texted, but I needed a walk. I didn't expect rain to blow in so early."

"Yes, I'd love it if you signed more books. We sold out of the first batch of signed copies. Come back to our break room."

Diego started to follow Jazzi. She motioned to Dawn that she was going there.

Once in the break room, Jazzi took a stack of Diego's cookbooks from an open box on the floor and set them on the table. Reaching into a cupboard, she produced a pen for him to use and set it beside the books on the table.

He didn't bother sitting on one of the folding chairs but stood at the table to sign.

"The other reason I stopped in," he began nonchalantly, "was to ask if you've seen Griffin."

That was an odd question for Diego to ask, wasn't it? she thought. Surely he and Griffin moved in the same circles. Then she remembered their interchange the night of Diego's restaurant takeover at Vibes. Maybe they did and maybe they didn't.

"I haven't seen Griffin for a while. But I have his cell number." She took her phone from her apron pocket. "Do you want to text him?"

Diego looked disappointed. "No. I have his number. But he's not picking up. I had Colleen try to call him, and he didn't pick up for her either."

Jazzi had intended to step away and let Diego sign books at his leisure. But now she stayed. "Do you think he's in trouble?"

"I hope not. But with Griffin you never know. He's not the most tactful person. And he does drink heavily at times."

She decided to fish a little. "I know Detective Milford asked Griffin and the other chefs to stay in town."

"Yes, he did. He called me a few days ago and asked me to return for more questions."

"He couldn't ask them over the phone?"

"I wondered the same." Diego closed the book he'd just signed and picked up another. "Apparently, the officer of the law likes to question suspects face-to-face."

That conclusion shocked Jazzi. Not that the detective wanted to question Diego face-to-face like any expert detective would. What surprised her was that Diego considered himself a suspect.

"You feel you're a suspect?" She couldn't hold in the question or her surprise.

He studied Jazzi in the dim light. "Do you want my opinion about this investigation?"

"I do. My roommate is affected by finding Finn's body. The sooner the killer is found, the better."

Diego selected another book from the stack and opened it to the title page. "I believe the detective's team is falling down a rabbit hole."

Jazzi moved closer to the table. She'd heard that term from her mother when Daisy Swanson had considered the police were following the wrong lead. "What rabbit hole?"

"Instead of pursuing one suspect, they seem to be proposing a conspiracy among the chefs." Diego gave an offhanded shrug of his shoulders.

A conspiracy would mean the killer had accomplices! "What would that have to do with Finn Yarrow, who *wasn't* a chef?"

Diego stopped signing to face her directly, with a line between his brows and a serious depth to his brown eyes. "That's a good question. Unless it has something to do with Finn wanting to take photos of all the chefs' foods and putting together a book of his own. Griffin and I had agreed to give Finn a try for our next projects."

Jazzi had never suspected a conspiracy. "If the police suspect a conspiracy, do they think someone was contracted to kill Finn?" She couldn't imagine it. How could Finn be a threat to any of the chefs?

"I do know they've obtained subpoenas to acquire all of our financials. I wanted to ask Griffin how he was dealing with it. I'm not happy about it. Next thing you know, the IRS will be auditing all of us. This bake-off has truly turned into a mess."

Jazzi agreed with Diego that the conspiracy theory was definitely a rabbit hole. Financial gain? Financial fraud? Finn knowing too much about something?

Or did one person have a grudge against Finn? That made more sense to her.

But what did she know?

Diego had left when Oliver entered the store. Jazzi felt her smile start and spread across her lips. When Oliver spotted her to the rear of the store, he headed that way.

She checked her watch. He'd soon have a lunch crowd to oversee. Her heart ran faster when she thought about their conversation on the lakeshore—the closeness she'd felt to him.

Since then, she'd warned herself not to read too much into sharing part of their backgrounds. But the thrill of excitement seeing him again said she wasn't buying what she was trying to sell.

He looked *good*. Slim indigo jeans. A pale blue shirt with its long sleeves rolled up his forearms. Sandals and socks that on him appeared to be the hippest style ever. Oliver didn't claim to be someone he wasn't. He was simply himself.

Jazzi turned toward him and dropped her hands into her apron's two pockets. "Hi, Oliver. Need a cup of tea?"

He grinned. "I think I can brew tea in my kitchen at the Kangaroo."

She felt embarrassed at trying for teasing and falling flat.

Reading her embarrassment, he quickly said, "But, of course, yours tastes better."

She laughed. "Good catch. If not tea, how about a book?" She wasn't going to assume he came in for more than that.

After one of his long looks, he cleared his throat. "Actually, I did come for a book Diego recommended to me." Oliver slipped a piece of paper from his jeans pocket and showed it to her.

She read it. *The Real Truth about Kitchen Service.*

"I know it's probably not a title you carry. Can you order it for me?"

"Sure. I can check if it's available through a distributor we use. Don't you already know all about kitchen service?" She tilted her head up to meet his gaze again. He was a good six to eight inches taller than she was.

"Sometimes we have a problem expediting. I have a terrific chef and good personnel, but the kitchen can always run smoother."

He was standing close enough that she could catch the scent of his . . . soap. She liked that, plus the fact he felt he could always learn more.

To channel her thoughts away from Oliver, she fingered the slip of paper he handed her. "Diego was just in here. Did you see him on his way out?"

"No. He must have left in the other direction. I'm surprised he's back in town."

No one stood or sat nearby, but Jazzi still lowered her voice. "The police asked or ordered him back."

"Diego is a suspect?" Oliver's voice was filled with shock.

"He's not sure about that. But he believes the detective is taking a circuitous way that leads to all the wrong places."

"What do *you* think?"

"I find it hard to believe there was some kind of conspiracy among the chefs and Finn. Diego wonders if it has something to do with photos Finn wanted to take of the chefs' food. I saw Finn approach Griffin about it. Maybe he was feeling out Colleen, Emmaline, and Diego too."

"And one of them killed him because—"

Jazzi shrugged. "*I* can't think of a motive." She'd learned through her mom's investigations that motives were as complicated and unique as suspects. Find a motive and you could often find the killer.

She was about to say that when she caught sight of Belinda Yarrow speaking to Audrey. Belinda followed Audrey's pointed finger, which directed her to Jazzi.

Jazzi told Oliver, "Belinda Yarrow is coming my way."

Understanding that their conversation was over, he nodded.

As Belinda joined them, they both expressed their condolences once more.

Belinda's brown hair hid her expression for a moment as she bowed her head. Then she swept it away from her eyes with one hand, and Jazzi saw the widow carried a book in her other hand.

She offered it to Jazzi. "I want to talk to you about this."

Oliver took his cue from Belinda. He said, "I have to be going. Jazzi, I'll see you—" He hesitated, then added, "Later."

Lifting the slip of paper she held between her fingers, Jazzi said, "I'll see if I can order this and let you know."

Belinda began to apologize for interrupting, but Jazzi quickly stayed the apology. "Oliver simply wanted to order a book. How can I help you?"

Extending the book she held once more, Belinda explained what it was. "A niche publisher agreed to publish this book of Finn's photos. Many of the photos I displayed on the screen at the memorial. The company is essentially a vanity press, but Finn wanted to put his photos into the world somehow."

Jazzi knew a vanity press was a publishing company that charged authors a fee to have their books published. Distribution was often left to the author.

After paging through the book Belinda had given her, Jazzi suspected the widow's purpose in handing it to her. "All of Finn's photos capture humanity or the beauty of the world as he saw it."

"Exactly. Would you consider letting Tomes & Tea sell the book as a memorial to Finn?" There were tears in Belinda's eyes.

"I'll talk to Dawn about it. We make decisions like this together. But I don't see a reason she wouldn't agree. She'd like to honor Finn too. You might be able to place some books in the other shops. The Dockside Bakery might carry them near their register with their tourist books."

"You wouldn't mind if they did that?"

"Of course not."

"I'm going to donate half of all sales to the scholarship fund," Belinda revealed. "It probably won't be much, but every little bit helps."

Jazzi laid the book on top of a bookshelf she was standing close to. "I'll text you after I speak with Dawn." She took her phone from her pocket. "Can you give me your number?" Bringing up her contacts list, she handed over the phone. "Tap in your number and I'll have it."

Belinda did and returned the phone to Jazzi. "I appreciate this so much."

Belinda looked so sad that Jazzi took her hand. "How are you really doing?"

Squeezing Jazzi's hand in return, Belinda said with a breathy sigh, "It's a lot. The missing is bad enough. I keep thinking Finn will walk in the door, I'll hear his laugh, or I'll see him pick up his camera to go on a shoot. But there's also his business to handle. There are still orders to be filled. Bookwork to keep. Appointments to cancel. His friend Claude, who's also a photographer, is helping me clear some of it. But . . . I can't imagine anyone is ever prepared for death and all it brings."

"I know you're right. Dreams and hopes fade away too."

"You *do* understand." Belinda looked as if she'd found a kindred spirit.

"If you need anything, let me know," Jazzi offered. "In the meantime, maybe we can send Finn's photos into the world."

Belinda gave Jazzi a weak smile.

Jazzi hoped Finn's widow would find more reasons to smile in the days ahead.

Chapter Thirteen

Early Sunday afternoon, the kayakers were lined up, ready to go. Jazzi adjusted her helmet and shifted in her life vest. After visiting Dawn in Belltower Landing when they were in college, Jazzi had taken to kayaking with as much ease as paddleboarding.

Jazzi took hold of the paddle shaft. She remembered when she first took an interest in the sport. Dawn had her sit in a straight chair while holding a broom. She'd learned to paddle from side to side. As she gazed at Dawn in the kayak floating beside her, the memory made her smile.

As Jazzi looked up, the perfectly powder-blue sky sheltered everyone in the shoreline under its dome. The mayor's nephew used a megaphone to shout to participants to take their positions. The colorful kayaks, in shades of salmon, yellow, orange, blue, and green managed to float into place.

This straight-line race wasn't Jazzi's preferred method of enjoying an afternoon of kayaking. She preferred smooth and silky water, gliding with a buddy, watching sunshine glint off silver maple leaves, willow branches, and the backs of ducks, enjoying the water as she went.

Scanning the line of kayaks, Jazzi spotted Diego. Maybe this event would help him relax. She also spotted Tim and saw Derek farther down the line as he waved to Dawn.

Dawn didn't seem to notice him though. As a matter of fact, she was staring at the fir trees on the shore as if they held the answers she needed. Dawn had been much too quiet, totally into her head. And Jazzi was worried. She'd hoped this outing today would help Dawn forget about Finn's murder.

Jazzi nudged Dawn's kayak with her paddle, and Dawn looked her way. Her friend smiled, but it wasn't Dawn's usual bright, ready-for-a-new-day expression.

Charles Harding, taking his megaphone in hand, called out to the crowd, counting down for the race to begin. With all the participants ready, the mayor shot the starting pistol.

Jazzi noticed Dawn recoil from the noise. But then they were off. Jazzi could see Dawn paddling as if her life depended on it.

The exhilaration of paddling, coasting over blue-green water, feeling the cool breeze against her cheeks, pushed any other thoughts out of Jazzi's head. For the next hour, adrenaline, the race, and its aftermath settled around Jazzi like an escape from the real world into one of laughter, excitement, friendly rivalries, and exertion that was pleasurable and welcome.

An area of the shoreline had been set up for racers and friends to mingle after the event. Some members of the book club gathered with coolers that held bottles of water, cans of soda, and lunch offerings like sandwiches, cheese, and fruit.

Derek opened a cooler and offered bottles of water to the group. "Did you have temps helping at the bookstore today?"

It was rare for Dawn and Jazzi to be absent from Tomes at the same time. "We do have temp help," Jazzi said. "There's a college student who's taking a year off to work to decide if he really wants to stay in college. I think he'll be a valuable addition to our staff. Don't you think so, Dawn?"

Dawn was fingering a cheese cube. She simply nodded.

Derek pressed, "That should give you more time off. I bought a new snowmobile. You just need a down jacket and boots that keep your feet warm."

Obviously expecting a smile or at least an expression of enthusiasm from Dawn, Derek appeared disappointed when she gave him nothing. He turned to Jazzi as if he expected her to do something about Dawn's mood.

Jazzi felt helpless.

There was suddenly a flurry of activity farther up the shoreline where several kayaks had been dragged in. Jazzi had wondered why their owners hadn't carted them off yet.

Parker came strolling over to them from the area of the kayak landing. He grinned. "Any food left for me?"

Derek made room for Parker on the blanket. "If you tell us what's going on over there."

Parker lowered himself to the blanket, sitting cross-legged. "Photos from the race. First, second, and third, runners-up. The mayor is there. He wants in the photo for the newspaper to spread his good cheer."

"And keeping his face front and center for the next election," Derek noted.

Parker nodded in agreement. "You have to admit, his events bring in tourists."

Derek again looked toward the group down the shore while he ate a few grapes. "Who's the guy with the camera? Is he from the newspaper?"

In a low voice, Dawn said, "That's Claude Fenton. He was . . . Finn's good friend . . . and took over jobs when Finn—"

The pauses in Dawn's speech had caught Jazzi's attention. When all of a sudden Dawn's words stopped, when she put a hand to her chest, Jazzi went on full alert. Fear stole through her as Dawn's pretty face grew taut with tension. Jazzi realized why. Her best friend was having trouble breathing!

Immediately, Jazzi began rubbing Dawn's back. "Are you choking on something you ate?"

Shaking her head vigorously, Dawn closed her eyes, her cheeks draining of color. Jazzi could feel her trembling.

Parker was on his phone.

"Are you calling 9-1-1?" Derek was beside Dawn now, looking helpless at what to do.

Moments later, Jazzi faced the shoreline past the kayaks and saw an emergency vehicle was headed their way. She remembered seeing it in the distance while the kayaks raced.

"I knew they were nearby," Parker explained. "Better to be safe. Dawn can yell at me later."

After the emergency bus arrived, Abe jumped out. Jazzi was so glad to see someone she knew. As EMTs gave Dawn oxygen to breathe and checked her vital signs, Abe told Jazzi, "We're going to transport her to the Urgent Care Center."

Dawn reached out a hand to Jazzi and squeezed hard. "Come with?"

Jazzi didn't hesitate. "Of course." She changed her focus to Abe. "Can I ride with her?"

He was busy transferring Dawn to a gurney but nodded his agreement.

Jazzi jogged alongside of them to the ambulance. Parker, running beside her, clasped Jazzi's elbow. "Should I call Dawn's parents?"

"Yes. Please do." Parker and his parents had known and been friends with the Fernsbys for years.

Jazzi glimpsed Parker's face as the ambulance doors shut her inside with Dawn and Abe. Parker already had his phone to his ear, his expression as worried as the fear in Jazzi's heart that something serious could be wrong with her friend.

The Urgent Care Center always seemed busy during the summer months—more sports, more tourists, more accidents, Jazzi supposed. Since the nearest hospital was forty-five minutes away, the Belltower Landing Urgent Care Center was state-of-the-art. The mayor solicited donations to update everything about the center, including the latest diagnostic machines.

An attendant had whisked Dawn away from Jazzi as soon as they'd arrived. Parker and Derek joined Jazzi a short while later.

When Dawn's parents arrived, though, the tension in the small room ratcheted up. Gail had rushed to the desk, demanding to see her daughter.

Jazzi heard the commotion and stepped outside of the waiting room.

Gail's green eyes were flashing with indignation as the receptionist spoke calmly in the face of Gail's upset. "Your daughter is having some diagnostic tests completed. As soon as those are finished, we'll ask if she wants to see you."

"See me?" Gail was breathing hard, and her husband stood beside her, looking as if he didn't know what to do. "I'm her mother. Of course, she'll want me back there with her. We want to know exactly what happened."

Taking a few steps closer to the desk, Jazzi softly said Gail's name.

Both Fernsbys turned in her direction. Jazzi knew that if she was smart, she'd just let the receptionist handle this. But Gail and her husband had been good to her, and she cared about them. "I was with Dawn."

The steam seemed to leak out of Gail all at once. "Of course, you were. I should have expected that. What did you pull her into? I swear, if she's hurt because of you—"

George Fernsby capped his wife's shoulder with his large hand. "Gail. Slow down. I'm sure Jazzi had nothing to do with whatever happened."

Her throat tightening, Jazzi attempted to keep calm while she explained. "A group of us were having a picnic on the beach."

A middle-aged couple with a teenager entered the center. The teenager's arm was wrapped in a towel, and Jazzi glimpsed a stain of blood on the terry cloth. She motioned toward the waiting room. "Derek and Parker are here too. Come into the waiting room, and we'll tell you what happened."

With a gentle nudge from her husband, Gail followed Jazzi.

After Parker and Derek greeted the Fernsbys, George sank down on one of the green vinyl chairs as if his legs wouldn't hold him up. "Tell us what happened. Don't leave anything out." He held out his hand to his wife, and she sat in the chair next to him.

"It happened after the race," Derek began.

"We were simply sitting on blankets and talking," Parker added.

"Dawn raced, didn't she?" Gail asked. She sent a pointed look at Jazzi. "She said you convinced her. Even found temp help at the store so you could both compete."

"I thought it would be good for her to be out of the store."

"Why did you think that?" George asked shortly.

"She's been quiet and in her head a lot. I thought sun and water and exercise would help."

"Parker told me she couldn't breathe!" Gail's face was red, and she looked ready to pop out of her chair.

Derek faced Gail. "We were just sitting there, watching the people around us, when she seemed to have trouble catching her breath. But as soon as the EMT came with oxygen, her color came back, and she was doing better. Has Dawn ever had a problem with asthma?"

Gail's answer was immediate. "No. Never."

"Even in her adult years?" Parker looked at questions from every angle.

Gail blinked as if she didn't separate Dawn's adult years from her childhood years. "I . . . I don't think so." Her breath hitched and she grabbed George's arm. "What if something horrible is wrong? What if the problem is coming from her heart?"

George soothed his wife. "Let's not get ahead of ourselves."

Ever since Parker had called for the EMTs, Jazzi had been considering what had happened. In the ambulance, when Dawn could breathe easily with the oxygen and no other obvious symptoms, Jazzi had weighed her friend's reactions over the past few weeks.

The problem *was* her heart. Only not in the way Gail meant. Ever since Dawn had discovered Finn's body, she'd been quieter, jumpier, less reactive to what was going on around her. Jazzi could remember a time when her mother had been like that. Her mom had had a panic attack in the middle of a murder investigation. Jazzi certainly wasn't a medical professional, but to her, Dawn's reaction had seemed very much like her mother's.

What had brought it on today? Seeing Finn's friend Claude taking photographs in Finn's stead? The workings of the mind and body were sometimes mysterious. But emotions could definitely affect the body's responses.

It was two hours later when Gail came out of Dawn's cubicle. She motioned to Jazzi. "Dawn wants to see you." She didn't look happy about it.

Parker gave a shrug and sipped on his third cup of coffee. "Go on. We'll wait for you."

Derek nodded in agreement.

As soon as Jazzi stepped into Dawn's room, she could feel the tension in the air between Dawn and her parents.

Looking forlorn, Dawn blurted out, "It was a panic attack."

"Now, honey. The doctor said he'd like you to have a couple more tests . . ."

"Mom, I don't need any more tests to tell me I'm stressed." Dawn turned to Jazzi once more. "He wants me to find ways to relax. Maybe take up meditation."

"He said there are apps for that," George contributed.

"There are apps for everything, Dad. And I'll try one even though meditation isn't my jam. I don't want everyone fussing over me. I'll take some time off work and go paddleboarding more as long as the weather holds. If Jazzi can't get away, I'm sure Derek or Parker will go with me."

"Dear, we can take you out on the boat," George suggested. "Sometimes having family in the mix stresses me out more."

Those words from her daughter seemed to wound Gail. She squared her shoulders and lifted her chin. "You'll have medication now you can take when you need it."

Dawn focused on Jazzi. "I don't want to rely on medication."

When Gail sank down on the side of Dawn's bed, she looked defeated. "Of course, you don't. But you might need to use it for a little while. Come home with us and we'll talk about it."

Dawn's head was already shaking back and forth vehemently. "No. I want to go home with Jazzi to our apartment and the kittens."

Jazzi had been silent up until now, knowing Gail could be combative when her daughter's welfare was the issue. "You'll have to tell me what you need. I'm sure our new temp help would like more hours. You can work shorter days—"

Dawn swung her legs over the side of the bed as if she couldn't stand to be there a moment longer. "Maybe some shorter hours. But I don't need more time to think. That's what makes me anxious."

"A therapist might help too," Gail offered. "I'll start researching and look for someone with a good recommendation." Gail's expression said she would do anything for her daughter.

"Maybe, Mom. But I know what I need most."

Jazzi, Gail, and George asked in unison. "What?"

"I need Finn's killer found."

The silent message behind that statement was obvious to

Jazzi, along with the directive in her friend's serious green eyes. If Jazzi could help with that, Dawn wanted her to make this nightmare end.

Zander and Freya slipped and slid over Dawn's lap. Jazzi was relieved to see a smile cross her friend's face as she sat on the floor in front of the couch.

Dawn had convinced her mother that she wanted to come home to her apartment, not go to her childhood home. When Gail had stepped out of the cubicle to consult with the doctor, Dawn had confided in Jazzi that she couldn't handle her mother hovering right now. She just wanted to be with her friends to talk as she needed to and to be quiet when that mood hit.

Gail had protested, but her husband had convinced her to give Dawn space.

Doing anything they could to help, Derek and Parker had picked up pizzas and salad while Jazzi had brought Dawn home.

Now with the food eaten—Jazzi had watched Dawn pick at a Greek salad—Parker stood. "I'm going to head home. Dawn, if you need anything . . ."

He mimicked putting a cell phone to his ear.

"I will," she agreed. "You're all too good to me." Her eyes misted with tears.

Derek reached over and took her hand. "We all care about you. We'll get through this."

One of Parker's eyebrows quirked up, and he nodded to the door as if he wanted to talk to Jazzi over there.

She said, "I'll walk you out."

After they stepped outside on the landing, Jazzi pulled the door almost closed. "You wanted to talk to me?"

"Do you think she'll be all right?" he asked.

"I'll keep a close eye on her. Before we left the medical center, I heard Gail tell George she would make an appointment for Dawn with her family practice physician. But I do think we have to listen to what Dawn wants."

Parker leaned back on the railing. "What's that?"

"She needs Finn's killer to be caught."

Parker started shaking his head. "There's nothing we can do about that."

Thinking back to all the times friends and family had asked Daisy Swanson to help solve a murder case, Jazzi returned quickly, saying, "I think there is."

"Jazzi . . ." Parker's drawl of her name was a warning.

"I can't just sit by and let Dawn go through this."

"There's nothing you can do. It's in the detective's hands."

"Maybe. On the other hand, maybe I can find out more about the suspects that could help."

"What suspects? Are the police targeting anyone?"

"They have to be looking at Griffin and Diego. Tim, Carl and Abe. Anywhere is someplace to start. Starting someplace is better than doing nothing at all."

"You almost got killed the last time you became involved."

"I can quietly poke around. Who knows what I can turn up?"

"Yeah, who knows," Parker said with a grimace. He put his hands on her shoulders. "Promise me you won't do anything alone. I'm a text away."

His hands conveyed a protective reassurance, and she couldn't help but smile. She tipped her head back to look up at him. "You don't want anything to do with investigating."

"No. I don't. But I won't let you jump into danger either. Let me be your voice of reason."

What Parker meant was—he'd convince her to play it safe. They'd just have to see about that.

Erica nudged Jazzi's shoulder on Monday morning as they stood at the tea bar filling orders. "The kids are loving this."

Jazzi's gaze shifted from the customers waiting for tea and baked goods to the section of the store where a face-painting artist designed butterflies, cats, horses, and ducks on the children's faces.

Planned special events at Tomes & Tea had raised the store's profile in Belltower Landing. When Dawn had suggested a Reading Is Fun week, all the staff members had become excited about welcoming kids and expanding their reading horizons.

Dawn had invited a face painter who was creative about painting animals. Tied into that, she had set up a display with all types of wildlife books, from fiction to nonfiction.

"We're selling quite a few books about animals too. Are you ready to teach kids origami tomorrow?" Tomorrow was craft day and Erica was spearheading that.

"I am. If kids don't want to learn how to fold paper into animals, I'll move on to folding paper into airplanes."

A children's author reading her new release would be the highlight of the week on Wednesday.

Jazzi heard the ding of the door opening, and she looked that way. Tim Blanchard's wife, Nan, shepherded two freckle-faced, red-headed boys into the store. They'd inherited her red curls.

The boys, who were about eight and ten, ran toward the face painter.

Nan lifted her hands in a "What are you going to do?" gesture.

Jazzi thought she looked a little disheveled, with her hair banded back from her face in tumbles of curls. She was wearing stone-washed jeans and a T-shirt that said MOMS RULE.

The customer line at the baked goods case had dwindled down to one. Jazzi asked Erica, "You got this? I want to talk to Nan."

"Go ahead. I'm curious how they're dealing with everything too."

Sometimes Jazzi suspected Erica could read her mind.

As she approached Nan, the woman smiled. But that smile wasn't genuine. It was hiding Nan's true emotions, which had caused shadows to form under her eyes and stolen laughter from her.

Nan motioned to her boys, who were already standing in line for their turn to be painted. "They'll probably ask for dinosaurs. Does she do those?"

Their artist could paint practically anything. "I'm sure she does. But she'll want your approval to do it first."

"This morning they can have whatever makes them happy." Nan gazed in the direction of her boys again, looking sad.

Listening for the message under Nan's words, Jazzi suspected it was her way of continuing their conversation in the direction she wanted it to go. The store was busy, but nothing required Jazzi's immediate attention.

"Are you okay? Are the boys okay?"

Nan sighed heavily. "The atmosphere at home is tense." She lowered her voice even though no one was in listening distance. "Tim's been like a bear. Any little thing and he snaps at the boys."

As soon as she said the words, Nan put her hand to her mouth and looked embarrassed.

Stepping closer to her, Jazzi lowered her voice too. "You're frustrated. Can you talk to Tim about his mood?"

"Not right now. He's wound up and angry with everyone."

"Because of what happened to Finn?" Suddenly, Jazzi wondered how often Tim Blanchard became angry and what happened when he was. He and Nan always seemed happy, affectionate, loving. But sometimes the outside packaging didn't reveal what was inside.

Nan slouched against a set of free-standing bookshelves. She could still see over the top to what was happening in the face-painting line. "Not just what happened to Finn, though that's bad enough. Finn and Tim were good friends. We often met up at each other's houses for a night of cards or a glass of wine. Finn knew someone with a cabin cruiser. We went out on the lake together earlier this summer."

"So Tim's really missing Finn?"

The leading statement brought an immediate reply. "He is. But Detective Milford is making Finn's death get lost in other concerns."

Jazzi waited.

A second later, Nan went on. "He's called Tim into the station for questioning four times." Nan was indignant as she blurted out, "Four! Early this morning was the latest."

"I suppose the detective wants to know everything about their friendship." Maybe Tim had confided to his wife why the detective was riding him so hard.

"Someone else has questioned Tim too. I don't know if they're doing the good cop–bad cop routine."

Considering everything Nan had told her, Jazzi thought about Detective Milford's mindset. Multiple interviews. Bringing in a colleague. Retracing the same territory. It sounded to Jazzi as if the detective thought Tim was hiding something. Was he?

"I'm sorry this is happening to you."

"We just want this to be over. We want the killer caught so we can go on with our lives."

That was exactly what Jazzi wanted too, so Dawn could find closure.

"This morning Tim is looking into lawyers. He's afraid he'll need one. But I don't know how we'll afford it. His business is already being affected. We've had cancellations. Our neighbor who has been a longtime customer called another plumber. Word has gotten out that he's a suspect!"

"That's hard to counteract unless the guilty person is caught." Jazzi wished she could sit in on a conversation or two at the police station. What if they were focusing all their attention on Tim and they were looking at the wrong person?

Suddenly, Nan's boys waved at her and called "Mom."

Glancing around Tomes & Tea again, Jazzi saw that Erica was watching her discussion with Nan.

Studying the baked goods tray, Jazzi asked Nan, "What are your boys' favorite cookies?"

Nan managed a small smile that was actually genuine. "Anything with chocolate."

"Good choice," Jazzi said with a laugh. "I'll package up a few chocolate with chocolate chips for you to take along home."

Before Nan crossed to her sons, she squeezed Jazzi's hand. "Thank you."

Jazzi squeezed back. She wished conversation and cookies could fix Tim and Nan's dilemma. They couldn't. But a deeper dive into the investigation possibly could.

Chapter Fourteen

Shortly after Nan and her boys left Tomes & Tea, Jazzi returned to the tea bar to work with Erica.

Erica motioned to the counter behind them. "I started another batch of mango tea. That one has been popular this week. When the sweetened green tea sells out, I'll brew more of that."

Glancing over at the baked goods case, Jazzi commented, "We might have to text Colleen to send another order of cookies. More chocolate or something else?"

"Since the kids will be driving those orders, I'd say more chocolate." Erica waited a few beats, then asked, "How is Nan?"

"She's worried about Tim. The detective has called him in a few times. Being a suspect is affecting him."

"Tim can't be a suspect. He wouldn't hurt anyone." Erica's demeanor, with her frown and drawn-together brows, was downright indignant.

"Are you sure about that? How well do you know him?" The questions slipped out before she could stop them.

Erica seemed surprised. "I have gut instincts about people, don't you?"

"Sure. But . . ."

"But what?"

Jazzi reached under the counter for more paper cups to serve tea. Then she met Erica's gaze head-on. "There has to be a reason Detective Milford keeps asking Tim for another interview."

"And what do you think that is?" Erica's tone reflected her mother-knows-best attitude.

Erica might be a couple of decades older than Jazzi, but she didn't know everything about Jazzi's life experiences. Jazzi had decided to keep her mother's murder investigations to herself. Her mom still had to answer questions about those years. Anyone who googled her mom could find out about Daisy's talents and the help she'd given detectives in Willow Creek. But nobody had. Yet.

"Detective Milford is probably questioning Tim over and over again because he thinks he's lying. Or he believes Tim is hiding something. Maybe about that fight he had with Finn. I don't know. But he's trying to unearth *something*."

Erica was silent as she moved about the counter, and Jazzi thought she'd offended her. "Erica, I'm sorry. You must know Tim better than I do. I didn't mean to offend you."

Erica sighed. "You didn't. I don't want to think someone I've known all these years could be capable of anything horrible."

"How long have you known Tim?"

"He ran around with my younger brother. They played football together in high school. He was in and out of our house a lot."

"So let me ask you this. If Tim is hiding something, *why* would he do that?"

Slipping gloves on, Erica took a few muffins from the baked goods case and added them to the globed serving dish atop the counter. "Maybe he's trying to protect someone. That would be like Tim."

The sounds of the bookshop played around them—children's

laughter from the back corner, the tapping of fingers on a lap-top keyboard at a nearby table, the low chatter of two women conversing at the sales desk. Sunlight streamed in the front windows, and neon blue and green lights glowed from inside the book cubicles. They shouldn't be talking about murder in this happy atmosphere. But they were.

Jazzi considered her conversation with Erica had come to an end when Erica said, "You know I care about you and Dawn like family."

All the kindness Erica had shown Jazzi since she'd hired her wrapped a loving band around Jazzi's heart. "I know you do."

"I don't want Dawn to have any more panic attacks."

"I don't either. It's why I'm going to do everything I can to learn what happened to Finn."

"The detective won't like you poking around."

"I know." Jazzi was surprised Erica's voice didn't carry disapproval.

Turning to Jazzi, Erica slipped off her gloves, opened the trash bin with the foot pedal, and tossed them inside. "What if I talk to Tim?"

"About the detective's interviews?"

"No. He'd probably clam up in spite of our friendship. I was thinking I could ask him what started that fight with him and Finn. After all, they were friends. It's a question anyone might ask. Maybe he just needs someone a little removed to talk to. He and Nan have a good marriage from what I've seen."

"She seems puzzled by the police questioning him so often. So I don't believe Tim has confided in her."

"All right. I think Mario and Tim are attending a softball game tonight with their kids. Maybe I'll just happen to tag along."

"Do you even like softball?" A smile crept across Jazzi's lips as she thought of Erica with the bill of a baseball cap keeping the sun from her eyes as she sat beside her brother and Tim.

"I've been to more games than I want to count. Little league games as well as high school matchups. I'm sure the men and kids will love it if I join them." Erica's smile held a bit of sarcasm.

"Just remind them you can pay for the snacks," Jazzi teased.

"True. They might welcome me then." The humor from Erica's words faded away. "I do want to help solve this for Dawn's sake."

Jazzi clasped Erica's arm. "Thank you."

"I should be used to you asking the tough questions after what happened in the spring. I'll see if I can find an answer or two."

Jazzi's conversation with Erica was cut off as a group of tourists—Jazzi didn't recognize any of them—stepped up to the tea bar.

The next few hours whizzed by until Jazzi's phone played. She'd been restocking books about crafts to fill in gaps from morning sales. Slipping it from her apron pocket, she found Oliver's name had popped up on the screen. Anticipation guided her fingertips as she tapped the green ACCEPT icon.

"Hi, Oliver." She tried to keep her enthusiasm for taking his call out of her voice. Friendly, she told herself. Just keep it friendly.

"Hey, Jazzi. Any chance we could meet up on the green in about half an hour? Or did you already take your break?"

"No break yet. We've been busy. We have a face painter working in our arts and crafts section. But the stream has slowed."

"I just happen to have a few bacon and cheese rolls to share for lunch. Are you interested?"

"You know I can't resist a bacon and cheese roll." *Or Oliver's Australian accent*, the devil on her shoulder added.

She heard his deep chuckle right before he said, "See you in half an hour near the bell tower."

＊   ＊   ＊

After Jazzi crossed Lakeview Boulevard, she headed for the green. Fortunately, the six-foot-long teak-and-stainless-steel bench closest to the three-story-high bell tower was empty. The large round-faced clock that faced the shops along the boulevard showed three p.m. The bell in the belfry resting on top of it chimed three times. A breeze seemed to be skimming across the lake today, brushing over the manicured green lawn and the tourists enjoying the sunshine.

As Jazzi sank down onto the bench, setting two water bottles on the greener-than-green grass, she could spot outboard-engine boats and the dots of sailboats against the blue topaz shade of the lake and sky.

Facing the lake, she couldn't *see* Oliver approaching. But those tiny hairs on the back of her neck prickled. She turned and there he was, striding past the brick bell tower, headed for her bench.

She sat up straighter and brushed strands of hair that had come loose from her low bun away from her cheek.

Oliver approached, carrying a box with THE WILD KANGA-ROO printed in red on top.

She could stare at Oliver's smile all day. She wouldn't, of course. She couldn't, of course. She was curious why he'd asked her to meet him here. Simply to chat?

He sat beside her as naturally as if he did that often and handed her the box. "Napkins are inside too."

She handed him a water bottle.

"Thanks. I didn't think about drinks," he said.

While he opened his water bottle, she lifted the lid on the box and heaved a pleasurable sigh. "My mother might be disappointed if I say this, but these bacon and cheese rolls are my favorite baked goods."

"What's your favorite dessert that your mom makes?"

"Have you ever eaten shoofly pie?"

Oliver looked perplexed as he repeated the term. "Shoofly pie? Seriously?"

After she took a bite of the roll, chewed it, and wiped her mouth with a napkin, she nodded. "It's a type of pie made with molasses and considered to be a Pennsylvania Dutch standby. It's also called molasses crumb pie. There are legends behind it. One is that flies buzzed around the sweet filling and cooks would shoo them away."

"Makes sense," he said with a grin.

They ate in silence and sipped water for a little while. Conversation soared toward them from near the bell tower arches. Built of red brick, the three-story-high bell tower was twelve feet wide and twelve feet deep. Arches were cut through the tower's base from front to back and side to side.

Two boys with the group who looked to be preteens tried to crab walk up the side wall of the arch. The man with them shooed them down and scolded them.

After a few gulps of water, Oliver brushed his hand over his mouth. "Rumor has it there's a locked trapdoor on the inside of the tower."

"I heard that too. Parker told me everything is mechanized for the clock and the bell. But there is a trapdoor with a ladder that pulls down. It's locked and only used for emergencies. The mayor is the only one with a key."

Maybe she was imagining it, but Oliver had seemed to go particularly still when she mentioned Parker.

He shifted, took the empty box from Jazzi's lap, and set it on the bench beside him. "Olsen has lived in Belltower Landing all his life, hasn't he?"

"He has. Except for his time away at college."

"Stanford, right?"

She nodded. At The Wild Kangaroo, rumors and facts flew about as easily as they did at Tomes & Tea. Maybe more easily with the addition of liquor.

"Are you coming to Movie Under the Stars Night on the marina boardwalk tomorrow night?" Oliver asked.

Jazzi blinked at the non sequitur and turned her focus in that direction. "I haven't talked about it with Dawn yet, but I was hoping I could convince her to go to get her out of the apartment." As soon as she said it, she realized she might have torpedoed her chance to go on a date with Oliver if he'd been about to ask her. Still, that didn't matter if she could do something to help Dawn relax.

Oliver seemed to take a beat. "Emmaline came in the Kangaroo yesterday. We weren't busy so I sat with her for a few minutes. The police have told her she can return home, but for some reason she's still hanging around. Whatever the reason, she seemed particularly melancholy. She heard diners at nearby tables talking about movie night and said she wished she had someone to go with. She doesn't want to go alone. I thought of *you*. You had lunch with her, didn't you?"

"I did. I meant to stop in to see her again, but time slipped away." She saw now where this meeting was going. Not about a date, but about helping Emmaline feel less alone. She admired Oliver for that.

"I have to supervise service tomorrow night," he explained. "There are a few new offerings as specials that I need to oversee. After the final service, I can stop here."

Oliver's brows were quirked in an unspoken question. She answered easily. "I'll give Emmaline a call. I'll ask her to join Dawn and me. We can pick her up."

"Bonzer!" Oliver's enthusiasm for her attempt to help Emmaline was evident. "You're the best."

Jazzi didn't need to speak Australian to realize Oliver's exclamation and wide grin told her he believed that she was.

Maybe she'd subconsciously hoped for a date invitation. But she enjoyed this connection they had, and that was good enough for now.

*   *   *

The final credits for *ET* were running up the giant outdoor screen when Jazzi, Dawn, and Emmaline arrived at the space set up on the green meant for viewing the next movie. *The Sound of Music* would begin in fifteen minutes.

Jazzi carried two folding outdoor chairs while Dawn carried hers. They spotted Colleen and set up next to her. After greetings all around, Jazzi noticed many families with children were leaving. But couples were arriving. It was a perfect night for an outdoor movie. Jazzi remembered sitting here for a concert in June by country singer Evan Holloway.

Chatter from the crowd was low-pitched as the sky became lit with dots of light and a crescent moon tilted up. Colleen spread her arms over the other three woman in their chairs. "You, ladies, are putting me to shame. You're all dressed up!" Colleen was wearing capri jeans and a white tee.

"I asked the girls what *they* were wearing, and this seemed appropriate." Emmaline looked a little flustered that she'd over-dressed for the occasion.

Seeing she'd made Emmaline feel uncomfortable, Colleen was quick to say, "Your caftan is beautiful. It looks like a Sandra Potts floral original. I've seen them in a boutique on the boulevard."

Emmaline didn't contradict Colleen but let the statement stand.

Jazzi had convinced Dawn to dress up, hoping that would lift her spirits. Jazzi had helped Dawn with her makeup, and Dawn had braided several braids around Jazzi's face while letting her hair hang free in the back. From the many fashion options in her closet, Dawn had chosen a smocked-bodice strapless dress in flamingo pink and white. Jazzi had worn a coral jumpsuit, keeping in mind she could possibly see Oliver later.

Emmaline's chatter with Colleen became lively as the women

discussed baking, popular desserts at The Dockside, and favorite movies. Not one whisper about Finn's murder passed their lips, and Jazzi was grateful for that.

Dawn seemed to be enjoying herself. Hopping up from her chair, she asked the group, "How about popcorn? I'll buy us a tub to share."

"Good idea," Jazzi agreed. "Do you want me to come with you?" The popcorn truck at the curb had a long line.

"No need. Don't talk about anything too important." Dawn gave a saucy grin and headed for the truck.

Dawn had only been gone a few minutes when Jazzi felt a presence behind her chair. She turned to see—

Detective Milford.

Jazzi automatically turned toward Dawn. Fortunately, she was occupied, speaking to a woman in line at the popcorn truck.

Standing, Jazzi moved around her chair. "Hi, Detective. Beautiful evening, isn't it?" Tonight, Detective Milford was dressed casually in jeans and a tan oxford shirt.

"It is. My wife is supposed to join me soon. She had an errand to run. I'm just making sure movie night goes off without any drama. I have a few extra patrolmen milling about. How's your roommate?" He looked Dawn's way. "I heard about what happened after the kayak race."

"I think she's doing okay. She'll be even better after the killer is caught."

"Working on it."

Jazzi could see he was getting ready to finish their conversation. But before he could, she said, "Dawn and I had an idea about Finn's murder that I wondered if you've considered."

"What's that?"

"Finn took video and photos at tons of events. What if he photographed or videotaped someone doing something illegal?"

She waited for the detective's answer.

"We considered that possibility and we're on it. We have Finn's computers. But it's taking time and manpower to examine all the files. It's tedious work." He shrugged. "Meanwhile, I'm pursuing other avenues." He nodded to the movie screen, which was suddenly lit up again. "You enjoy the movie. Stay safe and out of trouble."

Jazzi didn't agree that she would.

With a shake of his head, the detective left the area, maybe scouting for his wife.

As soon as Jazzi sat, Emmaline leaned toward her. "What did the detective say?"

"He was asking about Dawn. He heard what happened."

"He makes me nervous."

Jazzi was about to ask why Paul Milford made Emmaline jumpy when the soundtrack of the movie began.

Did Emmaline have a reason to be nervous?

On Friday, Jazzi took her break midmorning and rode her bike west on Lakeview Boulevard. She thought about the short time she'd seen Oliver last night. He'd appeared about a half hour before the movie ended. He'd sat on the grass in front of her chair. They'd mostly listened to and watched the movie. He'd hummed along with "Edelweiss" and so had she.

Colleen had offered to drive Emmaline back to her hotel. She'd brought her car to the curb near the bell tower, and Emmaline hadn't had to walk too far. When Oliver had bid them goodnight, he'd touched Jazzi's arm and said he'd see her soon. That had sent Jazzi's heart happily humming.

Nevertheless, the whole time she'd watched the movie and appreciated Oliver's presence, she'd thought about what Detective Milford had said.

"We have Finn's computers. But it's taking time and manpower to examine all the files. It's tedious work."

What if there was a way to make it less tedious? What if somehow there was an inroad to those files or at least some idea where to look? Had the detective grilled Finn's friends?

Jazzi didn't think it would hurt, and it might even help if

she talked to Abe. He might know something and not even realize it.

So . . . she'd decided to spend her break at the fire station. Word on the street was that it was a friendly place. Kids who stopped in Saturday mornings could sit in a fire engine. Often, tourists talked about asking for first aid there. Abe was a paramedic as well as a firefighter, and other personnel were too.

Because of the bake-off, Jazzi had access to Abe's mobile number. She'd texted him to see if he was free. He was . . . unless a call came up for first responder services.

The fire station was about a mile from the green, close to the community church, the post office, and the police station. Abe was outside waiting in front of the three engine bays, two of which were open. She could see firefighters wiping down one of the engines.

After greetings, he said, "You caught me at a good time. Ready to go back on shift in half an hour. Just finished a workout."

Abe had a towel slung around his neck. Sweat beaded on his brow and dampened his firehouse T-shirt on his chest and underarms.

"Do you have a gym here?" She checked out the brick building, which looked as if it had had a section added on in recent years. The gym and modern conveniences?

"We do. Locker rooms and a captain's quarters. Have you ever toured the original firehouse?"

"That's in the south section of town. I've never gone through it."

"It was built in the late 1800s, designed for horse-drawn steamer engines. Bays were too small when engines progressed. It's a museum now."

"Have you always wanted to be a first responder?" Abe's enthusiasm made her believe he had.

"Ever since I was a kid. Santa passed through town on a fire engine, and I was hooked."

The tradition of Santa riding through town on an engine, fire horn tooting, was a Belltower Landing holiday event that was held the weekend before Christmas.

Abe took hold of his towel at both ends and pulled it back and forth at his neck. He gave her an assessing stare. "I don't believe you came here today to ask me why I became a firefighter. What's on your mind?"

"I'm trying to help Dawn."

His gaze softened. "How is she doing?"

"She's learning strategies to control the panic attacks. But she needs some answers about Finn. We all do."

"I don't have any answers." It was easy to see he wanted no part of this conversation as he took a step back. "The police questioned me. *That* was an experience."

"Just once?" Jazzi asked quickly.

Tilting his head, he nodded. "Why?"

"If they only questioned you once and didn't bring you back in, they probably don't consider you a suspect."

"As if you'd know," he muttered. "They could be waiting to pounce. Look at how many times they've grilled Tim."

"Exactly."

Her one word conclusion must have surprised him.

With disbelief in his voice, he asked her, "Do you really think Tim is a suspect?"

"They're acting as if he is."

"It could be a ruse until they charge the real killer. Element of surprise and all that. I watch crime shows too."

"Tell me about Finn. Was he happy with his life?"

A kid of about ten came zooming by on his skateboard and yelled, "Hey, Abe."

Abe lifted a hand in greeting. "Take that to the park before the mayor tickets you."

The boy laughed. Everyone knew the mayor had a pet peeve about skateboards interfering with tourist pedestrian traffic.

Abe motioned to a spot of shade near the side of the building. They walked that way and when they stopped, Abe said, "Finn was a guy's guy, but he could relate well to women and kids too. That's what made him so good at photography. He could tune in to his subjects and coax out the best expressions or moves."

"Moves?"

"He photographed everything from pet adoption events to the ballet."

"Did he have hobbies?"

"Work was his passion, his hobby, and his life. He wanted to have kids, but I don't know what was happening with that."

"Do you think Finn could have taken video of someone doing something illegal and that could have gotten him killed?"

"If he filmed something like that, he would have gone to the cops." Abe's voice was filled with certainty.

"Are you sure?"

"What? You think he would have blackmailed someone? Never Finn. Dishonesty bugged him more than anything. On the other hand, one person can't right the world's wrongs."

"Meaning?"

"Finn could have captured all types of activity on film. That doesn't mean he could do anything with it. Still, if someone didn't even want him knowing about it . . ."

"The detective has all of Finn's work product."

"That would be time-consuming to sort through."

Studying Abe and listening to him, Jazzi believed he'd had nothing to do with Finn's murder. She also wasn't sure she'd gleaned anything from this conversation. That had to happen to the detective and his team over and over again.

"Thanks for talking to me. It could be a long while until anyone finds answers."

"You never know. Everyone makes mistakes. Including criminals. All of a sudden there could be a break in the case. Remind Dawn of that."

The way Abe said Dawn's name, she had the feeling Dawn could be more important to him than merely a patient he'd transported to the medical center.

"I will tell Dawn that."

"Is she dating anyone?" Abe looked a bit embarrassed as he asked.

"Not seriously. At least not yet. You could still have a chance if you ask her out."

"Good to know." Abe's smile hinted he might be calling Dawn soon.

As Jazzi said good-bye, went to her bike, and clasped her helmet on her head, she sorted through everything Abe had told her.

"Dishonesty bugged him more than anything."

If dishonesty bothered Finn so much, would he have tried to do something about it? That's what could have gotten him killed.

Chapter Fifteen

Rising around sunrise, Jazzi dressed, fed the kittens, made a note for Dawn on the eraser board on the refrigerator that she'd gone for a bike ride, and locked up the apartment. The sun was making its ascent as she rode down Lakeview Boulevard toward the marina. She rode a familiar route past the food trucks and into a development along the forested area of Lake Harding.

As she pedaled, she considered everything that had happened in the past few days. After sorting through her conversation with Abe—she really didn't consider him a suspect and doubted the police did either—her thoughts swirled around Dawn's panic attack, her conversation with Gail, and the fact that her roommate had dismissed her mom and given the impression she simply didn't want to be around her. Jazzi knew that Gail's feelings were hurt and she probably resented Jazzi's spot in Dawn's life.

To help Dawn, Jazzi and Gail had to be on the same page. Maybe *they* were the ones who should be talking. Dawn wasn't taking phone calls from her mom, simply texting that she didn't have time to talk but that she was okay.

Jazzi remembered a time in her life when she'd searched for her biological mother and then wasn't sure how to handle the two relationships of adoptive mom and birth mom. She'd been afraid the search and finding Portia was going to hurt her mom. Along with that, her birth mom had never told her husband that she'd given up a baby for adoption before she'd met him. That had caused problems in their marriage, and Jazzi had felt responsible.

Her mother had found her a therapist to help her sort it all out. Talking it through had helped, and her relationship with her mom had strengthened. Dawn needed Gail and Gail needed Dawn. They had to bridge that gap between them.

After her ride through the High Point development, Jazzi headed back to town. Instead of pedaling down the boulevard, she turned left onto Maple Street beside the food trucks, then turned right onto Boathull Road, which ran parallel to Lakeview Boulevard. After a few blocks, she stopped before Rods to Boards, Dawn's parents' outfitting store. It opened earlier than most other stores to suit sports enthusiasts.

The storefront was clean and modern, a rectangle trimmed in navy and black. The large plate glass windows allowed the outside world a peek at natural wood walls and utilitarian black shelves. A green paddleboard stood on one side of the electronic door's entrance and a kayak on the other. The sign RODS TO BOARDS stood out in black letters on a natural wood plank.

After braking her bike and removing her helmet, Jazzi locked her bike on a stand down the street from the store. Tucking her helmet under her arm and straightening her ponytail, she headed for the door without hesitation.

Passing by racks of hoodies and shirts, stands of sports shoes, and a rack of hats, she spied Gail speaking to a customer near a wall of fishing equipment. Jazzi didn't disturb her but rather waited. This should be a private conversation.

The customer must have decided not to make a purchase. After he strode toward the door, Jazzi approached Gail. Today

Dawn's mom wore her hair pulled away from her face with a wooden barrette. In a mint-colored short-sleeved hoodie and khaki shorts, she was attractive. Her look now, when she gazed at Jazzi, had a closed quality.

Gail was the first to speak. Going on the offensive? "Hi, Jazzi. What brings you here so early?"

Jazzi wanted to plunge right in, but she had to tread carefully. She lifted her helmet. "I was out for a ride and thought I'd stop by."

"Stop by?" Gail asked with a frown. "Do you need a sun shirt or a hat?" She motioned toward a rack.

Jazzi dropped all pretense of small talk. She wished she and Gail could return to their first days of easy friendship when Dawn had brought Jazzi home from college to introduce her to water sports and the unique aspects of Belltower Landing.

"I'd like to talk to you about Dawn."

"Does my daughter know you're here?"

Jazzi shook her head. She could easily see disapproval on Gail's face, in the tightness of her lips pressed together. But Jazzi also believed she saw curiosity in Gail's green eyes.

"No, she doesn't. I'll tell her when I get back. I know she's still upset from the ruckus she believes her panic attack caused. And I think you're probably still upset about the way she pushed you away at the Urgent Care Center."

"You have no right barging into our personal business."

"I live with Dawn. I care about her as if she was my sister. I don't think she wants to push you away."

"She's doing a good job of it," Gail muttered.

"I've done the same thing with my mom, especially when I was trying to decide what I wanted to do with my life. My mom thought I had my future planned—earn a master's, then a Ph.D. But suddenly I began to change my mind about what I wanted. Mom didn't understand at first. Moving here and buying the store was a risk. But she let me figure it out."

Gail looked across the store, then focused on Jazzi again. "You think I need to back off and give her space."

"It might help," Jazzi agreed softly.

"You're more independent than Dawn."

"Not always. I grew into it. Kids just want to please their parents or at least have their approval."

"And when they find what they want to do doesn't meet their parents' approval . . ." Gail added.

"A clash happens," Jazzi filled in.

Gail studied her fingertips, the store, the view out the front window where traffic was picking up. "I need to let Dawn find her independence even if I don't like it."

Jazzi remained quiet.

"Do you think Dawn still wants to find her biological parents?" Gail's moist eyes said she wanted the truth.

"She hasn't talked about it since spring."

"I suppose I have to let her find her independence with that too." Gail's grimace spoke for her on how difficult that would be.

"My mom did, and her support helped us to stay close." Jazzi respected her mom more than Daisy would ever know for that gift.

Gail unexpectedly held her hand out to Jazzi. "Truce?"

Jazzi shook Gail's hand. They both wanted what was best for Dawn.

The grumble of thunder drew Jazzi to the front window of the bookstore later that day. When she'd returned from her bike ride, she'd spoken to Dawn about her visit to Rods to Boards. No more secrets. Dawn had seemed pleased Gail and Jazzi had formed a truce.

Unfortunately, now at three in the afternoon, a storm had moved in. The gray sky, turbulent with black clouds, was churning out sheets of rain.

The in-store traffic had slowed as the beating of the rain increased. A few customers sipped hot tea—always a favorite on a day like this—while they sat at a table looking over a book they might want to purchase. As Jazzi turned into the store and away from the dreariness outside, one of her regular customers motioned to her.

Jazzi hurried toward Annette, a blonde in her forties who always chatted when she came to Tomes & Tea. Through their conversations Jazzi knew Annette was divorced. She was the mom of a nine-year-old boy named Trevor who enjoyed leafing through volumes about chemistry experiments. Annette tried to have an amicable relationship with her ex-husband for Trevor's sake. But the operative word there was *tried*.

It was amazing what Jazzi learned about her customers from simply listening. Since she wasn't needed anywhere at the moment, Jazzi took the white enamel chair across from Annette.

"I'm not working today," Annette said. "I took a vacation day. Wouldn't you know we'd have rain all day."

"Is Trevor at summer camp?" She remembered Annette enrolled her son in week-long educational camps throughout the summer.

"Not this week. He's spending it with his dad. I thought a vacation day would be good for me to do woman stuff instead of mom stuff. I'm getting a mani-pedi this afternoon at the Lotus Blossom spa. Ever been there?"

"No. I haven't." The problem with the spa, which offered everything from mud wraps, massages, and seaweed wraps, was that it was très expensive. Dawn's mom had made appointments now and then.

"I just need to relax today." Annette's brow creased from the stress she was probably trying to escape. "Insurance claims have been crazy. So many tourists are driving rental cars they're not used to and bumping into residents. It's worse than the snowfall months. And truth be told, I think drivers aren't watching where they're going. They're distracted by the murder. Another murder in Belltower Landing. Who would have thought?"

Who *would* have thought about it? One murder last spring was an anomaly. But now two murders in a tourist town known for its positive vibes and community events was bordering on city life—what tourists here were escaping from.

"I knew Finn," Annette revealed. "He did a family portrait when Trevor was a baby. I gave the photos to our parents and family members for Christmas presents. He was easy to work with and so good with Trevor."

"I hear he was a likeable guy," Jazzi prompted.

"He was! I mean, I saw him around at weddings I attended and at Belltower Landing's charity events. Some of his video was even broadcast on the local news when he captured something unusual that happened when no one else did."

"Such as?" The talk of video caught her immediate interest.

"I remember once he caught an argument between the mayor and his chief of staff. Another . . . he taped a newscaster giving his personal political views. He did video of good stuff too. He captured the chief of police helping a little girl find an egg at the annual Easter egg hunt."

The Chief of Police, Vince Caruso, seemed to stay out of the news as much as possible. Jazzi had only caught a glimpse of him a few times at the Santa parade and at the Fourth of July celebration.

Annette brought Jazzi's thoughts back to Finn. "When I heard that Finn and Tim Blanchard almost started a brawl, I was surprised."

"Everyone else seemed surprised too."

Two customers with umbrellas shook off raindrops, opened the door to Tomes, and left their umbrellas outside the door. Jazzi made a move to stand. Time to get back to work.

Annette glanced around the store. "I don't see Dawn anywhere. I wanted to say hello."

Dawn had left for a therapy appointment. To Annette, Jazzi said, "Dawn had errands to run."

"When I was in last week, she didn't seem like herself. She's usually so bubbly, but she didn't want to chat and looked . . . sad. I heard she found Finn."

Jazzi didn't want to prolong this conversation because she wouldn't gossip about her best friend. "She knew Finn. His death has been hard on her and everyone."

"I feel for Belinda. Finn and his wife were such a perfect couple."

This conversation with Annette had shown Jazzi how much Annette liked to gossip. Why hadn't she seen that before? However, something good had come from their talk.

Jazzi stood and smiled at Annette. "I'm glad you mentioned Lotus Blossom spa to me. I might have to try it." Or rather, she'd buy Dawn a gift certificate for a massage and mani-pedi. That might help her roommate relax.

After Jazzi said good-bye to Annette and wished her an enjoyable day off, she helped the two customers who had come in and started browsing. A few other customers rushed inside Tomes & Tea to escape the weather, and Jazzi found herself busy for the next hour.

Erica crossed to Jazzi and touched her arm. "Can I see you for a couple of minutes in the storeroom?"

Dawn had returned from her therapy appointment, and Audrey was serving tea at the tea bar. "Sure."

Once in the storeroom, Erica said, "I tried to talk to Tim at the softball game I attended with him and my brother. But he was closed off. He kept insisting he told the police everything he knows. But I've known Tim a long time. And he couldn't look me straight in the eyes when I asked him what he'd told the detective. He wouldn't say what his fight with Finn was about either. All he'd say was that they'd had a difference of opinion. I went at him about family, that he's only hurting his family if he doesn't tell the truth."

"What did he say to that?"

"He insisted more than family was involved. And then he stopped. Full brakes. But I'll keep working on him."

"Maybe Detective Milford should have *you* on his team. What do you think Tim meant?"

"I have no idea. But I do believe more than a difference of opinion is involved." Erica appeared as troubled about Tim as she would be about her brother.

A rap sounded on the door. Audrey peeked in.

Erica slipped out through the door when her daughter came in. Audrey told Jazzi, "Griffin Pelham wants to speak with you."

Jazzi and Audrey returned to the shop, where Griffin was waiting for Jazzi.

"Your partner said I have to talk to *you*." He looked indignant, as if all of his needs should be taken care of immediately.

Jazzi gazed across the store to where Dawn stood at the tea bar. Her partner just shrugged and shook her head.

"What can I help you with, Griffin?"

He almost shoved a stack of narrow pamphlets in her face. "I'd like you to put these brochures at your sales desk."

Jazzi took one from the stack and studied it. It was a sales brochure for Griffin's latest cookware. "We don't pass out sales brochures."

"You have my book for sale." His eyes were flashing as if they were throwing darts to convince her to his way of thinking.

"We are a *book*store. We don't sell cookware." She was not about to let him throw around his celebrity or bully her.

"Maybe you *should*. Maybe that would increase your sales all around. There's ordering info on the pamphlets. If you showcased a few display pieces—"

Jazzi cut him off. "No. I won't do that." She sighed. "But what I will do is insert a pamphlet inside each book. By the way, both Colleen and Diego are trying to get in touch with you. They asked me to give you the message if you came in."

He studied her. After he thrust the stack of pamphlets at her, he walked away.

She could definitely imagine Griffin Pelham murdering Finn.

Jazzi was washing down the tea bar as Dawn set it up again for the next day. It was almost closing time. Rain still ran from the gutters down the front window when the door opened and Abe Ventrus came inside. He wore a yellow rain slicker. Even so, his hair was wet as if he hadn't bothered with the attached hood.

Dawn had recently called Abe *hot*. And he no doubt was. He unbuckled the slicker, went to the door again, and shook it under the overhang. Then he propped it there against the front window's casement.

His grin was wide as he strode to the tea bar. Across the room at the sales desk, Erica's brows rose with her questioning look for Jazzi. Jazzi just shrugged.

Dawn didn't seem to realize he'd come to see *her*. She had her side to him as she straightened a stack of cups for serving customers the next morning.

Abe cleared his throat, looking slightly unsure. His dark brown hair, wet with rain, dipped over his left eye. He pushed it away. "Sorry if I wet your floor with my slicker."

Jazzi peered over the edge of the bar. "Just a few drops. No problem."

"Give me one of those paper towels and I'll wipe it up."

Jazzi could see he was serious. A man who cleaned up after himself could be a keeper.

Dawn finally faced him head-on as he wiped up the sprinkles, then straightened. "What brings you out in this mess? she asked. "I bet you were busy today with accidents."

"A few. A car went into a ditch on High Rock Road. The driver was knocked around a bit, and a passerby called it in. No serious accidents, thank goodness."

"No brewed tea left since we're shutting down for the day. But I have a few maple pecan cookies left," Jazzi offered.

"No, I'm good. I'm headed back to the station for chili."

Abe still hadn't told them why he'd stopped in, though Jazzi had an inkling. He wore a football-type jersey with jeans. His shoulders were broad, his jaw determined, and his brown eyes sparkled as his gaze fell on Dawn. Jazzi hoped her best friend didn't resist what he was going to ask her.

When he cleared his throat, Jazzi nudged Dawn's arm. Her partner hadn't seemed to be paying attention up until now.

Her gaze seemed to register who stood in front of her. Apparently, he wanted more than tea.

Jazzi stepped away from Dawn to the end of the bar and dumped tea stirrers into a basket for the following day. She was close enough if Dawn needed to be rescued but far enough to give her a little privacy.

Abe shifted from one foot to the other. "I didn't stop in for a book or tea. I came to see *you*."

Dawn's pointed chin quivered a bit. "You came to see *me*?"

She was usually talkative and bubbly, but that effervescence had appeared to vanish since Finn Yarrow's murder. Now she looked like a deer caught in headlights. Her green eyes had widened with her surprise.

"I'm off-shift the night of the Get Out and Dance night at the marina," Abe explained.

The advertising and publicity for the town's latest community event, to be held on Labor Day, had been pushed hard over the past two weeks. Their friend Delaney, who had been contracted as a consultant by Mayor Harding to get the word out on social media, had talked about the preparations at their most recent book club meeting. Canopies with string lights and music of all ilks should lead to a fun night for every age bracket. However, Dawn hadn't seemed the least bit interested.

Jazzi wanted to prompt Dawn or give her a nudge, but she

knew she should stay out of Abe's attempt to ask Dawn for a date.

When Dawn didn't respond to Abe's statement, he stepped closer to the bar. "I thought it might be more fun to attend it with someone I'd like to get to know better. Would you like to go with me?"

Dawn didn't respond right away, as if her surprise had made her mute.

Abe took a deep breath. "I understand if you're busy that night or have a date—"

Jazzi couldn't stand Abe's torture. She intervened. "Dawn, you're not busy that night, are you?"

Jazzi's question seemed to snap Dawn out of her trance. "No, I'm not busy. I haven't thought about going—"

Leaning toward her best friend, Jazzi whispered to her, "You could wear something glitzy. I hear an award-winning ballroom dancing couple are supposed to be there."

"What do you think?" Abe asked hopefully.

Suddenly, Dawn looked shy, and dimples appeared at the corners of her mouth when she smiled. "I'd like to go."

Abe jumped at her acceptance. "Can I have your number? We can text each other deets."

Not hesitating, Dawn slipped her phone from her apron pocket.

While Abe and Dawn exchanged numbers, Jazzi glanced over at Erica. Erica gave her a thumbs-up sign. Maybe Dawn was finally moving on from the murder. Jazzi hoped with all her heart that was true.

Dawn's closet wasn't roomy enough for all of her clothes. As Jazzi pulled two hangers with colorful dresses from the closet in Dawn's bedroom, she considered the other closet in her friend's childhood bedroom at the Fernsbys' house, which was also full. She switched her winter and summer clothes back and forth.

Dawn shook her head at both of Jazzi's choices for her date with Abe. Jazzi had suggested sorting through Dawn's closet tonight after supper to fuel her excitement about going out.

Zander jumped in and out of an open shoe box in the corner of the closet while Freya chewed on its corner. Jazzi lifted the black furry kitten away from the cardboard and tossed a puffy ball in the direction of Dawn's bed to divert the feline's attention.

"Neither of those feel right." Sitting cross-legged on her bed, Dawn's expression was thoughtful. "We're at the end of summer. Maybe I should wear something less—" She paused. "Less breezy. Do you know what I mean?"

Jazzi riffled through the closet once more. "Possibly."

"Or I could go shopping for something new." She shot Jazzi a mischievous smile, and Jazzi was glad to see it.

While Jazzi watched her personal budget carefully with her eye toward that rainy day, Dawn was apt to spend her discretionary income on makeup, skin care products, and clothes. At the end of the month, she often borrowed from her mom or her brother if a car repair loomed or she "needed" new sports equipment.

"You seem excited about this date." Jazzi pulled out a black jumpsuit with a halter top and little white dots patterned in the fabric.

"That's a possibility," Dawn agreed, unfolding her legs and sliding from the bed. She took it from Jazzi and turned it frontward and backward. "I *am* excited. Though I wonder what Derek will think about it."

Dawn and Derek Stewart were good friends. They participated in scads of activities together but hadn't officially "dated," much like herself and Parker.

Before Jazzi could respond, the doorbell rang. "Are you expecting anyone?"

Dawn shook her head.

"I'll get it." Jazzi left Dawn sorting through outfits.

As Jazzi went to the door and peered through the peephole, she saw a shadowy figure in a black slicker who was facing the lake rather than the door. The motion detector light above the landing hadn't switched on. That happened sometimes with heavy rain.

She turned the dead bolt, then opened the door a crack before the chain lock stopped the door from opening farther. As she did that, the person on the landing faced the door. She breathed a sigh of relief. It was Parker.

After she unhooked the chain, she opened the door. "Hey, Parker."

Instead of a greeting, he asked, "Did your phone run out of charge again? I texted but you didn't answer."

When she and Dawn had come in after work, she'd laid her phone on the counter intending to charge it as they made supper. She hadn't.

"I just wanted to stop in to see how Dawn was doing. I didn't intend to surprise you. She didn't answer my text either." His expression was so serious his forehead creased, the lines around his mouth deeper than usual.

"Dawn's deep in her closet. She has an upcoming date to look good for." Jazzi was smiling at her roommate's excitement and was sure Parker would ask questions about it. But he didn't. That and the sober depth of his brown eyes told her something was wrong.

"What's going on, Parker?"

He rubbed across the mole above the left side of his lip. After a moment of hesitancy, he spoke. "I don't want to alarm you. I could be all wrong."

"Wrong about what? If you tell me, I might be less alarmed than watching the expression on your face. Spill it, Parker."

His slicker was dripping on the kitchen floor. He didn't seem to notice or care. "Someone was standing at the base of your stairs, staring up at your windows and door. I stayed across the boulevard, wondering why that person didn't climb the stairs to your apartment. But they didn't. They just watched. I couldn't tell if it was a man or woman. Whoever it was wore a long dark raincoat with a hood."

"Maybe whoever it was ducked under the landing, hoping the rain would let up." That was Jazzi's reasonable head voice providing an explanation. But a creep factor was settling in at the back of her neck.

"No. The watcher didn't duck under the landing. They watched. And then they hurried away. I don't like the idea of you having a stalker, Jazzi. I don't like it at all."

Suddenly, Jazzi had goose bumps on her arms. She was hoping Parker was wrong. Yet deep inside she knew he wasn't wrong.

Just what was she going to do about it?

Chapter Sixteen

The following evening, Jazzi and Dawn were finishing a supper of egg rolls, chicken lo mein, and mixed vegetables when Dawn received a text. She lifted her phone from the table and read it.

"It's my mom. She and my dad want to stop by." Dawn made a face. "That can mean nothing good."

Jazzi stood and placed a leftover egg roll into a container and covered it. "You don't know that. You should see what they want."

"It's so awkward talking to Mom now. Will you stay?" Dawn stood too, closed the carton of leftover lo mein, and carried it to the refrigerator.

"I'll stay as long as it's not a private conversation between you and your parents."

Dawn rounded the corner and picked up a few cat toys littering the floor. "Maybe I should dust the living room really quick."

"Do you think that will help the conversation?" Jazzi teased. "I'll make a pitcher of iced tea."

Reluctantly lifting her phone, Dawn answered her mother's text. Her phone pinged again with a return answer from her mother. "She says they'll be right over."

A half hour later, Dawn had run a Swiffer cloth over the furniture when the doorbell rang. She crossed to the door at a slow-footed pace, then welcomed her parents inside.

Everyone stood around awkwardly until Jazzi asked the Fernsbys, "Would you like a glass of iced tea?"

"Sure would," George Fernsby replied. "With the rain stopping this morning, the temperature climbed up again."

Jazzi knew Dawn's dad's small talk was meant to ease into whatever conversation they wanted to have. She brought the pitcher of iced tea to the coffee table, where she'd laid a quilted placemat with nautical themes.

Dawn and her parents each took a seat while Jazzi poured the tea. Dawn sat on the sofa with her parents. Jazzi lifted Zander and Freya, who were nestled on the armchair, into her lap when she sat there.

To start some type of dialogue, Dawn asked, "Was Rods to Boards busy today?"

"It was," George answered quickly so they didn't have to sit in silence. His wife was usually the gregarious one, but she seemed to be waiting for the right time to speak.

He continued. "Lots of customers are here to enjoy water sports with the predicted fine forecast for Labor Day. Some of the wives seemed eager for the Get Out and Dance party at the marina tomorrow night. Outdoor events really call to the tourists."

Finally, Gail looked to Dawn and then Jazzi. "You will be going, won't you?"

"I'll be meeting friends there," Jazzi answered. "But Dawn has other plans." It was up to Dawn to reveal she had a date.

"What plans, dear?" Gail asked. "I hope you're not going to

stay in and watch a movie or something. These end-of-summer nights are so pleasant."

Before Gail could go on, Dawn picked up a glass of tea. "I'm going. I have a date."

"With Derek?" Gail looked intrigued.

"No. With Abe Ventrus," Dawn cut in.

"But wasn't he involved in the bake-off and the murder?" George seemed horrified.

Dawn simply said, "He's the paramedic who took me to the hospital during my panic attack. Let's leave it at that."

Gail nudged her husband's arm.

Apparently, Dawn decided to get to the point of the visit. "Mom, why did you need to see me tonight?"

Jazzi was quick to offer. "I can leave."

"Not necessary," George quickly said. "Gail and I wanted to talk to you both."

Dawn eyed her parents suspiciously. "What about?"

"Your dad went to a city council meeting last week."

Dawn's eyebrows hiked up and her eyes widened. "Dad, I thought you hate those meetings."

"I do." George nodded. "But I heard rumors that the councilors were thinking about bringing proposals to the chamber of commerce and the mayor. I wanted to find out what those proposals were."

Dawn exchanged a look with Jazzi as if asking what this had to do with them.

Gail jumped in. "The councilors think it's good business if stores pool their PR dollars. Sort of a buddy system. Of course, there will be pushback against that. Stores that operate mostly in summer won't care about doing it for winter. But businesses like yours and ours could benefit by working together, don't you think?"

Jazzi and Dawn had spoken about keeping their sales numbers up after the summer tourist season. That's why they'd worked hard on social media promotion as well as special events and increased traffic to their website.

"What do you have in mind?" Dawn asked cautiously.

With alacrity, first Gail and then George laid out their thoughts.

Gail pointed out, "You can have a winter sports book promotion when we have a sale on skis, for instance."

George added, "And we know a ski instructor who gives a class on pointers for beginning skiers. He has a training guide. He could do a signing at Tomes & Tea."

Full of enthusiasm, Gail was practically bobbing on the sofa. "We could even connect our websites."

That wasn't an idea Jazzi was ready to embrace.

When Zander stretched and hopped over to the sofa, Jazzi took that opportunity to nudge Dawn and check her expression. Dawn swung one of her gold dangling earrings back and forth, which was a tell of hers that messaged Jazzi that she was probably against the idea too.

As Zander hopped over Dawn's legs to settle on Gail's, Dawn stopped the flow of suggestions. "I don't know about the websites. But I do like your other ideas. And I'm sure we could come up with more."

It was possible that Rods to Boards and Tomes & Tea could provide links to each other's sales promotions. But Jazzi was certain that the two stores shouldn't converge too much. That would be asking for disputes and more of Dawn's involvement in Rods to Boards, which Dawn was set against.

George seemed to understand. "Our promotions would help each other. That's all."

As they discussed further ideas, Dawn seemed to relax with her parents. By the time they were ready to leave, there were smiles all around.

Dawn proceeded out the door with her dad.

Gail hung back. In a low voice, she asked Jazzi, "Do you think Dawn dating this Abe is really safe?"

"The dance will be in a public place. Abe has a reputation for being a good guy. He really helped Dawn through her panic attack. You have to trust her. I'm sure she'll be careful."

"You mean by protecting her drinks and that kind of thing?"

"I do. We know the drill. I'll check in on her by texting throughout the evening if we don't meet up."

"Gail, are you coming?" George called.

With that assurance of Jazzi checking in with Dawn at the dance, Gail went out on the landing with her husband.

As Jazzi waited for Dawn to return inside, she remembered what had happened outside last night with Parker. *Could* she have a stalker, as Parker had put it? He'd wanted her to call Detective Milford. But as she'd explained to Parker, there was no reason to call. Someone had stopped near the deck in the rain. Maybe they wanted to know if the apartment would ever be available to rent. Maybe they were wondering how many square feet it occupied. Maybe they stopped to catch their breath. Maybe . . .

No proof at all that the person meant anyone harm. Detective Milford would dismiss her concern. Or rather, Parker's concern.

She wasn't sure either of their concerns were legitimate.

Still, a little niggling voice had to wonder if Parker's concern should be for Dawn instead. Maybe the killer believed Dawn had seen something that could connect him or her to Finn's murder.

Stopping the runaway thoughts with action, Jazzi snatched her phone from the counter. Taking it to the sofa, she settled beside the kittens. They awakened and looked up at her. Zander yawned and returned back to napping. Freya washed a paw, swiped at her face, then toddled over to Jazzi's lap. Jazzi

ran her finger over Freya's ears, then tapped the icon for the social media site where she'd looked at Finn's professional photos
once before.

After Dawn closed and locked the door, she was smiling.
"What do you think of all that?"

"Your mom is making an effort to let you live your life. But
she wants to help. Is that okay with you?"

"Yeah, I guess it is. Do you like the idea of a joint promo?"

"It could help during the winter."

Sitting beside her, Dawn picked up Zander and cuddled him.
"What are you looking for? Isn't that Finn's page?"

Jazzi studied Finn's professional social media page photo by
photo. "It is. Do you know if he had a personal profile page as
well as a professional one?"

"Finn and Belinda had one together. I see their photos in my
stream."

"I'd like to look at them. Do you mind?"

"You could ask to be friends," Dawn suggested.

Jazzi thought about that idea. "Yeah, I can. But I'm sure Belinda has other things on her mind, and it might take a while for
her to see my friend request. Is the page in Finn's name or both
of their names?"

"Both," Dawn answered. "Friends are posting their condolences and stories about Finn."

Leaning forward, Dawn plucked her phone from the coffee
table. She'd soon brought up Finn and Belinda's personal page.
Handing it to Jazzi, she shrugged. "Take a look. I like seeing
the photos of Finn when he was smiling and joking around."

Scrolling down the photos, Jazzi learned that Finn was a social guy. He had loads of friends, judging from all the smiling
selfies. There were photos of him and Belinda interspersed
among others. In the casual photos on the shore of Lake Harding, in a canoe, and pulling a kayak onto a grassy slope, Finn

was shirtless. Jazzi noticed something about those photos, and she looked more closely at others.

She sank back against the sofa cushion. Awake now, Freya climbed up Jazzi's shirt to her shoulder and nestled under her hair.

Jazzi held out Dawn's phone to her. "Finn is wearing that gold necklace with the key pendant in all of these photos. Even those where he's not wearing his shirt. I can see the chain."

Dawn studied the photos. "I see. I told you he wore it in all his pictures and whenever I saw him."

Uppermost in Jazzi's mind was a question she needed Dawn to answer. "I don't want to upset you."

"I know you don't. But most things about Finn's murder upset me. What do you want to know?"

"Did you ever see the other side of that key?"

When Dawn closed her eyes, Jazzi hoped she wasn't thrusting her friend into another panic attack. But Dawn's breathing remained calm. After a few seconds, she shook her head. "I never did. It always laid flat. What are you thinking?"

"I'm wondering what the necklace meant . . . what might have been on the back." Was Finn keeping information in a safe-deposit box or somewhere else that got him killed?

There was something about the night sky, streamers, and colorful lantern lights that could make any outdoor event festive. Jazzi headed toward the boardwalk outside the community center and marina on Labor Day evening. In addition to orange, blue, and yellow lanterns, huge lit-up balls on the ground at least two feet in diameter lined the perimeter of the dance area.

Delaney and Giselle waved at her from one of the high round metal tables where they were drinking sodas and eating from snack bags. A station to sell sodas and water and another with packaged snacks were located outside the community center.

This Get Out and Dance event had been planned long before Finn's murder. Apparently, the community planning committee had decided to continue with it at this location to wipe out the memory of what had happened.

When Jazzi stopped at Delaney and Giselle's table, Giselle said, "Don't *you* look very boho."

Giselle's grin was wide, and Jazzi knew her friend wouldn't be caught anywhere in anything boho. Jazzi had dressed for a night out with her friends in a retro-print navy and coral casual dress with a lace-fringed neckline and fringed bell sleeves. It floated to her knees and would be comfortable for dancing.

"We all look like we're ready for a fun night out." Delaney was fashionably perfect in an orange sundress that fit her figure like a second skin. "I spoke to Charles this week. He approved everything the decorating committee planned. He hoped the lights and color would wipe out remembrance of the bake-off."

Music played softly from the huge speakers set up near the front door of the marina's store. Jazzi imagined the playlist would increase in volume as the night went on.

"Who's in charge of the music?" she asked. Right now, a Katy Perry song played.

Delaney grimaced. "Believe it or not, Charles's girlfriend is handling it. He insists she's a music afficionado."

Giselle's eyebrows raised and her lashes, which were loaded with mascara, fluttered. "As long as she plays a selection from old to new, it won't matter who chooses the songs. Especially when the bring-your-own-bottle-brigade arrives."

No alcohol was on sale tonight, but bringing booze on-site wasn't prohibited. It was a controversial policy with the town council, but no one seemed inclined to change it.

"I'm going to circulate a bit, then I'll be back," Jazzi said.

"Looking for anyone in particular?" Delaney asked, her expression teasing.

"No, I don't expect Parker to show."

"Too boisterous a crowd?" Giselle asked.

"Something like that." Everyone in the book club knew Parker would rather be out on his boat fishing rather than socializing.

"If you spot Derek or Addison, tell them to join us." Delaney said. "We can move to a bigger table."

"Will do." Jazzi moved away from Delaney and Giselle and strolled toward the tables surrounding the dance area, where a few people were moving to the rhythm of the latest song choice.

Jazzi hadn't penetrated much of the growing crowd when she spotted Abe sitting at a table by himself. Immediately, she wondered if Dawn was okay.

Abe smiled when he saw her. He was his usual first responder handsome self with a little more polish. He'd gotten a hair trim, and he wore a pale-green polo shirt and black jeans.

He motioned to the chair across from him. As Jazzi sat, he explained, "Dawn saw someone she knows. Addison, I think. She introduced her as a member of the book club. They went off to freshen up. I think Addison was upset. Something about her husband not wanting to come."

If Addison was sharing a tiff between her and her husband, Dawn could be a while. "Do you feel deserted?"

"Nah. I have two sisters. I know how they like to gab. Are you here alone?"

"Friends over there." She waved in the direction of Delaney and Giselle's table. Jazzi never would have barged in on Dawn and Abe's date. But now that he was here alone . . . She had a question about Finn that maybe he could answer.

Before she could ask her question, Abe nodded toward the community center, where Griffin and Tim stood talking. "Rumor has it that those two are the prime suspects in Finn's murder. They've been called back to the police station the most."

"The detective is probably trying to ferret out more information." That was true whether they were prime suspects or not. "Did you and Finn hang out much together?" That wasn't exactly the best way to broach the subject on her mind, but it would do.

"We were sports buddies. Nothing deeper than that. Sometimes we kicked around a soccer ball or shot hoops."

Glancing around, Jazzi didn't spot Dawn heading back to the table. She took her phone from her macramé purse. Taking Dawn's suggestion, Jazzi had messaged Belinda to ask to be added to her friends list. Belinda had answered Jazzi's friend request, and now she could access Finn and Belinda's personal page.

She tapped the icon to bring it up on her phone. She quickly found a photo of Finn with the key necklace. "Do you recognize the necklace Finn is wearing?"

Abe nodded. "I do. Finn always wore it. Even when he swam. Why?"

"I just wondered."

Abe gave her a perplexed look, then seemed pensive. "I heard you were involved in helping to catch a killer in the spring."

"Wrong place, wrong time," she answered glibly, as she usually did when the subject came up.

Eyeing her with a keen expression, he said, "If you say so."

"Do you know where Finn got the necklace or what it meant?"

Abe shrugged. "He never said. Belinda might have given it to him. There was an engraving on the back of the key. But I never saw what it was. He also wore a Breitling sports watch. Big bucks that."

Dawn hadn't mentioned the watch. Jazzi would have to ask her about that. Could the watch and necklace have been stolen for what they were worth?

The music turned up a notch as Dawn reappeared, approaching the table. Jazzi quickly rose to her feet and motioned Dawn to the chair.

Dawn said, "When you see Addison give her a hug. She and Mark had another fight. I shoved her toward Delaney's table."

"I'll do that. I'm going to buy some snacks for all of us. You two have a fun night." She was hoping Dawn would relax and find her happiness again tonight.

"Wanna dance?" Abe asked Dawn.

Her friend looked overjoyed Abe had asked. On Abe's part, he was looking at her as if he thought she was someone special.

On the way back to the table with her friends, Jazzi almost literally bumped into Nan Blanchard. She looked pretty tonight, as if she'd taken special care with her makeup, lip gloss, and dangling earrings. Her chartreuse dress fell above her knees. Jazzi was used to seeing her at Tomes dressed in shorts, trying to corral her boys.

Both women laughed as they stood apart.

"It's good to have a night out, isn't it?" Nan asked rhetorically.

"It *is* fun to meet up with friends."

"I'm hoping I can convince Tim to dance. I had to do something to keep him from brooding. He actually turned down jobs this week because he said everyone was talking about him."

"Do you think that's true?" Jazzi spotted Tim standing by the snack stand.

"Whether it is or isn't, Tim has to make a living."

Jazzi suspected Nan's attitude conveyed the message to Tim that she didn't understand what he was going through. From everything Jazzi had seen of Nan, she was a no-nonsense, practical woman. That could help Tim in the long run or make him feel worse.

After glancing around, Nan too spotted her husband. "Have

a good time, Jazzi. I'm going to coax Tim to dance." With a flounce of her skirt, Nan crossed the boardwalk to her husband.

Jazzi watched while Nan spoke to Tim and he took her into his arms for a slow dance that had begun playing.

Suddenly, Jazzi felt a tap on her shoulder. She swung around to find Oliver!

"Did you manage to sneak out?" she asked, surprised he'd come.

"I've been executing service all day, so my manager is closing. I was hoping you'd be here." Oliver's face after that last revelation told her he might not have wanted that sentiment to slip out.

"I'm glad you caught up to me."

"Not always easy to do," he joked. "You look nice tonight. You don't often wear your hair like that."

Wearing her hair down in a waterfall style, she'd spent extra care with the crown braids. Oliver's gaze was on her hair but her face too. Her breathing quickened and she wasn't sure what to say.

The song that had been playing switched to a slower country tune.

Oliver tilted his head and gave her an uncertain smile. "Would you like to dance?"

She nodded and smiled back.

As he took her into his arms, Jazzi took a deep breath, absorbing everything about the night—the lights glowing around them, the ballad, the murmur of voices. Oliver had changed from his standard work uniform of black slacks and a white oxford shirt. Now he wore chino slacks and a black Henley. And he smelled . . . good.

The warmth of his large hand seeped through her dress. She laid her head on his chest for merely a moment—

Old alarm bells clanged in her head—thoughts of her college boyfriend dumping her when she'd thought they were serious . . . misjudging a man's character as recently as this past spring. What did she *really* know about Oliver?

Yes, they'd been shot at. Yes, his accent made her want to listen to him whenever he spoke. Yes, he'd given her a kitten. Yes, they'd had a deeper conversation.

When she lifted her head to give herself a little distance, his blue eyes twinkled at her. "Have you been staying out of trouble?"

"As much as I can."

His forehead creased and his teasing smile slipped away. "Good trouble or bad trouble?"

They brushed past Tim and Nan, who were looking as if they were enjoying themselves.

"Dawn is in the middle of this investigation. I feel as if I have to do whatever I can to help her."

Oliver gave her a probing look. "How are you accomplishing that?"

"Mostly by keeping alert about what the suspects are doing."

"Asking questions?" He didn't appear either approving or disapproving.

"Mostly just in my head because I haven't gotten any real answers." She thought about the latest she'd been considering. "I have one for you."

His smile crept back onto his lips. "Am *I* a suspect?"

She shook her head, even though she knew he was teasing. "No. But I need a male point of view."

His hold loosened a little as he studied her. "About?"

"I've been looking over Finn's social media photos."

"I imagine they could be revealing."

"Not so much in the way you'd think. Or maybe I don't know enough about his life to see more than the obvious." She so much wanted to tell Oliver what she and Dawn knew about the crime scene. But she'd promised Detective Milford she'd keep it to herself. That didn't mean she couldn't ask Oliver a question that might help her find answers. She knew she could trust Oliver.

"Let's say you wore a necklace in the shape of a key," she suggested.

"I suppose this is hypothetical?"

"It is. Say there was engraving on the back of the key, and you never took it off."

"Okay."

She could tell Oliver was absorbing everything she said. That was something else she liked about him. He listened.

"You never take the necklace off. You wear it when swimming or working out."

"Got it," he assured her.

"I want to know possible reasons why."

They danced around in a circle, then Oliver answered her. "Three reasons come to mind. The first is that a man might like jewelry. That's not just a woman's thing."

"I thought of that."

"Number two. That necklace means something sentimental. He doesn't want anything to happen to it, no matter what."

"The same reason a woman treasures a locket with photos," Jazzi added.

"Could be," Oliver agreed.

"You mentioned three reasons. What's the third?"

"That necklace holds an importance a man might not want to share. You know that old adage—Keep your cards close to your chest. Or vest. Nothing anyone else should see."

Which reason was the most applicable? Especially if the killer stole the necklace.

The song they were dancing to ended. Jazzi and Oliver gazed at each other. Finally, he asked, "Do you want to take a walk?"

"I'd like that." Tonight, she'd forget about Finn's murder. Just for tonight.

Oliver took her hand, and they started toward the marina's docks. Tonight, she'd think about a part of her life she'd neglected since college, the side that could possibly include a man like Oliver. Possibly.

Chapter Seventeen

As Jazzi turned the CLOSED sign to OPEN, she was glad she'd convinced Dawn to go paddleboarding with her earlier this morning. The first water sport Jazzi had engaged in at Belltower Landing had been paddleboarding. She knew her mom and stepdad had missed her when she'd moved here, but Jonas and Daisy hadn't made her feel guilty for having a different life than theirs. Jazzi had been so grateful for their attitude. She'd had a talk with her mom about Finn's death soon after it happened. Her mom had acted as a sounding board. When Jazzi had asked Daisy for the best way to help Dawn, her mother had said, "Support her. Don't try to lead her."

That's what Jazzi hoped she was doing. Dawn's date with Abe last night had seemed to buoy her up and she was the one who'd suggested taking their SUPs to the lake this morning.

Maybe Jazzi was thinking about everything else besides her dance with Oliver. After their dance, they'd taken a walk, then sat with Delaney and Giselle and danced again for more upbeat songs. When Oliver had offered to walk her home, she'd accepted.

After Oliver had left her at her door with a nod and a smile, she'd wondered if she should have invited him inside. Now she regretted not doing it. Still, her mother's voice in her head seemed to say, "If you're not sure, don't."

As Jazzi turned toward the sales desk, Erica rushed inside. "Sorry I'm late. I had an errand to run. I want to talk to you about it."

"You're not late. I just unlocked the front door."

Dawn waved at Erica from the tea bar.

Erica waved back. "Can you come with me to the break room for a few minutes?" she asked in a low voice that wouldn't carry across the room.

"Sure. You don't want Dawn to hear?"

"No." Erica's answer was as firm as her expression was serious. She usually emanated calmness, but this morning, the energy around her seemed to be buzzing.

Erica deposited her handbag in a cupboard the staff members used for that purpose. Then she turned toward Jazzi, who was standing near the open break room door. Jazzi asked, "What's wrong?"

Shaking her head, Erica leaned against a stack of boxes. "I stopped by Tim Blanchard's house. I prayed about what I should do this morning and decided seeing him was best."

"You're worried about Tim."

"I am. He's not himself. Are you busy tonight?"

"Just the book club. Why?"

"I thought we could meet Tim at The Wild Kangaroo after book club tonight. I've convinced him to talk to you if not the police. I can't convince him to tell what he knows to them. Maybe you can."

"Why me?"

"Because you're close to Dawn and you know how the murder is affecting her."

"What did Tim tell you?"

"Just that he knows something about Finn that would surprise everyone," Erica disclosed. "I believe you can convince him that opening up would be best."

Did Tim really have information that could have led to Finn's murder? There was only one way to find out.

Jazzi and Erica were only a few minutes late as they opened the red door to The Wild Kangaroo. This gastropub was always busiest in the evenings.

Amid the clink of dishes and glassware, the chatter of pub goers at the bar and at tables, Jazzi headed for the table in a corner that was relatively secluded from others.

Out of habit, Jazzi's gaze scanned the brick serving bar that fronted dark wood shelves holding bottles and bar implements. The silver barstools were all occupied. The silver theme carried through the pub, with silver metal chairs at solid-black round tables, some higher than others. One of the distinctive elements of the pub was the large wooden kangaroo that hung in the center of the wall behind the bar, with smaller versions at intervals around the restaurant.

Jazzi didn't pay attention to the offerings on the large blackboard that listed tonight's specials. She and Erica aimed for Tim Blanchard. He looked as if he was ready to bolt.

Why? Why was he so determined to keep what he knew to himself? Perhaps even chance Detective Milford charging him for Finn's murder?

Jazzi quickly slid into one of the chairs, barring Tim from leaving easily. When she greeted him, he didn't look any more relaxed.

In fact—

Tim stared at Erica. "I don't know why you think this is going to do any good. Why should I tell *her* anything?" His face was becoming redder by the moment.

Jazzi wasn't sure this was a good idea either, but she trusted Erica's judgment. "I've heard about how many times you've been called to the police station."

"So what?" His belligerence was an outer shell that he probably thought protected him. But Jazzi guessed it was simply a cover for his fear.

Tim stood to leave. When he pushed back his chair, it screeched against the floor. Tim was a big guy, and the table wobbled when he pushed against it.

Out of nowhere, Oliver suddenly stood at their table. "Is everything okay here? Tim asked for a quiet table. Does this suit?"

Tim quickly resumed his seat. "Everything is fine," he mumbled.

Oliver turned questioning blue eyes to Jazzi.

"We're good," she said.

Oliver gave them all another long look. "I'll send a server over right away."

Jazzi watched him go to a desk near the bar, and a male server came to take their drink orders. Erica and Jazzi ordered frozen pink lemonade drinks. Tim ordered Scotch, neat. As if they'd made a consensus, they all waited for the drinks before saying a word. As soon as the server set down their glasses, Tim picked his up and knocked back the Scotch.

Erica frowned. "How often have you been doing that?"

"None of your business," he groused.

Erica touched his arm. "Tim, I'm not the enemy. I've known you for years. I care what happens to you and Nan and your boys. Jazzi, tell Tim to be honest with the detective."

"I *was* honest with him," Tim protested, obviously trying to keep his temper in check. "I told him Finn and I fought about our recipes."

"I doubt *that's* true." Erica took a swig of her drink through its wide straw.

Finally, Tim seemed to relent. "I don't think Milford believed me either."

Watching Tim's back-and-forth with Erica, Jazzi listened to the emotion in his voice, and she considered the best way to encourage him to talk to them.

Appealing to his sense of compassion, she asked, "Erica has told you what Dawn's going through, right?"

Tim nodded and looked down at his glass as if he wished it held more Scotch.

"Do you remember the mess I was involved in last spring?" Most of Belltower Landing didn't know all the details, but Erica and Audrey did, and their friends probably did too.

Whether Tim knew the details or not, she went on. "I misjudged someone until it was too late. I should have gone to Detective Milford with everything I knew, but I wasn't sure the information was important."

"Oh, I know *this* is important."

Jazzi kept going. "I was almost killed, and the same thing could happen to *you*."

Tim looked away at one of the kangaroos hanging on the wall. "I don't want to put myself in danger. Or Nan and the boys. What I know might have nothing to do with Finn's murder. And there are ramifications if I talk about it."

Jazzi and Erica waited and sipped their drinks.

"Okay. I'll tell you what I know. If you believe it's important, I'll tell the detective."

Jazzi held her breath.

Tim scanned the area around them to make sure no one could hear and sort of hunkered down in his chair. He started slowly. "I . . . I was doing plumbing work." He paused. "At Finn's house. I found a pinhole camera in the bedroom and wondered if Finn was spying on his wife. Or else, maybe the recording was for his own purposes. I've heard all kinds of things about the dark web and sites with porn videos. But that couldn't be Finn, right? Not Finn."

Jazzi was so astonished she couldn't find words. The expression on Erica's face—her wide eyes, brow creased—told Jazzi her friend felt that same surprise.

Tim added, "I didn't know if I should tell Belinda, let alone the detective."

Finally, Jazzi's words tumbled out. "Did you tell Belinda?"

"No. But maybe I should tell both. What if Finn did that elsewhere? It's not hard to set up those tiny cameras. His photography gigs took him into people's houses just like my plumbing jobs do. *What* was he doing?"

Tim's revelation could have smaller ramifications, involving only Finn's wife. Or whatever Finn was doing could ripple out to include many more people than him and Belinda. What sort of man *was* Finn?

Jazzi had no doubt that Tim's knowledge about that camera could blow the case wide open. "Tell the detective. Let him decide if you should tell Belinda."

Tim raised his hand to gain the server's notice. He pointed to his drink for a refill. To Jazzi and Erica, he said, "I'll go to the police station first thing in the morning."

Jazzi hoped he wouldn't change his mind.

It was midafternoon on Wednesday before Jazzi took her break. She grabbed a peach and pecan muffin and an iced tea to go from the tea bar and headed for the town green. On her way back, she'd run up to her apartment and feed and play with the kittens.

Traffic was heavy as she waited to cross Lakeview Boulevard. At the green, she turned right toward the bell tower, then aimed straight for her favorite bench near the lakeshore. The first bite of her muffin made her smile as a preautumn breeze ruffled a nearby maple tree. The lake water shimmered with afternoon sunlight.

Jazzi had just finished her iced tea and crumpled the cup when she heard her name called. Then she heard it called again.

"Jazzi!"

She turned from watching a sailboat skim the blue-green water to see Belinda Yarrow running toward her, her long brown hair flying behind her. When she reached Jazzi, she was out of breath. She was a tall, willowy woman. Thin before Finn's death, she looked as if she'd lost weight. Her white shift dress seemed to hang too loosely on her.

Standing, Jazzi asked, "What's wrong?" It was obvious something was from Belinda's woebegone facial features. She looked as if she'd been crying, with tear streaks through her makeup.

"Erica told me you were here. I *have* to talk to you."

Jazzi motioned to the bench. "Sit and catch your breath."

After sinking down to the bench, Belinda closed her eyes. She seemed to be having trouble finding words. "Tim talked to . . . to the police this morning. He found—" She stopped. "The police came to my house. Tim was with them. He asked if he could come along to tell me what he found. He said he told *you*."

"He did. Last night. The detective moved fast. Did he simply want to talk to you?"

"He let Tim tell me what he'd found. Then Detective Milford questioned me while his men searched the house for that camera and if there were any others."

"Oh, Belinda. That had to be so upsetting. First, that Finn would do that. And then to have the police there."

Belinda wiped a stray tear from her cheek. "They just found the one. I can't believe—" She abruptly cut off her words.

"I don't know what to say."

"No one but Tim knows about this, and I want to keep it that way. It would harm Finn's good reputation. Will you give me your word you won't tell anyone?"

"Erica knows too." Jazzi thought she might as well prepare Belinda for how this might play out. "And if the detective had his team there, leaks are always a possibility."

Rubbing her hands over her face, Belinda shook her head. "I don't know how this happened. Finn and I had some problems. I'm his business manager. It's not always easy working together. How could he possibly think I'd have an affair?"

Belinda seemed more concerned about that idea than the camera itself.

"Wait a minute," Jazzi said to slow Belinda's thinking. "Is that what the detective believes this is about?"

"He asked if I was seeing anyone. But . . . but he also asked if Finn had done anything like this before. Maybe for his own viewing pleasure." Belinda's cheeks were red.

"Some men . . . some couples do that," Jazzi offered.

"I never considered Finn would do anything like that. The detective asked me if any of Finn's clients complained or seemed angry with him."

"Did they?"

"No. His customers always seemed satisfied. I mean, payment was delayed now and then. But photographs aren't cheap, and couples have to save up for their wedding packages."

"Is it possible Finn had clients you didn't know about?" This case of Finn's murder had broadened past celebrity chefs and the bake-off.

"Finn did go out of town. He went where his work took him."

In other words, even though Belinda was Finn's office and financial manager, she could be in the dark about much of Finn Yarrow's work life.

*   *   *

Out for a bike ride early the next morning, Jazzi pedaled to-ward the marina. She smiled when she spotted Oliver standing with his bike in the walkway between businesses at The Wild Kangaroo. He hopped on his bike as she passed and joined her.

He called, "G'day, Jazzi."

"G'day to you too," she tossed over her shoulder. His accent along with his greeting made her morning much brighter. She'd thought about that camera and Belinda's feelings of betrayal most of the night.

Today, she and Oliver didn't talk as they pedaled, even when they rode through some forested developments. The silence with the early morning breeze sweeping by them, the sun rising higher in the blue sky, was comfortable.

They were nearing the marina area on their way back when Oliver called to her. "Do you have time for breakfast?"

"Sure," she said. "I have time."

After they stood their bikes at one of the picnic tables and removed their helmets, they headed for the waffle truck. They both ordered the waffles topped with fresh strawberries and whipped cream. Oliver ordered coffee, but Jazzi plucked her bottle of water from her bicycle's basket and set it on the table.

They had settled on opposite sides of the table when Jazzi noticed Oliver's expression. His hair had been smashed down from his helmet, and he'd run his hand through it. A few blond strands spiked up. He lifted a forkful of waffle to his lips but sent her a side look that said he had something on his mind. A dollop of whipped cream fell on his black Henley shirt when he lifted his fork again.

Jazzi had grabbed a few napkins. She handed one to Oliver. He grinned, thanked her, and swiped at the whipped cream.

Jazzi offered him her water bottle. "This might help."

He shook his head. "I have spare shirts at the Kangaroo. I'll change when I get back. After all, I can't greet diners in bike shorts."

She laughed. He could indeed greet diners in bike shorts. A lot of women would enjoy that. And she was one of them. Digging into her waffle again, she didn't want Oliver to guess how much she *did* enjoy it.

After Oliver took a swig of coffee, he said, "I want to run something by you."

Okay, she thought. This might have been his reason for having breakfast together this morning. "What's on your mind?"

"I heard something at the bar last night about Finn Yarrow."

Uh oh. Could news of Finn's camera have spread around town already? "From a credible source?"

"That's a solid question. The two men work with Tim Blanchard. They're on some plumbers softball team."

Jazzi considered Belinda asking her to keep the new information about Finn quiet. Had she asked the same of Tim?

"What they were discussing seems unbelievable. They were talking about a hidden camera Tim had found in Finn's home. And then the possibility that Finn put cameras other places than his house. Could that be possible?"

"Other than being a voyeur, what if he put the camera there for security reasons?" Jazzi offered. "I know about it. I spoke with Tim and Belinda. I didn't ask Belinda if they kept valuables in the bedroom like Belinda's jewelry, important papers, even cash."

"Did they have a front door camera? Maybe he was merely security conscious," Oliver suggested.

"I'll have to ask her. She's searching for a reason to think the best of Finn. I'm wondering if the detective found videos of anything other than weddings, charity galas, and family photos." Jazzi dug into her waffle again.

Finishing his waffle, Oliver observed, "If Finn had years of videos on his computer, they would take the police hours and hours, maybe even days, to search through. His murder might never be solved. That happens."

Picking up her water bottle, Jazzi took a swallow. After she set the bottle down, she admitted, "I trust Detective Milford."

"He was a few steps behind *you* solving the last murder."

"But only a few steps," Jazzi acknowledged. "The problem with police searches and police interviews is a common one."

"And that problem is?" Oliver was looking at her with all of his interest.

"Regular people sometimes don't trust the police or they're afraid the detective will get it wrong and then *they* will come under suspicion."

"That sounds as if you might like to do something about that."

"And if I did? To help Dawn?"

He reached across the table and took her hand. "I'd say you're a very brave young woman."

She let Oliver wrap his fingers around hers. Brave or foolish, she was going to talk to the contestants and maybe the judges once more.

That evening after Jazzi had closed the store and had a light supper with Dawn, she went to the garage for her bike and pedaled toward the marina. Dawn was streaming a movie and didn't ask questions when Jazzi told her she was going for a ride.

Jazzi had kept the address and number of Carl West's office. She'd remembered it was open until eight p.m. A boat fitter kept unusual hours. But the receptionist she'd spoken to earlier in the day had explained he was usually back in the office before closing to finish his notes on the boats he repaired that day.

The noise and foot traffic of the daytime was changing into a muted flow as tourists and residents entered and exited restaurants and night spots. A group of laughing teens flowed out of an arcade. Jazzi soon passed the marina's store and aimed for the docks.

Jazzi found Carl's office, such as it was, by the docks past the marina. It was more like a fishing shack with an attached storage shed. The lights shone inside, and the OPEN sign hung in the door. Jazzi parked her bike, opened the door, and stepped inside.

Carl West sat at a beat-up wooden desk, peering at his laptop screen. He looked up. "Hi, Jazzi." He grinned. "Do you have a boat for me to repair?"

"I might own a rowboat someday."

"I can get you a bargain on one with a leak," he joked.

Carl was stocky, with russet-colored hair that stuck out from his fisherman's cap. He wore a waffle-textured T-shirt and worn jeans. His boots were fashioned for practicality on the docks, with rounded steel toes and a zipper up the ankle. He didn't appear to mind being bothered.

"I hope you don't mind me barging in." It was almost eight.

"Not at all. My eyes are getting blurry from the screen. How can I help if you don't need a boat fitted?"

"Dawn and I were talking. She's still shaken up about finding Finn's body." Maybe she could segue into a discussion on Finn's murder to find out what she wanted to know.

"I heard about her panic attack after the kayak race. I hope she's okay." His gray eyes were filled with compassion.

"She's getting better. I have a question. Dawn said Finn shot your wedding video. Did anything unusual happen when he did?"

Carl swiveled on his office chair. It squeaked as he came around to face her. "Nothing unusual happened with Finn taking photos and video. We were all having a great time, and we have it all to watch again and again. He cut the video so we could afford it."

"Cut it?"

"Sure. He charged by the minutes on the finished product."

"I suppose he owns the rights to it all?" She'd learned that was a common practice.

"That's what our contract said. He could use our stills and video for promotion."

"Do you know if he did use it?"

Carl shrugged. "I never asked. Something odd did happen at the reception but not with Finn."

Was this the anomaly she was searching for? She held her breath as she listened.

"We had a wicker basket at our reception for cards and money gifts. After we returned from our honeymoon—Hilton Head is the best if you're ever interested," he added with a sly smile. Then his smile disappeared. "Two guests who are close friends asked which appliance we bought with their gift cards. My wife and I never received their cards."

"Did you look into the missing cards?"

"Sure did. We asked more questions. We found out we hadn't received other gift cards."

Jazzi's mind was spinning the details. "So what gifts in congratulations cards *did* you receive?"

"No gift cards. The only cards we received besides good-wishes ones had checks and cash included."

"Did you report this to the police?"

"We did. But there was no way to know exactly how much we didn't receive. The officer I talked to said any of the guests or serving staff could have rummaged through that basket and felt the gift cards in the envelopes. There was no way to know."

"Where did you have your reception?"

"We had an outside wedding at that farm on the north side of the lake that hosts receptions. Why?"

"I wonder if there were security cameras."

"Not outside. We couldn't afford to rent the banquet room. We just had a dessert reception in the garden. My wife could tell you more about the place, if you're interested."

Jazzi *was* interested. But not in the reception venue. Just what were the chances that Finn had recorded whatever happened to the missing gifts?

Chapter Eighteen

After her talk with Carl, Jazzi pedaled home to discuss what he'd told her with Dawn. She didn't want to keep secrets from her best friend.

Once inside, after grabbing a bottle of water, she told Dawn what Carl had revealed to her.

Dawn was incredulous. "Someone actually stole Carl's wedding presents?"

"It seems like it. Carl said he and his wife could have really used what was stolen. The first year of their marriage was tough financially."

"You don't think Carl could have killed Finn?"

"I really don't think so. But there is someone else I want to talk to." Jazzi sank into the yellow armchair near Dawn.

"Who?" Dawn sat on the sofa with her leg pulled up under her.

"Claude Fenton. I can go talk to him at his photography studio on Pine Street. Belinda had mentioned him at the memorial."

Dawn looked worried. "Are you sure you should delve

deeper into this? Don't you think the detective will have talked to Carl and Claude?"

"I don't know. But he won't tell me if I ask. I'm sure of that. Ongoing investigation and all that." Jazzi let her fingers drift back and forth over the arm of the chair. She knew the time had come to reveal to her best friend what no one else in Belltower Landing besides Detective Milford knew.

Dawn watched her as if she knew Jazzi had something on her mind. "What's wrong?"

"Nothing's wrong exactly. Except I don't want you to be angry with me." She looked into Dawn's pretty green eyes. No dimples were visible now on her cheeks.

"Why would I be angry?"

Jazzi swung around in her chair to face Dawn more squarely. "There's something I haven't told you ... about my past ... my background."

"About you being adopted?" Dawn looked confused.

"No. I told you everything about that."

"What, then?" Dawn swung her legs to the floor as if this conversation might be too serious to just sit back and take in.

"It's about my mom."

"Your mom is sweet. Sometime I want to visit Daisy's Tea Garden in Willow Creek. I've never been to Amish country. I know from your photos that part of Pennsylvania is beautiful. Lots of farmland." Dawn smiled at the thought.

Jazzi could either jump right into this revelation or proceed with caution. Maybe the beginning was the best place to start. "Mom moved us to her hometown after my adoptive dad died."

"Right. You were in high school when she opened the tea garden." Dawn already knew that portion of Jazzi's story.

"I was fifteen when my Aunt Iris started dating." Jazzi paused, then considered jumping right in would be preferable to drawing out this background. "One evening after closing, that man was murdered in the tea garden's backyard."

Dawn's hand covered her mouth. "Oh, Jazzi. How awful! No wonder you haven't wanted to talk about it."

"I wasn't there when it happened. Mom and Aunt Iris were. They both came under suspicion for the murder, but especially Aunt Iris. Since the detective was grouchy and antagonistic, my mom started following clues herself. She and Aunt Iris ended up facing down the killer, and he was caught."

"Wow!" Dawn's eyes were huge and her mouth was rounded. After she'd absorbed what Jazzi had disclosed, she murmured, "Something like what happened with you."

"Something like," Jazzi agreed. "But that's not all."

"What more could there be?" Dawn's question was full of astonishment.

Zander zipped under the table and stopped short at Jazzi's feet. She scooped him up and set him in her lap. She needed to stroke his cottony fur right then. "If you search 'Daisy Swanson' on Google, you'll find the Daisy's Tea Garden website. If you keep searching, you'll find articles about my mom solving murders."

"Murders?"

"Yes. Not all of them were written about, but she helped the police solve ten. My aunt is now married to the retired detective who my mom ended up working with on many of them."

Dawn seemed to be speechless as she absorbed everything Jazzi had revealed. Finally, she asked, "So the detective accepted her help?"

"In a fashion. My mom grew up with an Amish friend named Rachel, so she understood the Amish community. Rachel's friends and family talked to her much more easily than the police if Amish were involved."

The silence in the room was only broken by Zander's little purrs. Until Jazzi spoke again. "I wanted to make a life here on my own without bringing my mom and the past into it. Don't get me wrong. I'm proud of my mom and everything she did to help people she cared about. But I didn't want to be known for what my mom had done. Do you understand?"

"You say Detective Milford knows?"

"Last spring when he questioned me, he already knew about my mom. Police circles have chatter too. He warned me to stay away from his investigation. And I tried to."

"But you know how this is done. And what questions to ask because of your mom," Dawn said, suddenly seeming to realize Jazzi's point.

"Sometimes I helped her with research. And I saw how she handled a reporter friend. I watched how Jonas helped too. After all, as a former homicide detective, he had skills."

"Skills," Dawn repeated.

"You're my best friend, Dawn. I wanted to tell you . . ."

"But you don't want your history, your mom's history, to spread around Belltower Landing. No one else knows?"

"No. But that doesn't matter as much now. I want to help you if I can."

Rising from the sofa, Dawn gave Jazzi a long, tight hug.

Jazzi had taken the day off. She and Dawn tried to do that once a week on separate days. Her plans were simple—clean the apartment, play with the kittens, make sure her MINI Cooper purred when she ran errands. Today one of those errands was a visit to Claude Fenton's photography studio.

Thinking about last night made Jazzi grateful for Dawn and her acceptance. Now she'd see where a meeting with Claude Fenton would lead.

Claude's office and studio were located south of Lakeview Boulevard. The rows of houses on the oldest streets of the town running parallel and perpendicular from Lakeview were grand in their vintage beauty, mostly Victorian styles mixed with Dutch

Colonial architecture. The Dutch Colonial houses wore distinct features of gambrel roofs and overhanging eaves.

As Jazzi drove down Silver Pine Road, she began watching the numbered addresses. Claude's studio was located at number 407. When Jazzi had called the studio to discover if Claude was there, the receptionist told her he had scheduled photograph sessions for the entire day. But he had a break between one o'clock and two.

Jazzi had no idea whether or not Fenton would be cooperative. All she could do was try to find out more information about Finn. If they'd spoken friend-to-friend or photographer-to-photographer, Finn might have revealed something important.

The house she stopped in front of had a dark green roof, lighter green siding, and dark brown shutters. The front stoop extended across the breadth of the house. After she parked, Jazzi climbed the few steps and stopped before the dark brown door. Then she opened it and stepped inside.

Last night Jazzi had studied Claude Fenton's website, which included samples of his work along with his bio and photo. Some of those same framed photographs hung in the reception area. She recognized Claude as soon as she stepped inside. He was sitting on the corner of a massive hand-carved desk, showing wedding prints to his receptionist.

He was saying, "The Godfreys ordered ten of these originally, but now they'd like ten more."

Jazzi stepped in closer to the desk.

Claude looked over at her. He appeared to be around forty but was prematurely gray. His brown eyes were questioning. "Can I help you?"

His receptionist chimed in, "If you need a sitting for a photo shoot, I can set you up."

Jazzi smiled back. "Thanks. But I wondered—" She turned

her focus to Claude. "Could I talk to you for a few minutes? I'm Jazzi Swanson."

Whether her name clicked with him or not, she couldn't tell. After a moment, he nodded to an open door behind the desk. "C'mon in to my office."

Jazzi followed him, with the questioning look of the receptionist going after her. Once inside the room, she glanced around at the computer setup, a gray metal desk stacked with folders, file cabinets, and a credenza that resembled a coffee bar.

He sat on the corner of his desk. "You have a recognizable name. My wife shops at Tomes & Tea. She was quite thrilled to get a signed photo of Evan Holloway when he stopped in at Tomes."

Pulling some strings, Jazzi had hosted the country singer at the store to up their social media image. "Evan didn't have time to sign many. I'm glad she was one of the lucky ones."

Claude studied her. "So what can I do for you?"

Jazzi decided to be blunt. "Dawn Fernsby is my partner and roommate. She found Finn Yarrow's body."

The photographer looked shocked, as if he hadn't expected *that* subject to arise. Finally, he said, "I'm so sorry. That must have been awful for her."

"It has been. She's taking this hard, and I thought finding answers could help."

He blinked. "What kind of answers? I'm sure the police are on this."

"Maybe they are," Jazzi agreed. "But they aren't revealing anything to anyone."

"That makes sense," he said with a shrug.

"I understand you often backed up Finn."

"We watched each other's backs. We were longtime friends. Totally different photography styles, though."

"I'm somewhat familiar with Finn's work." She motioned to the reception area. "Yours are quite artistic."

"Thank you. Finn preferred a down-to-earth style."

"Have the police interviewed you?"

"They have, but I don't believe I was much help."

"I suppose they went over the timeline up to the bake-off to see if you could add anything?"

Claude shifted on the desk until he was altogether sitting on it, his long legs swinging down. "The Monday before the bake-off, Finn and I managed a round of golf. We both let off steam with the walking, driving, and concentrating. Sometimes we talked business. Sometimes we didn't talk at all. We're constantly dealing with clients, and that can get noisy, as you probably recognize with running a store."

"I do understand. I bike ride or paddleboard for relaxation." Claude seemed like a nice guy. The more he revealed, the more she could gauge what kind of man he was. "Can you tell me if Finn had any enemies?"

"Detective Milford asked me that. I told him in our business, we have complaining clients. But no enemies. That said, I don't know everything about Finn's life, but—"

"But . . ." she pushed.

"The couple of golf games before Finn's murder, something was on his mind. I could tell because he wasn't as relaxed on the course, as if he was working something out in his head. He clammed up that last game."

"Did you ask if something was bothering him?"

"When I asked, he said he had a decision to make. He didn't say any more. Finn and I didn't poke into each other's heads. He wasn't made that way, and neither was I."

Claude's watch gave off a signal. Either an alarm, Jazzi surmised, or a text coming in. He glanced at it. Then he hopped off his desk.

"Sorry," he said. "I have a client coming in fifteen minutes, and I want to ready the set and backgrounds."

Jazzi suspected she wouldn't coax any more info from

Claude. After she thanked him for speaking to her, she left his office and the building. Sliding into her MINI Cooper, she had to wonder if Claude and Finn had truly been friends. Or had they been rivals? That led to the question: Was Claude Fenton capable of murder?

Still reflecting on her visit to Claude, she returned to her apartment to play with the kittens and do that cleaning. Zander chased the feather duster and Freya hid from the sweeper. As she cleaned, Jazzi considered the suspects—the chefs, the contestants . . . and Claude. Detective Milford and his team no doubt were conducting interviews with all of them, maybe looking into bank records and phone histories. Yet Finn and his camera seemed to be a predominant theme. Did Finn's profession fit into the murder? There were so many threads to pull that might unravel the investigation.

Jazzi was sanitizing the kitchen area when she heard the door that led from her bedroom to the storage and breakroom downstairs open and the jingle bells ring.

A minute later, Dawn appeared in the kitchen. "Break time," she explained. "I was hoping you were back. How did it go with Claude?"

Jazzi recapped what Claude had told her, ending with "They were friends and colleagues. It's hard to tell if there was a serious professional rivalry."

Dawn went to the refrigerator and pulled out strawberries and cottage cheese. "Abe dropped by the store this morning."

Jazzi watched a pleased smile spread across Dawn's face. "Is another date in your plans?"

"It is, but—"

"But what?" It had been obvious at the dance event that Dawn liked Abe.

"I'm having trouble setting boundaries." She carried her dish of cottage cheese and berries to their small table.

"What boundaries? Whether to kiss on the first date?" Jazzi teased.

Dawn pulled out a chair and sank onto it as she put a tiny dot of cottage cheese on her finger and offered it to Freya. The kitten lapped at it. Straightening in her chair, she picked up her spoon. "Abe is easy to confide in. We couldn't help but talk about Finn."

Jazzi was concerned about the confidences Dawn might have shared. "Detective Milford specifically warned against talking about the crime scene."

"I know. And I changed the subject when Abe brought it up. But I'll never forget the sight of the two kitchen stools knocked over, Finn's prize-winning Black Forest cake on the floor as if someone had tossed it at his face. His eyes . . ." Dawn shook her head to rid herself of the images. "I hate keeping it all under wraps. But I almost let my memories slip to Abe."

Jazzi's suspicions were activated. "Did Abe specifically ask about the crime scene?"

Dawn shook her head. "Not specifically. We were just talking about coping with trauma. Abe sees a lot of it in his occupation."

Jazzi supposed that was true. And if he cared about Dawn, it made sense he'd ask questions. "So your next date is set?"

"He's going to take me to a driving range. It sounds like fun."

Would Dawn be able to keep her boundaries set? Or would her growing interest in Abe remove any and all filters?

The more Jazzi thought about the crime scene, the more she considered the chefs as suspects and what they'd seen and heard that day as important details. She remembered Emmaline talking to Finn between rounds. Maybe she'd invite Emmaline to tea. Jazzi picked up her phone from the counter and texted Emmaline, hoping she'd discover some answers rather than more questions.

*   *   *

Jazzi had intended to go to Emmaline, but the older woman insisted she needed to get out. She'd come to the store, she said. Watching for Emmaline now, Jazzi hoped the woman wouldn't change her mind. Emmaline sometimes appeared to be flighty.

An Uber let Emmaline out of a midsized silver vehicle around eleven a.m. Jazzi went to the door and ushered the chef inside.

"It's good to see you again," Jazzi said enthusiastically.

Emmaline had used a purple hair band to keep her hair away from her face. Her dress was a lilac cotton with an embroidered bodice. She still carried her red tote. She looked to be part hippie and part *Little House on the Prairie.*

Emmaline's large rings clinked as she took hold of Jazzi's hand. "I'm going to browse a bit and then we'll have that tea."

That was fine with Jazzi since a group of customers had walked in.

Fifteen minutes later Emmaline looked ready to have tea and talk. Taking her break, Jazzi escorted Emmaline into the break room with two cups of tea and muffins on a plate.

They settled themselves at the table where staff members ate quick lunches. Early this morning Jazzi had spread a pale blue cloth over the table and set a vase with a rose in the center.

"Isn't this lovely," Emmaline said in a low voice. "Did you do this just for me?"

"I did. This is more private than the store proper." Jazzi set the tray on the table beside a small wicker basket that held packs of sugar and honey.

They both fixed their tea and turned to the cinnamon-swirl muffins. Jazzi asked conversationally, "How are you enjoying Belltower Landing?"

"I like it more than I thought I would. It might be a tourist town, but it has a small town feel to it. I lengthened my stay even though the detective said I could leave so I could explore a little more."

Apparently, Detective Milford had released the out-of-town suspects. Did that mean he was concentrating solely on Tim? Had that changed since Tim's revelation?

"It must feel good that the detective feels you're in the clear. No more interviews." Jazzi lifted her muffin from the plate and broke it in half.

Emmaline withdrew a pack of honey from the basket, opened it, and stirred it into her green tea. "I wasn't really worried. After all, I didn't know Finn Yarrow well."

Jazzi asked, "But did you talk to him at the bake-off?"

Emmaline focused on her tea, maybe stirring it more than necessary.

"I did. Actually, I was familiar with him before the bake-off."

"Really?" Jazzi prompted.

"There are all types of occasions when one runs into a photographer who is widening his professional boundaries," she stated, as if she might have been questioned about that before.

Jazzi stirred sugar into her tea. "And Finn was doing that?"

"I have attended charity functions in Ithaca—galas and the more mundane fundraisers. Sometimes Finn was there with his camera. Ever since I closed my business, those community events keep me involved, and I receive speaking invitations just from being around town."

"You like to stay busy."

"I do. But . . ." She paused. "I'm slowing down. That idea that seventy is the new fifty is rubbish." She took a huge bite of her muffin, obviously enjoyed the flavor, and swallowed.

They spoke about the community, books, and recipes. But whenever they came near to the subject of Finn, Emmaline redirected the conversation. Did she think Jazzi wouldn't notice? Or was she counting on Jazzi's respect for her elders not to push?

Emmaline ran her hand through her white curls and sighed. "This was such a nice visit. But I should let you get back to work."

Before she revealed something she intended to keep to herself?

"When will you be returning to Ithaca?" The chefs were scattered now. Except for Colleen, they might not be handy for Detective Milford to reach.

"Next week. I've decided to sell my house in Ithaca. In fact, I'm thinking about moving here to Belltower Landing."

Way to go dropping a bomb at the end of their visit!

Seeing Jazzi's surprised expression, Emmaline added, "I'm not getting any younger. The time to downsize is now. After all, just how important are our earthly possessions?"

Jazzi's gaze went to Emmaline's red designer tote bag on the floor beside her chair. Her gut instinct told Jazzi that Emmaline's desire for downsizing had more to do with something other than selling off earthly possessions. But she might never know what that reason was.

That evening, Jazzi pan-fried a piece of salmon and stir-fried vegetables. After she and Dawn ate, Dawn said she had a few errands to run, so Jazzi settled in with her laptop to check website sales. Their website sold books and tea in souvenir boxes. She was deep in sales figures when her phone played. It was Belinda. They'd exchanged numbers when Jazzi had decided to sell Finn's book at Tomes & Tea.

"Hi, Belinda. How are you?"

"Something has happened, Jazzi." Belinda sounded breathless and maybe a little upset.

"What's going on?" Jazzi knew Belinda was contending with a lot between her grief and managing Finn's office.

"I found a phone I didn't know Finn owned. It looks like a burner."

This could be the break the police were looking for. But why was Belinda calling *her*? "The police didn't find it when they searched Finn's office?"

"It wasn't in his office. It was here in a closet in a shoebox. The thing is—" Belinda made a full stop. "I'm not sure I want to turn it in to the detective if it has videos of *me* on it from the camera Finn set up. Do you know what I mean?"

If Finn had shot the videos for his own use, it could be embarrassing at the least to have the police department viewing them.

Before Jazzi could respond, Belinda asked, "Jazzi, will you view them with me?"

Chapter Nineteen

The Yarrow house was located on Seneca Avenue in an older section of town. Jazzi didn't pull into the driveway but parked at the curb in front of the house. It looked to be maybe a three-bedroom, two-story with an enclosed porch along the side. Black shutters framed the front windows, and white siding made the structure look fresh and clean. Boxwood hedges lined the front yard, leaving a cement path clear from the street to the side-lighted front door.

Belinda was waiting for her. Sustained energy seemed to buzz around her. Dressed in navy shorts and a red boat-necked top, she pulled the top lower and ran her hands down the sides of her shorts.

She opened the front screen door as Jazzi ran up the three steps to the porch. "Thank you for coming, Jazzi. I didn't know who else I could call. Friends wouldn't understand if the video is just too embarrassing to watch."

That *was* a dilemma. Especially if Belinda had friends who gossiped. "You didn't take a peek?"

"No. I felt better waiting for you." She led Jazzi inside to a small living room. Stairs on the left rose to the second floor while the living room on the right led into a kitchen large enough for a round table with four chairs in one corner.

As they made their way through the kitchen, Belinda showed Jazzi to an office located in the back.

"It's a mess," Belinda said with a sigh. "At his studio, I kept Finn's office organized. But here, I let him have free rein, and I worked around his stacks of photos and files."

The office wasn't in as much disarray as Belinda claimed. Yes, there were stacks of folders here and there, what looked like piles of receipts, and books about photography toppled over on a table. Framed photographs of landscapes, cityscapes, and pedestrians walking near the bell tower decorated the walls. This looked to be the work Finn enjoyed most since he kept it around his personal space.

Belinda noticed Jazzi studying the work. "He photographed couples, families, and weddings because that brought in the income. But if he could have transitioned, his portfolio would have been very different from weddings."

Crossing to the empty L-shaped desk with a keyboard tray, storage shelves, and monitor stand, Jazzi guessed why it seemed deserted. "I suppose the police confiscated Finn's home computer too?"

"They did. For the most part, that's all they took. The rest didn't seem to interest them." Belinda went to the desk and opened a side drawer. She plucked out a phone.

It was a facsimile of a smartphone. But even Tracfones could be password protected. "Did you have trouble getting into the phone?"

"No. I was lucky. The passcode is our anniversary date. It was the start of our life together." A tear slipped down Belinda's cheek, and she swiped it away. "I don't know what to think, Jazzi, about the hidden cameras and secret videos."

"Let's take a look," Jazzi said softly. "So you can stop wondering."

Belinda led Jazzi to the table in the kitchen. After they were both seated, Belinda tapped the passcode into the phone. The phone opened to a still scene of Lake Harding with a sailboat front and center.

Belinda touched the photo. "Finn wanted to own a sailboat like that soon. I guess the photo manifested that into the universe."

After she pressed the icon for the video folder, they both peered at the small screen.

Finn's voice sounded before the video began. Jazzi heard Belinda's catch of breath as Finn simply said, "Carl West's wedding reception."

"That was three years ago," Belinda murmured.

They watched sights and sounds from the reception. Jazzi quickly remembered the report Carl had given about gift cards being stolen from their gift basket. She watched the video of the garden wedding carefully. The focus changed from Carl in a tuxedo and his wife in an off-the-shoulder lace gown to the wedding cake table. The white-, pink-, and yellow-flowered two-tier confection sat next to a pile of gifts wrapped in colorful paper and silver foil. Beside those stood a small wicker basket with a handle.

Belinda exclaimed, "Is she stealing that?" as a server in a black skirt and white blouse swiftly lifted the gift basket and rushed out of sight. "She shouldn't have her fingers anywhere near the presents."

"Do you know her?"

Belinda stopped the video. "I do. She's the head caterer at that venue—Joanne Greenburg. Certainly someone would have noticed the basket missing."

"You know how busy receptions get. Everyone is focused

on the bride and groom. Carl recently told me someone stole gift cards from that basket."

There was a time lapse. Not long after the first segment, the caterer returned the basket.

Belinda leaned back into her chair. "You mean Finn never told Carl about this?"

"No. Carl said they didn't know who did it, even though they made a police report. No follow up."

"I'm almost afraid to see what's next," Belinda murmured.

On the edge of her seat, Jazzi leaned forward as Belinda started the next video.

"Oh, I remember this event. Roscoe Choi was retiring. He passed his HVAC business down to his son at the dinner."

There were the usual sounds of the dinner breaking up and groups of friends gathering to chat. Suddenly a blank screen showed. Was the video over? A moment later two men came into view in a quiet corridor.

"That's Roscoe's son, Leland," Belinda noted, pointing to the man on the left of the screen.

Audio began. Leland, in a burgundy pinstripe suit, asked the man beside him, "Do we have a deal?"

"What's your old man going to say?" the second man asked.

"It doesn't matter what he says. Choi HVAC is mine. We signed the transfer papers yesterday. Your purchase will fund my new life in Hawaii. No more cold winters for me. Just surfing those waves."

Belinda shook her head as if she didn't believe what she was seeing. "Roscoe spent his whole adult life building that company to leave as a legacy."

"What do you think Finn was going to do with this?"

"No idea. Not much he could do if the deal was done."

Belinda pressed the icon to play the next video. Jazzi suspected Finn's wife wanted to shuffle through them to make sure she wasn't depicted in one of them.

The video on the screen began with Finn's voice declaring, "Frisco and Jennifer Gorman's wedding reception."

"I remember them. Cute couple. Young, midtwenties. Frisco sells boats. They had a beautiful wedding at the golf resort."

Jazzi had no idea what was coming but almost dreaded watching the video. These weren't positive clips from life events.

Only about a minute of the couple's reception video showed the wedding party. Then—

Down a hall, near the rest rooms, Frisco and Jennifer's maid of honor were passionately kissing.

Belinda made a disgusted sound. Jazzi had to look away. At his wedding reception!

Jazzi could feel Belinda tense beside her as another segment of video ran. With a glance at the widow's face—her locked jaw and pursed lips—Jazzi saw that Belinda merely wanted this viewing of the videos over with.

When the video began, Finn's voice was loud and clear. "At the silent auction for Friends of Art Appreciation in Ithaca."

Belinda leaned closer to Jazzi. "I don't remember this. He often did clips and stills for his website and any papers covering the event."

She sounded relieved that she knew nothing about this video.

Recognition of the person being videoed was instantaneous for both Jazzi and Belinda.

"That's Emmaline Fox!" Belinda's eyes were glued to the phone screen.

Items for auction were displayed on three tables. Beside each item lay a card. If a donor wanted to bid on a purse, a pillow, or a ski trip, they just had to mark the card with their name and their bid.

Watching closely, Jazzi saw Emmaline, dressed in a paisley midlength dress and carrying her red tote bag, swiftly swipe a porcelain vase from a table and stuff it in her tote!

Turning to Jazzi, Belinda asked, "What did we just see?"

Jazzi had questions of her own. Had Emmaline known Finn had shot this video? Did that make her a credible suspect? And what about the people in the other videos? Were they all suspects now?

Jazzi imparted to Belinda the only advice she could give. "You have to turn the phone over to Detective Milford. Any one of the subjects in those videos could be a person of interest."

Belinda nodded. "That was the end of that video. Thank goodness I wasn't in any of the videos. I'll call the detective now."

The following day, Jazzi set up a lunch to meet Delaney at the food trucks. The walk to the marina under the sun-filled sky helped her think. Last night she'd gone with Belinda to take the phone to the police station. They'd briefly met with the detective and then left. But to Jazzi's dismay, Charmaine Conner had been stationed outside. She'd run over to them from her car and scowled at their combined "no comment." Jazzi still wondered if Charmaine had been the one looking up at her apartment the night Parker had spotted someone there.

Thinking about the videos now as she walked toward the marina, Jazzi had a feeling that the news of them would start percolating around town. Or could the police keep a lid on it? Not with Charmaine outside their door.

Delaney was waiting at one of their favorite food trucks, looking as if she'd stepped from a fashion catalog. She wore a huge smile. "I was at a meeting at the mayor's office this morning. What are the chances I won't spill the corn-jicama salsa on my blouse?"

Said blouse was a silky toast color. "I'll pull extra napkins." The chicken tacos could be messy, with the guacamole and corn and bean salsa toppings, but they were delicious and even healthy. "Why were you at the mayor's office?"

"PR problem again. Apparently, Detective Milford uncovered new evidence, and the mayor is planning how to spin it."

"Are you talking about the videos?"

"How did you know?" Delaney's question was filled with astonishment.

As Jazzi and Delaney picked up their tacos and carried them to a picnic table, Jazzi explained how she knew.

"The mayor is set to downplay them, saying they were simply Finn's work product and they don't carry much weight." Delaney frowned. "But he's most worried about Emmaline's video and the one of the caterer."

After dabbing the toppings on her taco, Jazzi took a bite, then wiped her mouth. "I can't believe Detective Milford would let the information out."

Delaney tucked a napkin into her blouse's neckline. "He didn't. The chief of police did. He and Mayor Harding are tight."

Jazzi couldn't help but wonder if Charmaine had gotten a whiff of what had happened.

More food truck customers were milling about. Lunch to sundown was when the trucks did the most business. A family of four asked if they could share Jazzi and Delaney's table. They welcomed the parents and two teens, and the discussion about the videos stopped.

Jazzi was learning that the tourists were visiting from their home state of Virginia when a police siren sounded, the vehicle heading to the marina and nearby docks.

"What's going on?" one teen asked, jumping up from the bench. The dad stood too, and both headed closer to the marina while the wife shook her head, admonishing them to stay here. They didn't listen.

Jazzi was curious but she'd soon have to head back to Tomes & Tea.

Maybe ten minutes had passed when the dad and his son

jogged back. He explained, "Not much going on. Just a lot of shouting. Someone called 9-1-1."

"Shouting about?" Delaney asked.

"Some guy at the dock shouting at a woman that he wanted her to pay back every cent she stole from him and his wife. She was begging him not to press charges."

"This was at the dock?" Jazzi asked

"Yep. The guy was working on a boat," the dad answered.

So it could be Carl and his caterer. Had the police already questioned the new suspects? That must have been their first order of business this morning.

Jazzi had just finished her taco when her phone played. She expected it was Erica, asking if she'd be back soon.

But her caller wasn't Erica. It was Emmaline.

As Jazzi watched the tourist family devouring their chili dogs, she answered. "Hi, Emmaline."

Delaney's brows quirked up.

The scone chef said to Jazzi, "I need a huge favor."

"I'll help if I can."

"Something awful has happened." The scone baker sounded dejected.

"The video?"

"You know already. Soon everyone will know." Emmaline sounded near tears. "I want to explain, but—" She stopped and caught her breath. "I'd like you to drive me home to Ithaca tonight. I'm meeting with an auctioneer first thing in the morning, and a real estate agent. I must sell my house. Detective Milford said it's okay if you take me. You can call him to verify. I need to spend a few days there to get my affairs in order. Just in case—"

She didn't have to finish, and Jazzi felt sorry for her. She wouldn't pass judgment about anything until Emmaline could explain.

"Would you mind if Delaney Fabron came with us if she's free? She also knows about the video. I don't believe my car would be comfortable for you. She has a sedan."

There was a moment of silent debate. "Soon everyone will know. I like Delaney. She was my contact for the bake-off. Go ahead and ask her."

"She's right here with me. Hold on."

Jazzi made eye contact with her friend. "How would you like to drive Emmaline and me to Ithaca tonight? Supposedly Detective Milford approves."

An interested light shone in Delaney's eyes as her false eyelashes fluttered. "Let's do it!"

In the rear seat of Delaney's red sedan, Jazzi watched Emmaline, who sat beside her and seemed nervous. She wrung her hands together and stared out the side window, not saying much. The drive to Ithaca took about an hour. The city was known for Cornell University, the Ithaca College School of Music, Theatre, and Dance, and its waterfalls. This evening, they were headed to Emmaline's favorite Chinese restaurant to pick up takeout to eat at her house. Jazzi wanted to make sure Emmaline had food in her house when they left her there.

Delaney parked at the curb in front of a two-story stately brick house that presented with European styling. The slate peaked roof defied the ivy that was wildly climbing up the brick on both sides of the centered windows on the first and second stories. A rounded arch led to the inset door. The front garden, like the ivy, appeared overgrown. The limelight hydrangeas looked as if they needed staked. The rose bushes between them under the front window had yellow-spotted leaves and branches that stretched too high until they mingled with the ivy. One of the most striking features of the house was the copper gutters and downspouts. Once upon a time, this had been a luxurious house.

Emmaline was slow to emerge from the sedan as she used her cane to stand. She peered at the five brick steps leading up to the front yard from the curb.

Jazzi had gathered the bags of food. She'd also stopped in at a convenience store beside the Chinese restaurant for a quart of milk and a jug of iced tea.

Delaney stood beside Emmaline. "Do you need help up the steps?"

"Maybe if I can just hold on to your arm," Emmaline answered in a low voice. "A few of the bricks are loose."

Jazzi followed the two women and heard Emmaline say, "The double brick walls were imported from Holland."

"It's a beautiful home," Delaney replied.

"It once was . . . before my husband died. He kept everything in perfect condition. I did too. Until I couldn't."

The inside of Emmaline's house was as classic and old-world as the exterior. Jazzi knew about good construction from her stepfather and her sister's father-in-law, who was a contractor. She would bet the interior walls of the house were plaster on metal lath. The hardwood floors were scuffed and dulled with age but still beautiful.

As Delaney returned to her car for Emmaline's luggage, Emmaline directed Jazzi through the living room. Jazzi caught a glimpse of a sofa table with C-scrolled legs and a sunburst pattern on top along with damask furniture coverings in rose and olive. As they passed through the dining room, she noted that the seven-piece set showed wear. But the herringbone inlay on the top of the table and carved detail in the legs and chairs spoke of excellent craftmanship.

Jazzi heard Delaney drop Emmaline's travel bags at the foot of the stairs in the foyer. When she joined the women in the kitchen, Delaney blurted out, "This is thoroughly modern!"

Emmaline pulled out a chair at the huge rose-granite-topped island and sank onto it. "I moved to London after culinary school. I was drawn to teatime foods and the ceremony around them. I worked as a scone baker in a tea shop there. I met John there when he was on a business trip. When I moved back here from London, we married and bought this house. John insisted we redo the kitchen for my scone enterprise. The appliances are older now but are still fabulous."

The Viking refrigerator and freezer, double oven, and many-burner stovetop attested to the quality Emmaline used.

Never one to be shy about asking personal questions, Delaney asked, "What did your husband do?"

Emmaline laughed. "You're wondering if he bankrolled me? He did. He worked in finance. Hedge funds and venture capitalism. He was away a lot, but we had a good marriage. After he died, I soldiered on. But now—"

Finding glasses and plates in the cupboard, Jazzi set them on the island. "Let's eat. Then you can tell us what you wanted to talk about." Jazzi had assumed this trip to Ithaca hadn't been merely about giving Emmaline a ride.

Jazzi chose two egg rolls and a cup of egg drop soup. "Delaney told me you once had grand parties here."

Emmaline spooned beef and broccoli florets onto her plate. "We did. Lots of John's colleagues enjoyed my scones and desserts, though we had appetizers catered. Those were different days. Now, I don't even know my neighbors. Folks move on. The truth is . . . I don't have spare funds for parties. I don't even have funds for upkeep on the house or daily expenses."

"No money from your husband?" Delaney prompted.

Emmaline pushed around a broccoli floret with her fork. "We had a high old time for a while. But before he died, he made bad investments. My scone business was keeping us afloat. After I closed my bakeries for my personal health reasons, I only had savings to work with, and they dwindled quickly. My medications alone eat up my Social Security."

"I'm sorry to hear that," Jazzi said. Then she asked the question that she and Delaney considered most important. "Just how did Finn enter into your circumstances?"

After scooping up a forkful of fried rice, Emmaline poked it into her mouth. She looked from Jazzi to Delaney as if considering what to say next. Finally, she heaved a great sigh. "I've gone to silent auctions and stolen high-value pieces I could sell. There's a pawn broker who handles them for me. The objects don't bring in grand amounts. Usually, they are someone's white elephant they donate to clear their basements. Anyway, a few here and there keep me in groceries."

"Emmaline, stealing is stealing," Delaney pointed out.

"I know. I know. For the past year, I didn't want to admit I needed help. Now I have to. Thank goodness the police only have one video of me stealing something."

"Finn didn't try to blackmail you or anything like that?" Jazzi was looking for motive for Emmaline to hit Finn over the head with a cutting board.

"I knew Finn was the photographer at some of the galas and auctions I attended. I never considered he shot *me*."

"So you had nothing to do with Finn's death," Jazzi pushed.

Emmaline sighed. "Absolutely nothing except voting for his Black Forest cake. Jazzi, really. I have rheumatoid arthritis. My muscles and joints hurt. Sometimes I can't lift my arm shoulder high. The detective knows this. I had my medical records sent to him. Yes, I stole a Ming vase, an antique watch, and a sterling candlestick. But I could never physically hurt another person."

Jazzi could believe that. Emmaline's love language was baking. "Now that you've realized you need help, what are you going to do?"

After a swallow of iced tea, Emmaline looked into the dining room as if envisioning the parties she'd once given. "I'm going to sell this house and everything in it. I've already sold off some antiques."

Jazzi didn't begin to understand Emmaline's thinking about

all of it. How could she steal someone else's property instead of using her own? Had it been a game to see what she could get away with?

Tears came to Emmaline's eyes as she said, "I'm so sorry about all of it now. I think after John died and then I had to close my bakeries, I went a little daft. Now I have to face it all. I guess Finn did me a favor."

Jazzi shifted in her chair to make eye contact with the older woman. "What *are* you going to do?"

Emmaline didn't look away. "After I sell this house and everything in it, I'll look at the over-fifty community in Belltower Landing. I might buy one of those little villas with no maintenance. Maybe I can make friends and join a bridge club right there."

"Maybe when you talk to the detective again you can figure out a repayment to the charity you stole from." Emmaline seemed to need to be pointed in the right direction and find a caring group to support her.

"If you move to Belltower Landing, you'll have us as friends," Delaney said.

Emmaline was sitting with Jazzi on one side and Delaney on the other. The scone baker took hold of each of their hands and squeezed.

Jazzi didn't take a break at Tomes on Monday. Rather, she left the store a half hour early before closing so she could take a bike ride. With the days easing into fall, dusk swept over the lake earlier. She hurried to her apartment, changed into lime-green biking shorts and a yellow T-shirt, fed the kittens, grabbed a protein bar, and hurried out back. Taking a breath of the early evening air, she jogged down the steps. After she slid the wooden door to the side, she went into the garage for her bike.

The bike sat tilted against the wall with her helmet hanging on the handlebars. She fastened it under her chin and pulled the bike upright. As she wheeled it to the alley, she considered how much she needed this ride. Emmaline had been on her mind all day. She hoped the baker's meetings with a real estate agent and an auctioneer had gone well.

Emerging from the garage, Jazzi stopped short when a tall man stood in her way. His stance seemed confrontational. Her heart beat faster.

"Jazzi Swanson?" he asked in a gruff voice. "The man at the sales desk told me I might be able to catch you back here."

That must have been their temp help. She doubted the women would have given out her whereabouts. "How can I help you?"

He took a step closer. "I don't need anything from your store. I need something from *you*."

She didn't like the sound of that and didn't ask what because she suspected that was coming.

"You and Belinda Yarrow watched a video I starred in."

There was conceit in his words as well as a tone of menace. "I already warned Belinda she should keep her mouth shut. I want *you* to do the same."

Now Jazzi recognized who was confronting her—Frisco Gorman. She didn't deny she'd seen the video. There wasn't any point. "The investigation is supposed to be confidential."

"Yeah, well, I have a jetskiing buddy who's also a cop." The smugness in his tone irritated her. But any man who cheated on his bride at the wedding reception was bound to do more than irritate her.

She lost her filter and couldn't keep the snap out of her voice. "What was on that video was unfortunately not criminal."

"Oh. You're one of *those* women."

Although he took a step closer, she held her ground. "I believe a man should keep his promises and his vows." The words merely slipped out. At Frisco's expression, goosebumps broke out on her arms.

Rage seemed to suffuse his face as his cheeks reddened. He balled his hands into fists. "I won't have my reputation, or my marriage, ruined by the likes of you. You'd better stay out of my business, or you'll be sorry."

Frozen in place, Jazzi didn't respond. She didn't have to. Frisco turned and quickly strode up the path that led alongside the bookstore.

Shaken, Jazzi felt like collapsing onto the stone-covered alley. But she didn't. She took out her phone to call Belinda. The call went to voicemail.

Wheeling her bike back into the garage, she decided she didn't want to go back to the apartment. She wouldn't upset Dawn when she returned from Tomes.

After she closed the garage, she walked quickly toward Lakeview Boulevard. Maybe Oliver would have a few minutes to talk to her. She texted him as she walked.

His reply was immediate.

Table in the back is yours.

Five minutes later Jazzi was sitting in The Wild Kangaroo's dining room. She hardly had time to look around when a server came to take her order. She ordered a peach and mango smoothie along with a bacon and cheese roll. She'd count carbs tomorrow. Right now, she wanted comfort food.

The server had brought her drink and roll by the time Oliver came to her table. He pulled out the high chair at the cocktail table beside her. "I'm sorry I couldn't just come to you. I'm keeping my eye on a new sous chef."

"No need to apologize. I hadn't eaten supper and—" She stopped and looked down at the bacon and cheese roll. "I probably shouldn't have come."

Oliver laid his hand on her arm. "What's wrong, Jazzi? You're here now, so tell me."

Oliver gave off a sense of confidence and authority. She was well aware that she didn't ever dine at the pub in bike shorts. However, he didn't seem to care how she was dressed. His eyes were filled with a kindness she needed tonight. And she realized she was going to do exactly what Frisco had warned her not to do—tell someone about the video.

She took a breath. "Are you sure you have time?"

"I do. I've got to admit if a fire starts in the kitchen, I'll have to attend to it." His deep voice was teasing, coaxing her to relax.

"Understood." Then she began. She explained how Belinda had found the burner phone and asked Jazzi to view the videos with her. She detailed each of them, ending with Frisco's.

Oliver's scowl was deep. "I know him. He comes in several times a week for happy hour. Flirts with any woman who will flirt back. Doesn't wear a wedding ring."

Jazzi knew Oliver often tended bar with his bartender, especially during summer evenings when business was brisk. "I was ready to take a bike ride tonight when he appeared at our garage."

"At the back alley?" Oliver's full attention was on her face. She was only aware of him, not the servers carrying trays and setting steaming entrees on tables or the bartender shaking cocktails.

"Yes. He'd gone to the store. Our temp help told him he might catch me there. He warned me not to tell anyone about the video. He doesn't want his reputation or his marriage ruined."

Oliver scoffed. "All his wife would have to do is come into the Kangaroo with him." Obviously thinking over what Jazzi had revealed, Oliver said, "He didn't ask you kindly, did he?

That's why you needed a smoothie and a bacon and cheese roll?"

"No, not kindly. His warning that I'd be sorry disturbed me. But I think I overreacted. I tried to call Belinda . . ."

Oliver's hand on hers stopped her. "I'm glad you came here. Consider the Kangaroo a port in the storm."

All too aware his hand covered hers, she didn't pull away. Not this time.

Chapter Twenty

The next evening, Jazzi was trying to forget about her encounter with Frisco. Or maybe she was remembering all too well Oliver's hand covering hers. "Consider the Kangaroo your port in the storm," he'd said.

She kept turning her attention back to the movie she and Dawn were watching, a bowl of popcorn between them, when her phone pinged. The text was from Oliver. As soon as she saw his face on her phone screen, she felt like a teen with her first crush. Not good.

His text read:

I took care of Frisco. No worries.

After reading the text once, she read it again and pushed the bowl of popcorn into Dawn's lap.

"What?" her roommate asked.

"No need to worry?" Jazzi repeated Oliver's text. "What did he do?" She'd filled Dawn in on her confrontation with Frisco and talking about it with Oliver.

"I'm sure Oliver didn't do anything physical." Dawn's reassurance didn't carry much weight.

Jazzi remembered Oliver helping to separate Tim and Finn at the bake-off, his height, his muscled biceps, his strength. "I don't want a man fixing *anything* for me."

Jazzi disturbed the kittens, who'd been snuggled together, when she quickly stood. They blinked up at her and Zander yawned.

"Where are you going?" Dawn set the popcorn bowl aside.

"To the Kangaroo."

Ten minutes later, as she hurried along, Jazzi hardly noticed the tourists on the street. She'd texted Oliver she was coming to the Kangaroo. He'd texted back:

???

His response added steam to what she was feeling, though whatever that feeling was, it was complicated. She'd been dressed for a night of relaxation in harem pants and a crop top. Her black hair flowed loose around her shoulders as she opened the red door.

After she entered the pub, she took an end seat at the bar. The bartender, named Jeff, who mixed drinks most evenings asked, "What can I get you, Jazzi?"

She was surprised he knew her name since she didn't sit at the bar when she came in. Without a second thought, she answered, "Oliver."

Jeff blushed as if she'd just asked for the moon. He'd turned to the kitchen doorway when Oliver came through it.

He looked like he always looked—ready for anything that might happen. Yet there was curiosity in his eyes, as if he couldn't imagine why she'd come. That jangled her nerve endings more than they were already jangled.

Stopping by her barstool, he asked with a touch of humor, "Are you craving a peach mango smoothie?"

The fact that he knew that drink was one of her favorites irritated her more. He knew that but not the most important thing about her. She was an independent woman.

Seeing Jeff was mixing a drink yet seemed to have one ear tilted toward them, Jazzi kept her voice low. "Can you explain your text?"

Oliver seemed perplexed that he had to. She could tell by the crease in his forehead, the tightening of his shoulder muscles. "I thought it was self-explanatory. You don't have to worry about Frisco bothering you."

Her low voice held more force. "Why not? What did you *do*?"

Oliver's eyes widened, and she saw a twitch of a smile on his lips that actually fueled her irritation with him more.

"What? Do you think I took him out back all aggro and socked him?" That turn of a smile was still there.

Had she been stupid for even considering that Oliver could do that? Feeling a flush from her neck flow up into her cheeks, she admitted, "I didn't know if it was a possibility. So, what happened?"

His smile vacated the corners of his mouth. "Frisco came to the bar like he usually does for happy hour. I took him aside and told him I'll proclaim his sins to the world if he ever waylays you again."

"First of all, your threat told him I spoke to you about the video."

"Slow down." Oliver's stance became straighter, as if he believed he'd done the exact right thing. "He had no right telling you what you could or couldn't do. He's a cad. I've seen him flirt and even escort women out who aren't his wife. I haven't taken an oath of confidentiality not to spill my customers actions. Though I never do."

Trying to lighten the atmosphere, Oliver pointed to Jeff. "He can attest to that."

She didn't want Jeff involved in this. Again, keeping her tone not quite a whisper, she tried to make her voice devoid of emotion. "I fight my own battles, Oliver."

Finally studying her as if he was reading what was going on in her head, he lifted a hand in understanding. "*That's* what you're all steamed up about?"

Taking a huge bolstering breath because Oliver's complete lack of understanding was so disappointing, she stated her feelings clearly. "I learned how to stand on my own two feet years ago. After my dad died, I saw my mom take life by the horns, move me and my sister to where she'd grown up, and shoulder a new business. I wanted to be just like her someday. She didn't need a man to help her raise us or smooth her business concerns. I'm on that same road. If I need help, I ask. But I don't like to ask. You stepping in makes me seem weak, that I lack confidence to handle my life. I don't. I guess I showed you a moment of weakness, and now I'm sorry I did."

She slid off her stool, turned, and headed for the exit. He didn't call after her. Would she have turned back if he had?

She didn't know. She only knew her heart hurt.

Tomes & Tea was hopping with tourists the next day. Jazzi and Dawn had decided to run a Selfie Sale. Anyone who purchased books received five percent off if they took a selfie in the store and posted it on their social media. In the midst of helping customers, Jazzi spotted Belinda Yarrow come in.

Belinda stopped at the sales desk. "I just came in to see how Finn's books are selling. Talk a bit?"

Erica had overheard. She bumped Jazzi's elbow. "Go ahead. Audrey can help me here." She motioned to her daughter, who was across the store.

To Belinda, Jazzi said, "I'll meet you at the break room door in the back."

When Jazzi did meet Belinda there, Belinda said, "I can see how busy you are. I won't hold you up. Only three of Finn's books are left. Would you like more?"

Jazzi leaned against the door. "I would. The artful side of Finn is becoming more appreciated."

"I just placed a few of his landscape photographs in a gallery in Ithaca."

"That's wonderful. How are you doing other than the business side?" Jazzi knew grief came in waves and could sometimes be overwhelming.

"I'm okay. If Frisco Gorman doesn't bother me again. I suppose I was naïve to think the word about the videos wouldn't get out. He came to the house and warned me not to say anything about it to anyone."

"I had a visit too. My guess is the police questioned him to see if Finn had blackmailed him or anything like that."

Belinda looked heavenward. "Finn wouldn't do that. At least, I don't think he would." After a somber moment Belinda made a request. "How would you like to come over tonight for a chat and a glass of wine? I'm lonely. Evenings are the worst."

Jazzi thought about her argument with Oliver. Dawn had thought Jazzi overreacted. Had she? It made sense to talk it over with Belinda. "I'd like that. See you around eight?"

"Eight is good." Belinda smiled. "I'll chill a bottle of red."

As Jazzi drove her MINI Cooper to Belinda's house, dusk had fallen. Instead of thinking about her argument with Oliver, which had been on her mind all day, Jazzi considered having fewer daylight hours as fall turned to winter. She still looked forward to autumn overtaking Belltower Landing, when the forests surrounding Lake Harding would be breathtaking riots of orange, yellow, and russet against the blue of the lake. She'd still be able to paddleboard for a while into October. Though she'd have to find a buddy other than Dawn to go with her. Dawn didn't like to be cold.

Jazzi had left Dawn curled on the sofa with the kittens and

talking to Abe. Jazzi wasn't sure Dawn had heard her when she'd told her where she was going. Dawn and Abe could soon be labeled a dating couple. Jazzi smiled, hoping love had found her best friend, though she didn't know what the Fernsbys would think of their daughter dating a firefighter and first responder.

After Jazzi turned onto Seneca Avenue, she drove down the street and again passed the Yarrows' driveway and parked at the curb in front of the house. The porch light had been turned on.

Since the front door was closed, Jazzi pressed the button for the doorbell. She could hear the chime sound inside.

Seconds later Belinda was at the door, welcoming her. She looked pretty tonight . . . younger . . . with her long brown hair fastened in a messy topknot. She wore gray jeggings with a batwing-sleeve brick-red blouse that knotted to the side of her waist. Jazzi had worn a tunic over black leggings, her hair in a loose braid. They were two women sharing conversation and a glass of wine. It was nice to think about something other than her tiff with Oliver.

"It's good to see you," Belinda said. "C'mon in. Let's settle in the kitchen. I brewed a strawberry pomegranate green tea that I bought at Tomes and iced it. I have lemon drop cookies from Dockside too."

"That sounds great," Jazzi responded, following Belinda to the table in the kitchen. Two long-stem wine glasses stood by two square white dessert plates.

"I thought we'd have tea with cookies, then have the Cabernet Sauvignon. I bought the bottle to celebrate Finn's next gallery showing—" She stopped and bit her lip. "That never happened, but I'm hoping there are more gallery exhibitions in the future. You putting his book in your store and selling it online has helped promote his photographs." Belinda poured them both tumblers of iced tea from a mason jar pitcher on the counter.

"Finn's work deserves to be seen," Jazzi said.

Belinda's kitchen, in bold colors of orange-patterned wallpaper on one wall and pale green paint on the others with white quartz countertops, told Jazzi that Belinda had her own sense of style. "Did you design your kitchen or did Finn?"

Belinda laughed. "Finn wouldn't take the time for something as mundane as decorating the kitchen. Except for me adding his photo, of course."

A landscape photograph of children flying colorful kites on the green hung above the doorframe. Finn's photos could definitely entrance anyone who saw them.

"I heard you pretty much designed your apartment above the store." Belinda pushed the lemon drop cookies toward Jazzi.

She took one, then sipped at her tea. After she set the glass back down, she offered, "Dawn and I designed it together. The store wasn't in the best shape, and the apartment above was even worse. Before we bought it, we had the structure checked out. That and the original plumbing were sound."

Belinda turned her tumbler in a circle. "The store had been some kind of souvenir and vintage comic book and baseball card shop, hadn't it?"

After taking another cookie, Jazzi nodded. "That's right. The downstairs was easy to turn into the bookstore. My stepfather and my sister's father-in-law, who's a contractor, helped. I don't know what we would have done without them. Dawn's friend Derek Stuart, who flips houses, helped us choose practical flooring and finishes. Tomes & Tea was really a group effort."

"I take it you and your stepfather get along? I had a stepfather, and I avoided him as much as possible. My mom always agreed with him, so I mostly felt on the outside."

Jazzi wasn't sure how deeply she wanted to lean into her history with Belinda, but she explained how Jonas had helped find her birth mom. "We had a connection before my mom started dating him."

"Makes a difference."

Jazzi and Belinda talked about running a business in Belltower Landing. Jazzi admitted how fortunate she'd been to have been given a financial start by her grandparents.

Belinda confided, "I worked long hours waitressing at the golf resort after Finn and I married. He was just starting out. Those tips from rich tourists helped."

As if she didn't like thinking about those times, she motioned to the bottle of wine. "Let's move into the living room and break open that bottle. I'll bring the corkscrew."

Although the living room was small, it had a set of metal industrial-style bookshelves behind a modern three-seater curved sofa in an ecru bouclé. It was punctuated with ball cushions and matte-black metal legs. A matching lounge chair, a tree-type floor lamp with ball lights, and a drum-shaped black table finished the room.

Belinda switched on the tree lamp with a remote and then sat in the armchair with the wine bottle and corkscrew. Jazzi had carried in the wine glasses, and she set them on the table beside Belinda.

After she opened and poured the wine, Belinda handed Jazzi a glass. Jazzi knew she was only going to have one because she was driving. She swirled it a little, then brought the glass to her lips. She could taste a bit of blackberry and wood. Preferring sweeter wine rather than dry, she was certainly no expert.

Belinda took a swallow of wine while Jazzi took a sip. Then her host held her glass tightly. "I should tell you something."

Jazzi set down her glass, her full attention on Belinda. Was this the reason the photographer's wife had asked her here? "I'm listening."

"You do listen well, don't you, Jazzi?" It seemed to be a rhetorical question because she went on. "I'm the one who told Carl about the video on Finn's phone."

Jazzi relaxed, not even realizing she'd tensed. "You felt he should know?"

"I did. The detective could have held on to the video, never revealing what was on it."

Jazzi thought that the video of the caterer stealing Carl's wedding gifts would have been revealed at some point because it depicted a crime. But she said, "So he knew about it before the caterer went to him asking him not to press charges?"

"Yes. I never expected there would be such a ruckus from it." She took another sip of wine. "Do you know if Carl *will* press charges? I haven't spoken with him since then."

"No, I haven't seen him. Just Frisco." Jazzi picked up the ball pillow and set it in her lap. Thinking about that confrontation at her garage gave her goosebumps.

Belinda dramatically shivered. "He was scary. And stupid. Even if he silenced us, the news of what was on that video would get out. Maybe I should have called the police about Frisco's visit. Have *you* since it happened?"

Jazzi rolled the ball in her lap. Thinking about it and how it led to what Oliver had done upset her more than she wanted to admit. "No. But—"

"But?" Belinda's prompt was all Jazzi needed.

"I told Oliver Patel about it." She was embarrassed about how easily she'd confided in him.

"The pub owner? Whatever for?" After studying Jazzi's face thoroughly, Belinda said, "I wouldn't need Finn to photograph your expression to know Patel is more than a pub owner. Are you dating?"

"No." That word came out more vehemently than Jazzi liked. She tried to explain, "He's been around when things happen. We sometimes bike together."

"There's something you're not saying."

Belinda was reading her too well. Hadn't she accepted her invitation *because* of the argument with Oliver? Maybe venting to Dawn hadn't been enough. Maybe Belinda's outlook on the situation would help.

"After I told Oliver—" She stopped, then went on. "He knows and sees so many customers at the Kangaroo. Frisco's a regular at Happy Hour. He removes his wedding ring and flirts. Sometimes he even leaves with someone he flirts with."

"His wife probably suspects. She might pretend to be blind, but I doubt she is if he's that blatant." Picking up her glass, Belinda emptied it in a few swallows.

"Maybe nobody else at the Kangaroo pays attention. But Oliver does. After I told him about Frisco's threat, he confronted him. Oliver told him if he ever messed with me again, Oliver would spread the word so far and wide about his behavior that his wife would be *sure* to know."

A smile crept across Belinda's face. "He was defending you."

"I don't need him to defend me. I fight my own battles. I was so annoyed—"

"So you argued?" It was easy for Belinda to follow point A to point B.

"We did. And I'm trying to forget about it. To forget about *him*." Jazzi was honest. "But I keep seeing his caring blue eyes . . ." Tossing the pillow ball aside, she shut *her* eyes.

"Oh, Jazzi. I understand." Finn's wife leaned forward. "Don't you realize how lucky you are to know a man who wants to protect you? That's rare. We all have wanted women power for so long. And we have it. But we can't make it be a concrete wall that doesn't let a man in."

Was that what she had done? Built a concrete wall around her heart because of past hurts? "Maybe you're right."

"I'm about ten years older than you and definitely have had

more life experience. I know I'm right. Now with Finn gone, I wish he was here to defend me. When I think about him in that kitchen with the stools knocked over, his prize-winning cake smashed on the floor—"

Like a severe storm coalescing over Lake Harding, Jazzi's thoughts seemed to be shot with lightning. The sips of wine she'd drunk slid back up into her throat. In a flash of total recognition, she remembered her discussion with Dawn about Finn's crime scene, her roommate's remembrance, the detective's admonition to Dawn and Jazzi to tell no one what Dawn had remembered—black forest cake all around Finn . . .

Maybe someone had related the scene to Belinda. But the detective had been so adamant about keeping quiet. Belinda suddenly was Jazzi's number one suspect. She should text Dawn she was here.

Jazzi mumbled something like "That's hard even to picture." She slid forward on the couch and slid her hand into her pocket for her phone. "My phone just vibrated. I'd better check it."

But by the time she pulled it from her pocket to text Dawn . . . or anyone, Belinda was standing over her, recognition for what Jazzi had realized glaring from her eyes. She looked like a different woman now. The cold look in her eyes and on her face—

As the full understanding that Belinda had likely been Finn's killer unnerved Jazzi, she pressed the side buttons on her phone to call emergency services. Seeing what she was doing, Finn's widow knocked the phone from her hand.

When the phone flew, Jazzi instinctively grabbed the wine bottle to use as a weapon. Jumping up from the sofa, she pushed Belinda away and sprinted for the door. With her hand on the knob, she understood she'd rather run out of there than fight with a murderer. She'd done that once before.

However, at the same time Jazzi had run, Belinda reached into a side drawer on the drum table, removed a revolver, and pointed it at Jazzi. "Stop there. You're not going anywhere."

Swallowing the cotton ball that had seemed to form in her throat, Jazzi took a breath and turned to try to reason with her. "How would you explain shooting me? And why would you even think about doing it?"

"It's simple, Jazzi. You *do* listen too well. And every expression on your face manifests what you're thinking or feeling. It's that youthful innocence you're still blessed with. But in these circumstances, it will get you killed. I'll say I thought you were a burglar."

Jazzi remembered breathing exercises a therapist had taught her when she was a teen. She often called on them in stressful situations. This was definitely one of them.

Jazzi pulled in a breath, held it, then let it out. "If you're going to kill me, I deserve to know why you killed Finn." She might have to pretend bravado, but she needed to buy time.

"You deserve to know? That's rich. I asked you here tonight to find out exactly what you *did* know."

"I never suspected *you*." Jazzi's limbs were trembling. She firmly told herself to get a grip. She had to be ready to swing out the door.

"Of course, you didn't. Unfortunately, I became too involved in our sharing fest. I must say you are a natural at coaxing people to open up. I've seen it in your store. I was going to visit you one rainy night at your apartment to poke around, but decided not to. I knew your roommate would probably be there."

The longer Jazzi stalled, the better chance she'd have to make it outside. "So what did Finn do that was so horrible?"

Stepping forward, Belinda closed some of the distance between them. After all, what was a wine bottle compared with a gun?

"Finn was a sneak. He set up more than *one* camera in this house. Last year on our anniversary, he gave me a framed photo of the two of us. That frame had a camera in it. Remember I told you women always know if a husband is unfaithful? Smart men know too." Belinda's last words were spit out with venom.

Jazzi could hardly believe this was the woman who had pretended to be grieving for her husband . . . who set up a scholarship fund in his name. Right now, her brown eyes weren't filled with grief but with a blank soulless stare.

"What happened when you found the camera?" Jazzi was sure that was what happened. Her fingers slid tighter around the wine bottle.

Belinda's laugh was decidedly wicked. "I left it there. But I realized it was too late. The man I'm seeing and I had made love on the floor of the living room. I knew that's why Finn's attitude had been so cold lately. The night before that silly bake-off, he asked for a divorce."

One of Jazzi's legs began to wobble. She straightened her knee to stop it as her mind kept whirling. "Why not get a divorce and be free to start over?"

"You *are* naïve," Belinda almost yelled. The revolver shook in her hand. "I could have ended up penniless. Finn brought in the business. He made the money. What did I have to start over with? Part of his 401(k)? He not only wanted a divorce, but he was going to change his will to leave all his photos and videos to Claude Fenton. I'd have nothing."

"What happened to those videos of you and your lover?" Jazzi wasn't sure where to go with this subject, but she had to go somewhere. Either the moisture from the cold bottle was making it slip or her hand was sweaty. Still, she wasn't releasing the doorknob with her other hand.

Looking smug, Belinda said offhandedly, "I deleted them from the burner phone. His app for the home cameras was on there too."

If the detective's IT guy was examining the phone, he still might be able to find those videos. Did Belinda believe they'd stopped looking because of the other videos and suspects? She might be right.

Lowering the gun a bit as if it was too heavy in her grip, Belinda asked, "Any more questions? This is getting tedious."

Belinda was acting as if she had all the time in the world before she shot Jazzi. If it were later at night, would the shooting seem more plausible? Detective Milford was smarter than that. And Jazzi wouldn't give up the chance to escape this killer.

She thought of the last question concerning Finn's murder. "Did you steal the key Finn wore around his neck?"

"How did you know I did?" Finn's widow seemed genuinely shocked.

"Social media. Finn was wearing it in all his photos. But Dawn—" Jazzi stopped abruptly. Had she just put her best friend in danger from this murderer? Now she *had* to escape this house however she could . . . whatever she had to do.

"Ah. But Dawn saw Finn's body and remembered it was gone. You *are* a sleuth. I'll tell you the secret no one else knew. That key had a number engraved on the back. Finn would never tell me why. I thought maybe it was a safe-deposit box. But I took care of all Finn's financial paperwork and never saw a yearly charge. I knew it had to be important. And it was. It was the passcode to unlock his burner phone. Everybody thought I just guessed it. After I found the phone and got in, I changed it to the date we were married. That made a good story to tell the detective. And . . ." she added, ". . . I stole back the watch I'd given him. It would have just laid in the P.D.'s evidence room until they decided to give it to me. Who knows what would have happened to it?" With those final words, Belinda lifted the gun and pointed it straight at Jazzi's heart.

No time to dither, as Jazzi's Aunt Iris would say. Belinda must not have handled the gun or shot it often. Maybe it was

Finn's. Whatever the case, when Belinda tried to pull the trigger, the safety was still on!

Jazzi took advantage of that infinitesimal moment and tossed the wine in the bottle into Belinda's face. It splashed into her eyes. Belinda dropped the gun to swipe her hand over them.

Jazzi tossed the bottle at her for good measure, opened the door, and ran out.

Seconds later, Belinda shot from the open door. The first bullet went wide, but the second whizzed by Jazzi's shoulder, and she felt the burn. It felt as if a hot poker had stabbed her.

Dashing behind her car, Jazzi ducked low. Bullets kept shattering her passenger-side windows. When the destruction stopped, she raised herself up enough to see Belinda, standing on the lawn, realize she was out of ammunition and run back inside. Jazzi tried to imagine what Finn's widow would do next.

Jazzi heard a siren scream not too far away. Maybe her call had worked. Maybe a neighbor had heard the shots and called 9-1-1 too. Next she heard the sound of Belinda's garage door going up. There was only one thing to do.

With her shoulder throbbing, she climbed into her car and slipped her key fob from her pocket. First she hit the panic button. Then she started her car, ignoring the glass shards scattered on the seats and floor. Wasting no time, she pulled her car across Belinda's driveway and quickly climbed back out, running to the curb behind a neighbor's car for cover.

Belinda backed out of her driveway, probably fully intending to smash Jazzi's MINI Cooper to bits, when patrol cars hopped over the Yarrows' lawn, blocking her path. Two officers were out of their vehicles, service revolvers drawn, and Belinda's car screeched to a stop.

Minutes later she was handcuffed and directed into the back seat of one of the patrol cars.

※   ※   ※

A half hour later, Jazzi had given her statement to Detective Milford and was still sitting on the back of an ambulance. Abe had cleaned and bandaged the graze of the bullet on her shoulder and let her use his phone to call Dawn.

Detective Milford pushed his suit jacket away from his waist and stuffed his hands into his pockets. "We were closing in on her. Videos are never deleted. She had motive. We had a partial print that hadn't been swiped from the cutting board. I don't know how you became this involved. Because of your roommate?"

"I didn't come tonight suspecting *anything*," Jazzi reminded him.

"So you said."

A hunter-green SUV drove up with more speed than it should have on the usually quiet street. It pulled in front of Jazzi's MINI and had hardly parked when Oliver jumped out.

He ran over to her, concern written all over him as he asked, "Are you all right? What happened is already on the news. The report said someone was shot. And a neighbor uploaded cell phone footage to the local news channel. It showed Belinda Yarrow shooting at *your* car."

"She has a grazed shoulder," the detective answered him. "Make sure she gets checked by her physician tomorrow." He must have thought his neutral tone would calm Oliver.

Oliver bent over, hands on his knees, like a sprinter who'd run too far. After a few long breaths, he straightened and sat next to Jazzi on the back of the ambulance. "I'm sure she'll take care of that herself."

He and Jazzi shared a look, then Oliver swung his arm around her. "From what I heard, you didn't need any help. Good job."

Oliver had raced to her, not to extricate her from a jam but to make sure she wasn't alone.

"Dawn called me," he murmured. "Thanks to heaven she did. If I'd have seen you on the news, I would have stroked out."

Leaning against Oliver's shoulder, Jazzi let her head rest against his. His arm around her was so comforting. But most of all, his support felt right.

Epilogue

Two weeks later, Jazzi carried a hobnail milk-glass table lamp into a one-bedroom cottage at an over-fifty development on the east side of Lake Harding. Emmaline was moving in.

Delaney entered the bedroom after Jazzi, carrying sheets to make up the bed. Dawn followed her, toting a bedspread.

As Jazzi plugged in the lamp, Delaney said, "The guys are working hard emptying the moving pod."

It had been much more economical for Parker, Oliver, and Abe to drive to Ithaca and load the furniture Emmaline had decided to keep into the pod. The company's flatbed then brought the pod to Belltower Landing for the three men to empty. Jazzi couldn't wait to see Emmaline settled into the community. Fortunately, her house had sold a few days after it was listed to make the move possible.

Emmaline herself, who had been sitting on a lawn chair directing and watching, wandered into the bedroom. "You must let me help."

Jazzi exchanged a look with Dawn. To Emmaline she said, "With four of us doing this, we'll be done in no time. Are you still worried about coming into town without having a car here?"

Jazzi knew Emmaline had sold her car too. Everything left in the house would be offered soon for public auction.

"Not worried at all now," Emmaline responded. "One of the Rocky Creek Community's board members just told me about the van that goes into town twice a day. Isn't that marvelous? I won't even have to spend money on Lyft or Uber."

"When are you setting up the classes you're going to teach?" Delaney asked as she unfolded a sheet and let it billow across the bed.

Emmaline caught an edge on the other side and began slipping it over a corner of the mattress. "I submitted my schedule to the board. I think I'll be teaching residents how to bake everything from scones to biscuits to shortbread cookies every Wednesday morning."

A few days ago, Emmaline had confided in Jazzi that she and Detective Milford had come to terms. She was making reparations for the vase she had stolen by teaching the classes stipend-free. Emmaline felt guilty about everything she'd lifted from silent auctions, and this was her way of making amends.

Delaney and Dawn were hanging curtains and Emmaline was fluffing pillows into pillow cases when Jazzi slipped out of the bedroom into the open-concept section of the cottage. Parker and Oliver were positioning the damask-covered sofa into place. Abe carried a wing chair in rose velvet. They'd already set up Emmaline's kitchen table and chairs.

"You've done such a good thing for Emmaline. Your help will change her life." Jazzi felt emotion clogging her throat.

Oliver crossed to her. "You give us too much credit. Moving furniture flat out beats lifting weights."

When Jazzi looked up at Oliver, her heart sang a little. Since the night Belinda had tried to shoot her, he'd been texting her often to check in. So had her mom. She'd video chatted with her mom and Jonas after her confrontation with Belinda. Daisy Swanson could understand better than most how Jazzi had gotten pulled into the whole situation.

"I have news about Belinda if you want to hear it," Parker announced. He was looking from her to Oliver curiously.

As an IT guy himself, Parker had connections and also knew his way around the Internet better than anyone Jazzi knew.

"I'm ready to hear whatever you found out," Jazzi said.

"I found the charges against Belinda. Murder in the second degree, second degree assault, and reckless endangerment in the first degree. In a divorce, she was right about losing everything. Finn held all the cards. They also found Finn's key necklace and his watch in her jewelry box. Now that's a stupid killer."

Abe sank down on the ottoman that accompanied the wing chair. "No one will know what Finn was going to do with those videos. Maybe there were backstories to them. Maybe, for instance, he'd looked into Emmaline and her need for grocery money. The same with the caterer. We'll never know. He was such a good dude. He built up his business and life for both of them. I don't get how Belinda thought she could wipe him out and her problems would be solved."

"I don't think Belinda was rational. She was soulless that night." Jazzi cringed, and Oliver hung his arm around her shoulders.

Dawn came charging into the room. "My parents texted. They've invited us all out on their pontoon boat. Emmaline declined because she insists she needs to nap after the excitement of moving. How about the rest of you?"

Automatically, Dawn's gaze had shifted to Abe.

Jazzi thought about Dawn's parents, who always stood united, who had been married for twenty-eight years, who worked together at Rods to Boards and still enjoyed each other's company. She thought about her mom and stepdad, their romance, their wedding, their life that always included helping others. She considered her Aunt Iris, who'd found love late in life and was growing older with her retired detective husband. Then there was her sister and her husband, who had taken a risk and still looked at each other the way they had when they'd first met. And she couldn't forget her grandparents.

Not that she was ready for a serious commitment.

"Earth to Jazzi. Do you want to go on a boat ride? You look as if you were miles away." Dawn was standing in front of her expectantly.

Jazzi *had* been miles away. She was not going to dwell on Belinda and Finn's broken commitment. Instead, she'd remember all the healthy couple relationships she was fortunate to witness in her own life.

"How about it, Jazzi?" Oliver asked. "Are you free for boating tonight? I'm off for the day. So I'm free."

They were both free. She liked the idea of riding the lake together. Smiling up at Oliver, she said, "Boating sounds perfect."

Oliver gave a satisfied nod, and she knew she *could* be embarking on a new adventure. With him.